Too Many Miracles

A Novel

TOO MANY MIRACLES

A Novel

ERNEST L. SCHUSKY

SUNSTONE
PRESS

SANTA FE

Sunstone books may be purchased for educational, business, or sales promotional use.
For information please write: Special Markets Department, Sunstone Press,
P.O. Box 2321, Santa Fe, New Mexico 87504-2321.

Book and Cover design › Vicki Ahl
Body typeface › Plantagenet Cherokee
Printed on acid-free paper
∞

Library of Congress Cataloging-in-Publication Data

Schusky, Ernest Lester, 1931-
Too many miracles : a novel / by Ernest L. Schusky.
p. cm.
ISBN 978-0-86534-511-9 (softcover : alk. paper)
1. Clergy--Fiction. 2. Mexico--Fiction. I. Title.
PS3569.C55546T66 2012
813'.54--dc23

2012007832

WWW.SUNSTONEPRESS.COM
SUNSTONE PRESS / POST OFFICE BOX 2321 / SANTA FE, NM 87504-2321 /USA
(505) 988-4418 / ORDERS ONLY (800) 243-5644 / FAX (505) 988-1025

Dedicated to
Mary Sue

PROLOGUE

"We've done it, Carlos! We've done it." Hector loomed over Carlos' back as the secretary finished adding his figures. Carlos bent over a desk littered with splinters. Smoke from two candles at the desk's edge mingled with the sweaty aroma of a dozen bodies gathered in the warehouse.

"No more of the Sickness." Carlos and Hector spoke in unison.

"No more of the Sickness," a dozen voices echoed.

"A hundred thousand pesos, Father." Carlos' voice trembled. "El Hidalgo has entered the twenty first century. Not as much as with tomatoes in a good year. But enough for next season's seeds and fertilizer and a dividend to get us through the year."

The men around Hector and Carlos laughed, slapping each other on the shoulders. They reached in to pat Hector, a few hands reaching his shoulders, one patting his lower back.

Hector had never felt so delighted, at least not since his ordination twenty years ago. His years as an undergraduate studying agronomy and extension services had paid off. The work in El Hidalgo proved that poor Mexican farmers could make a living growing corn and beans rather than tomatoes or strawberries shipped to the North.

Without intensive application of insecticides, and whatever other poisons their contracts with Cultiva Grande called for, the villagers were free from the Sickness.

"We'll announce official results to the village in the morning," Carlos said. "My wife is preparing a feast. Tomorrow night we'll celebrate like never before."

"I'll go to Hermosillo for fireworks," Hector said. Given the results, he felt less guilty about using grant money for a few cheap rockets if he could find any in Hermosillo. A celebration would accelerate the village efforts at sustainable agriculture, ending dependence on large growers who contracted for cash crops.

Hector's dreams of becoming an agricultural missionary had been fulfilled. He could spend the rest of his life in surrounding villages, proving to Mexican farmers in the highlands that they did not have to raise chemically dependent crops for export. But for the moment, he'd have to survive the dancing and feasting of a village festival.

Hector left early the next morning for Hermosillo. It wasn't far, but since the washboards in the road only stopped when canyon size ruts took over, the drive took hours. He believed he knew every one of the ruts, but a gap between two of them caught him unaware. He shifted his jeep into four wheel drive to escape the road's clutches. The gear shift trembled in his hand.

On the outskirts of Hermosillo, he stopped at his favorite store. The owner checked off Hector's list and joked about the order having an "abundance" of sacramental wine. When Hector asked for fireworks, the man scratched his head. He stocked them but didn't remember if any were left. The owner disappeared into a back room, then appeared in a few minutes with a dusty box. "Some rockets. A Roman Candle. I don't remember its colors. A few pinwheels. I can't guarantee any of them."

"I can't afford much anyway," Hector said. "How much are they?"

"You can have them. I'm glad to get rid of such a fire hazard." He brushed his hands together producing a dust cloud. "Besides, for a customer who buys so much wine why shouldn't he have a bargain once in a while."

Hector's sneeze hid his own laugh. "A thousand thanks," he said. "Come out to El Hidalgo tonight. We'll feast you, and you can watch your fireworks."

The man chuckled. "I've driven that road, Father. It's bad enough during the day."

The two smiled their goodbyes.

Hector returned to the village and shuffled to his office that served as his bedroom. He stood before his desk wondering what could go wrong. No matter how many successes, he always anticipated misfortune if not disaster. His misgivings were interrupted by a dozen aromas from the nearby plaza. He scrubbed away the grime from the trip just before the El Hidalgo band called people to the plaza.

"Band" was perhaps an exaggeration. Two elderly men, whose hats must have been even older, sawed away at violins. An even older man plucked at what passed for a bass. Hector knew that a young man would join them in what he claimed was a *mariachi* outfit. He called his trumpet "the horn of a thousand notes" but everyone else called it a thousand dents. Hector noticed he found more right than wrong notes until his second drink when the ratio reversed.

Hector saw the musicians had taken their places on the plaza bandstand. Its platform lacked a roof, but the rare politician who found his way to El Hidalgo promised money for a proper gazebo. Villagers would have voted for anyone who paid to paint the platform.

Hector rinsed out his enameled plate and cup, decided his fork and spoon were clean enough, and rummaged through a drawer for a bandanna to serve as a napkin if the need arose.

When he reached the plaza in front of the church, he found it ringed with green, white, and red banners except for a gap filled with red, white, and blue pennants. The banners did a better job of catching the breeze than did the pennants.

A long rickety table graced one side of the plaza. A platter of roast corn was followed by pails of stew. No doubt, the women would assure him that the bits of goat meat savoring the blend were beef.

He took an ear of corn and stood with Carlos who munched one ear while holding a second. As Hector peeled the husk, steam rose to his chin. A golden brown grain with flecks of black stared back at him. He marveled at the villagers' skill to roast corn to perfection. He was half way down the ear when Carlos turned to him.

"You have worked a miracle, Father."

"It was your hard work and how the village worked together, my Son."

"But it was a miracle that you came here with your knowledge of plants and helped us organize a cooperative. I've never seen the people of El Hidalgo work together like they have the past year."

"You must have faith in each other," Hector said.

"And faith in God," Carlos answered. "You've brought that, too. We seldom had a priest to serve mass." Carlos reached to put a hand on Hector's shoulder as he looked up into his eyes.

Hector felt the blood rushing to his face. He blinked away a tear. He would miss the comrades he'd made in El Hidalgo

"Let's get our beef stew," Carlos emphasized beef and the two laughed.

"You must eat quickly if you're going to dance with every woman in La Paz."

Hector gritted his teeth. At his first celebration he had been asked his favorite dance. He'd answered the polka, unable to think of anything else. Hector found himself dancing with every unmarried woman in the village and some of the señoras safely in seniority.

Moments after he and Carlos finished gnawing their beef stew, the band struck up a polka. The young man with the trumpet joined other band members. He must have practiced. The first eight notes came out right.

The señoritas waved pleated skirts of red and green in time with the music. Their laundered white blouses failed to hide their wear until the sun set.

When a young girl started toward Hector, he found a place for his tableware. He knew she must have been teased into asking him to dance since she was so shy. The other young women lined one side of the plaza. From the way they were giggling and eyeing him, Hector knew he'd be avoiding toes the rest of the night.

The next woman didn't hesitate in beckoning him to the plaza floor. Hector guessed the girls assumed he couldn't ask women to dance so it was acceptable that they approach him.

She gazed up into his eyes until he felt his face afire.

She laughed. "Father, where did you get such green eyes and red hair?"

Hector brushed the reddish-brown mass back with his hand. He knew he needed a haircut. Even after a trim his hair appeared to need cutting.

"They say my ancestors were French soldiers who deserted from Maxmilians's army."

"Who was Maximilian?" The girl looked as if she were more interested in conversation than an answer.

"He was sent here by Napoleon the Third to rule Mexico."

"You know so much, Father. You're so educated!" The girl sighed her admiration.

"But we Mexicans threw him and his army out because we love our Independence."

"Speaking of love, Father," the girl stepped closer to bury her head in Hector's chest, her face turned upward.

Before she could say more, the trumpet saved Hector. Its dented notes ended the dance, and Hector sent the girl on her way with profuse thanks, welcoming the next in line.

"You're the tallest man I've ever met, Father. They say you had to be a priest because you're so close to heaven."

Hector forced a laugh. The quip was funny the first time he'd heard it.

"I'm six foot, six inches, my child. But we all have the same chances of entering heaven." Hector spun the girl.

"You're not going to ask why I haven't been coming to confession, are you?" The girl blinked long eyelashes. "I can explain."

"No need. Tonight's a time to celebrate. Enjoy yourself."

The girl threw herself into the polka with abandon. At the next confession she'd beg forgiveness for stepping on Hector's feet because she moved so close to him.

The band reached the limits of its endurance before midnight. The trumpeter had deserted an hour earlier, or more likely passed out, judging from his final notes.

Hector scurried to his fireworks along with Carlos. Both men leaped back when they lit the first rocket. It fizzled out with a whimper. The next five lifted off as if destined for heaven, bursting high in the sky into bellowing greens and reds. The last one included a series of explosions. A dozen dogs howled their appreciation. Hector lit the Roman Candle and held it as far away as possible. It shot out fire balls of green, white and red. The spectators cried out. "Long live the Tricolor!" Carlos sneezed in the cloud of fumes. Hector breathed deep, associating the acrid smell with victory.

Carlos had nailed half a dozen cartwheels to wooden posts, and the spinning sparks concluded the celebration. There could not have been a more fitting conclusion to Hector's success. Surely, now, nothing can go wrong, he thought.

✝✝✝

Hector finished correspondence while waiting for the bishop to assign him to other highland villages. The church hierarchy had failed to appreciate what he had done in El Hidalgo and assigned him to teach agricultural extension at a small university. At the end of a boring and unrewarding year, Hector came across a newspaper account describing a miraculous salvation for El Hidalgo. The government was paving the road to it, and a North

American consortium intended to build a spa. Villagers would be trained as hotel workers.

Hector cried. Surely the bishop knew of the development and had failed to notify him. He imagined a dozen different ways to confront the man, ending with threats to leave the priesthood. But in the back of his mind, his fantasies concluded the bishop would welcome his resignation. He turned to prayer, beseeching Divine help in convincing the bishop to make the best use of Hector's talents.

1

After Hector composed himself, he called the bishop to make an appointment. He was surprised by the late hour the secretary scheduled, but elated when told he could stay overnight with Edwardo Valdez, a friend from seminary newly appointed to the bishop's staff.

Hector packed his belongings. Everything fit into his jeep, even his books, which took up half the space. He kicked the tires, shaking his head. He knew the gesture proved nothing, but the ritual was ingrained. As a child he assumed the car wouldn't start until his father had kicked all four tires.

Hector had driven half way to the bishop's when he saw two women beside the road with a flat tire. The older woman's immaculate dress kept her from changing a tire. The younger lady's blue and white striped sweater showed off every inch of her breasts. Her tight skirt would prevent her from bending over. Hector parked on the shoulder in front of them.

"Oh, thank God," The older one uttered but with no conviction behind the Lord's name. "I thought it would be dark before anyone stopped." When Hector drew close enough to show his collar, she exclaimed with a hint of conviction. "God did send us help like I prayed for."

"I tried to read the directions, Father," the younger one said, "but I can't locate where the jack goes."

"These new cars aren't user-friendly," Hector said.

"You look perfectly capable," the young one purred, her eyes lingering over Hector's reddish brown locks.

Hector brushed back his hair while he opened the instruction pamphlet. The directions were in English. In the fading light, Hector struggled to read them.

"I believe the jack goes here." He took the tool from the girl and reinserted the handle. "Let's get out the spare before we raise the car."

The trunk was a jumble of camera gear along with a torn bag of potting soil. Its contents had leaked into the tire well. Hector's hands were black by the time he retrieved the tire. He rolled it to the fender, engaged the jack, and removed the flat. In straining with the spare, he braced his head against the fender. He felt a layer of dirt stick to his forehead.

When he straightened, the young woman laughed while she dabbed at his face with a handkerchief. Hector's nose wrinkled from the smell of gardenia perfume.

"I hope you aren't going anywhere important or else you'll need a shower."

"I'll manage," Hector said, but the dirt under his fingernails felt encrusted. "I'm curious. Where did you collect so much dust?"

"A terrible road in the mountains. We heard about a miracle at San Miguel and thought there might be a story." The young woman's voice bubbled with enthusiasm.

"We couldn't pass it up," the older one said. "My daughter's studying photojournalism."

"And my mother is a journalist!"

"I'm sure you make a fine team." Hector began to worry about his appointment.

"Do you know about any miracles at San Miguel?" the daughter added. "It's a tiny village." Before Hector could answer, she continued. "We heard it's a place of miracles." She failed to conceal a condescending smile. "All kinds of miraculous cures, I suppose."

"Actually, no one in the village would tell us much. Rude people." The mother wrinkled her nose. "Well, not so much rude as secretive."

"Oh, Mother. That one man, Andres or Alejandro, tried to be helpful."

"Well, he did answer my questions, but he never volunteered a thing."

Hector laughed to himself. Given the fit of the young woman's sweater and the shortness of her skirt, no man in any mountain village would talk long to this pair if his wife or her relatives were anywhere about.

"But someone told you about the miracle?" Hector asked.

"Andres explained a little," the older woman said. "It seems the villagers are building a new church. I don't know why. The old one is lovely, even if ancient. Looked like a fort more than a church. But I guess it's progress. Although Andres suggested someone else was building it."

The younger girl added, "It's just a foundation, Father. They've built a

14

kind of chapel or something. And his name is Alejandro, Mother, I'm sure. You should have it in your notes."

"We saw crutches and leg braces in the chapel." The mother was consulting a small notebook.

"I shot hundreds of pictures of whatever the building was. These new digital cameras are so wonderful. I must have a prize winner with so many."

"How do crutches prove a miracle?" Hector asked.

"We'd heard how a man who had used them for years made a pilgrimage to San Miguel," the mother said.

"From a friend's maid in Culiacan," the daughter said. "Her family lives in San Miguel."

"She told how a holy man blessed the cripple, and he walked away without them." The mother looked at Hector quizzically. "Don't you think the holy man had to be a priest?"

"Isn't is awesome?" the daughter exclaimed.

"What have you heard, Father?" the mother continued. "Surely the miracle's been reported to the church. Don't you people investigate?" Before Hector answered, she added. "Can I quote you?" She flipped to a new page in her notebook.

Hector shrugged. "I haven't heard anything. Of course, the church investigates claims of miracles. But, I'm an agricultural missionary. Miracles are out of my realm."

"Agriculture sounds interesting," the mother said, but her look suggested she could not imagine anything more boring.

Hector tossed the flat into the trunk. He neglected to screw it into place, trying to imagine how the two used potting soil.

"Father, I know you won't take money but give this to your favorite charity." The mother thrust a hundred peso note at Hector.

"No," he said. "You give it to your favorite charity."

"I wish I could give it to that San Miguel church," she said. "It must be historic and ought to be preserved."

"I think the Jesuits built it," the daughter said. "It was like a fortress. It had a round building attached to the church that must have survived siege after siege."

"Perhaps, I'll visit it someday. What were the farm fields like?"

The two women stared at each other, helpless to answer. Finally, the daughter said, "I guess they were like the others."

Hector chuckled. "Not many people pay attention to what farmers grow."

"What's your name, Father?" The mother evaded Hector's inquiry.

"Hector Cardenas."

"Cardenas! Are you related to the past President?"

"No," Hector said. "I wish I could claim a link."

"Oh,"

Hector couldn't tell if the woman was disappointed by the lack of a relationship or his suggestion that he favored Cardenas's liberal policies.

The woman searched through her purse. "In any case, here's my card." A flowery smell breached Hector's nose. "Please write me if you learn anything about the miracles at San Miguel."

Hector glanced at his watch again. "I certainly will." He put the card in his pocket.

"We are so grateful, Father." The girl looked as if she were about to hug him. "We'll make a generous donation to the poor." She stepped closer. Hector extended his hand to shake hers, then her mother's.

"It was a pleasure to meet you. Go with God, now." Hector waved to the back of the car as the two women drove off, wondering how he'd get himself presentable for the bishop.

✟✟✟

Hector stopped at a new fast-food restaurant on the edge of the city and cleaned up. He felt compelled to buy a meal but paid no attention to what he ate.

As he drove into the neighborhood of the bishop's residence, the quality of new houses surprised him. The neighborhood had looked substantial ten years earlier; now it looked prosperous. He parked on the street and strolled the grounds. The cathedral had been renovated with an expanded parking lot. On his way to the residence, the smell of new cut grass delighted his nose.

The bishop's residence gleamed with a fresh coat of off-white paint. Hector could choose between the old brass knocker with its intricate design or a new door buzzer. The traditional knocker tempted him, but he clenched his teeth and buzzed. He resolved to convince the bishop about the importance of sustainable agriculture in Mexico's development as well as the dangers of harmful chemicals.

A woman with lackluster gray hair but a bright red apron opened the door and led Hector to the bishop's dining room where a fugue on the intercom filled the air. Hector tried not to listen.

"You're right on time." The woman glanced at her watch. "The bishop said he'd meet you here." She gestured to a small table that seemed out of place in the large dining area. It was covered by a linen cloth, modestly plain but of fine weave. A long table, with hand-carved wooden chairs, occupied the middle of the room. The far wall featured a built-in bookcase from floor to ceiling. Hector stared at the table setting of china and silver, trying to fathom a use for the extra spoons and forks. The smell of something not quite chicken did nothing to relieve his uneasiness.

He stood beside the table, pondering whether or not to sit. The bishop's entrance decided him to stand.

"So, Hector, how have you been?" The words echoed in the room as the bishop extended his hand while staring at Hector's hair. Hector feared he'd missed a smudge, but he recalled the bishop had stared the first time they met. Hector wondered if the man envied his thick waves since the bishop was bald.

The two exchanged pleasantries, the bishop took his seat, and Hector knew where to sit.

"My doctor has advised me against hard liquor, but perhaps a glass of wine before dinner?" The bishop smiled. "We're having quail. Would you like to begin with a white or a red?"

Hector shrugged. He seldom drank. "Whatever you recommend, your excellency."

"A parishioner gave me a delightful burgundy. Then we'll switch to a white. I find either goes with quail."

Hector imitated his host in swirling the wine, studying its color or whatever it was that required studying, and copying the bishop's sniffing the glass. When the first course was served, Hector's stomach reminded him of his fast-food meal. The serving of ceviche satisfied him. As he toyed with later courses, he tried to bring up his assignment, but the bishop postponed Hector's duties until the housekeeper served a flan.

Hector made an excuse to stand so the meal could find a place in his innards. He went to the bookcase and perused the volumes. Most of the titles were unfamiliar, none appealing.

"What's your favorite book, Hector?" the bishop asked.

Hector didn't have to think. *Los de Abajo*." he replied.

The bishop laughed. "I might have known. You live up to the Cardenas name. I suppose you'd like to work among the rebels in Chiapas."

"I serve at your pleasure, sir. Anywhere in the mountains makes a better use of my talents than teaching."

"That's not what your chair thinks. He'd be happy for you to return."

"He was happy for a grant I received. The overhead the university charges is outrageous."

The bishop chuckled. "So you know about budgeting? I could use you here."

"I'd be worthless." A chill went down Hector's spine at the suggestion.

The bishop enjoyed a moment of silence before he changed the subject. "I understand Edwardo Valdez is a friend of yours. He's joined my staff, and you could work with him."

"Perhaps he could come to the field with me. He has a lot to learn about farming." Hector would do whatever the bishop felt necessary, but work in agricultural extension made the best use of his training.

"Edwardo has many contacts with well placed people here. With your looks and charm you could captivate the wives and widows. Our budget always faces a shortfall."

Hector's stomach churned. It would be bad enough to be confined to a city, raising money would be a living hell. "My numbers never add up," Hector stammered. "I had a difficult time tracking expenditures with my grant."

"How do you feel about your experience in the mountains?" The bishop studied Hector's face with his change of subject.

"It paves the way to independence for Mexican farmers!" Hector's face flushed. "We had a profitable year with sustainable crops—with sustainable methods. We used a little chemical fertilizer but no pesticides. Mexico can be less dependent on exports when we reach more farmers." Hector took a deep breath. He had to bring up El Hidalgo. "Surely, not all farms can be converted into resorts."

The bishop laughed. "No one could foresee a spa coming to El Hidalgo." The bishop stroked his chin. "The situation reminds me of an American film I saw on television. Did you see it?"

"I read the book. *The Milagro Bean Field War* portrays a tragedy similar to what happened in El Hidalgo."

"Well, the El Hidalgo development might be for the best. Tourism creates employment, contact with the larger world, regular employment."

Hector gritted his teeth. The bishop obviously didn't know about pride in coaxing seeds to fruition. Nor did he grasp the importance of sustainable agriculture.

"I know you're itching to get into the field. Edwardo assured me you're not happy any place else. There is an opportunity . . ."

The pause caused Hector's throat to tighten. The bishop must have been teasing him earlier, but he still seemed to have something in mind rather than agriculture. Hector put his hands behind him and rubbed aching fingers.

"Many mountain villages have been without priests for so long they are developing practices—how shall we say it?—that deviate too far from orthodoxy."

"Like miraculous cures?" Hector thought to tease the bishop.

"Cures and Madonnas crying." The bishop continued without a smile. "It's reached the point where it isn't wholesome."

"Would you like me to start in San Miguel?" Hector intended to describe his encounter with the two women as coincidental to what was on the bishop's mind, but the bishop's face paled.

"How could you know?" Then he laughed. "Oh, you've been talking to Edwardo."

"No, I haven't had a chance. But on my way here, I ran into two reporters who had covered a miraculous cure in San Miguel."

"Oh, no," the bishop sighed. "The media will make it a national joke."

"They called themselves journalists, but they didn't seem to have much of a story. I took them for amateurs."

"That's good to hear." The bishop stroked his chin. "A friend told me. His wife's maid can't stop talking about it."

"The reporters got wind of it from a maid who came from San Miguel," Hector said.

"That village used to report record numbers of miracles, but their committee stopped writing a while ago."

"Perhaps they could use a miracle worker to help them farm?" Hector meant to joke, but the bishop frowned.

He interlocked his fingers over the crescendo of a stomach. "I've sent Edwardo to look into the matter. You know Edwardo is a city boy so he never found out much, but he arranged living quarters for you. I want you to convince the San Miguel congregation that God isn't showering them with miracles. After all, the value of miracles is in part due to their rarity."

Hector tingled. His knowledge of science could help him explain the natural basis for most 'miracles' while he concentrated on introducing new farm methods. He jumped at the chance.

The bishop seemed disappointed when Hector declined to sample more of his wine, told him where to find Edwardo, and assured him he'd have a few months to bring San Miguel back into the fold. In his mind, Hector expanded the opportunity to a growing season.

✝✝✝

Hector found Edwardo's office door open, his back to him. Edwardo concentrated on a computer keyboard. Hector snuck behind and grabbed him in an headlock to give him a Dutch Rub.

"You depraved giant," Edwardo shrieked. "Your armpit smells as bad as ever."

"If you were a little shorter, you wouldn't reach my armpit." Their joking had started in undergraduate days. Hector released him, and they embraced.

"How have you been?" Edwardo stepped back but continued to hold Hector's arm.

"I'm great now. I should throw a party for you. My reassignment couldn't be better."

"I wasn't sure you'd like it. This business about the miracles, I mean. Cures. Crying Madonnas. A long history of who knows what else."

"Tell me about the farms. What were the people like? How long were you there?"

"Just over-night. Takes a day to get there. What a road! The farms are what you would expect. A little irrigation. You have a room adjoining the church, and I got you a cot. A so-called store across from the church has more empty than stocked shelves. The owner will cook for you—when or if she feels like it. Ask for Rosa."

Hector was disappointed that Edwardo had spent so little time in San Miguel, but it was better than nothing. "What's the church like?"

"Small but mighty. The Jesuits built it to protect against Indians. I'd guess even Apaches from the States raided the village."

"What about the new foundation? Do they really plan to build a new church?"

"What are you talking about?"

Hector raised an eyebrow. "Didn't you see any new construction?"

"No. The church is so old, it's got one of those round enclosures attached to it. Served as a fortress, I guess. That's your room and office. I slept there to break it in. I even used the outhouse." His nose wrinkled.

"You mean Alejandro had you sleep there?"

Edwardo's jaw dropped. "How? I didn't use his name in my report."

"It's the miracle of my telepathy," Hector said.

"Come on. What do you know?"

Hector related his encounter with the two women and what they had told him. He asked again about new construction.

"Come to think of it, I saw a concrete footing over by a large house that seemed out of place." He scratched his chin. "No evidence of any miracles— like abandoned crutches." Edwardo laughed. "Or like four inches of leg cut from an overgrown giant to make him normal."

"You want another Dutch Rub?" Hector threatened.

Edwardo threw up his arms, pretending to defend himself.

"What about Alejandro?" Hector asked. "How did he strike you?"

"Slow to relate to outsiders. He may be very shrewd. When he found out I represented the bishop, he listed ways the bishop could help San Miguel. That's the name of the church as well as the village, by the way. I'd guess its population is less than a hundred people. Shouldn't take you more than a month to convince twenty or so families that miracles are rare events."

"The bishop said I had more time than that."

"You don't want to spend months without a decent meal or a toilet, do you?"

"It will take at least six months to explain miracles," Hector said.

Edwardo gasped, then offered a lopsided smile. "Six months just happens to coincide with a growing season."

Hector smiled as he shrugged. "What can the bishop do if I overstay? I can get by without my allowance."

"With your good looks, he'll send you to a school for development."

"That's great, Edwardo. Development is my life."

Edwardo snorted. "In the bishop's vocabulary, development means raising funds."

Hector's shoulders sagged.

"Look, the bishop isn't going to support you in San Miguel for more than a month or two. He's never been convinced that the church has any role to play in farming. I doubt he even understands sustainable agriculture."

"Why his support in changing beliefs about miracles?"

"The press has been hard on Catholicism lately. He fears ridicule."

"Then you'll have to convince him I'm accomplishing a lot in education."

"Oh man, you've always gotten me in trouble. I'll do what I can, but there's no way to convince him you need six months there."

"I'm sure you'll work a miracle for me!"

2

Hector scooted his seat all the way forward to fit a trunk into the jeep. At his first stop to stretch his legs, he reviewed his friend's directions to San Miguel. The turn-off to the village was where he had helped change the flat tire.

No sign marked the turnoff. At first, Hector thought the road might lead to a hacienda. Once the way led into the mountains, he felt reassured. A flooded stream forced his second stop.

Hector pounded a stick into the water's edge to measure its progress. He sat and watched clouds hover over a mountain range, contemplating how he'd explain weather patterns to people in San Miguel. The vagaries in this part of Mexico often caused flooding in one valley while the next suffered drought. He mused that the right amount of rainfall spread evenly over the land might be considered a miracle.

An hour later, Hector's marker showed the stream receding. He finished leftovers from a generous breakfast at the bishop's. By the last bite, the stream was low enough to cross. He guessed San Miguel must be close, but a series of sharp hairpins and a stretch of washboard road kept him in second gear. Twice he stopped to roll away wandering boulders that barricaded the road. A storm-downed tree threatened a hernia when he wrestled it to the side of the road. He sucked at a splinter lodged in his thumb.

As he worried again about being on the wrong route, he reached a summit that gave a view of a village at the road's end. Hector pulled to the shoulder to stand beside the jeep, unable to see if the recent rain had blessed what must be San Miguel. He prayed that if this storm hadn't, the next one would.

A cloud of dust spiraled on the curve below to reveal the earlier rain had bypassed this village. On the lower hairpin, a black Leviathan of an SUV growled uphill. When it turned in his direction, two men in the front seat, their faces masked by dark sunglasses, stared straight ahead. He waved, hoping they might tell him something about San Miguel, but neither man raised a hand nor turned a head as their vehicle growled past him, enshrouding him in dust. Despite their frozen masks, Hector felt their hidden eyes had pried inside his thoughts. His mind raced to imagine what brought them and their SUV to San Miguel.

He shook off his trepidation to concentrate on a road growing ever bumpier and narrowing at each turn. When he breached the final bend, he wiped beads of sweat from his brow. The road led straight to the village, a dry, dusty place that the rain had bypassed more than once.

Hector parked his jeep in front of the church and breathed deep as he got out. Cobble stones that shone with wear paved the road in front of San Miguel. Opposite the church, adobe houses lined an earthen plaza. A larger building, also of adobe, faced the church, doubtless built for government offices. Now, a worm eaten sign announced it as 'Rosa's Grocery.' He wondered which would succumb first to nature's ravages, the sign or the building. Hector guessed the stores' shelves bore more dust than food. In the plaza center a would-be gazebo ended in a platform. Two posts suggested misplaced hope for a roof.

Hector walked around the jeep, inspected the tires, killing time while waiting a greeting from villagers. When none came, he walked up the few steps to the church. Sun glistened on a bell in the finished tower. The typical half-finished tower opposite it, sagged in comparison, as if bemoaning its bareness.

Patches of whitewash suggested the church once gleamed like a lily, but much of its upper surface now sprouted a rustiness that refused to be labeled a color. Adobe mud bricks probed through original plaster to dominate the lower part of the church facade. Instead of soaring to the heavens, San Miguel squatted like an aging warrior prepared to spring from ambush on whatever predators came its way.

Oak planks in its massive doors showed off their grain despite centuries of weathering. Iron hinges hadn't fared as well. Rust had ravaged them and streaks of orange sneaked to ground level. A small door had been cut in one of the larger doors. Hector found it open, pushed, and was greeted with a squeal that pinched his ears.

He squinted. His first thought was that the only light came from an opening behind the altar. As his eyes adjusted, he treaded forward. What he thought to be a beam of light was actually a reflection off a Madonna, illuminated by rays of the sun filtered from apertures between roof and walls at least thirty feet overhead. He wondered if any documents existed that chronicled the clever architects who designed such lighting while building a fortress. From the moment he entered, he had felt the thickness of the walls and the strength of the roof beams.

When Hector reached the altar, he dropped to his knees without thinking and begged for help, not sure if he beseeched God or the Blessed Virgin. When he looked up, a sparkling ray of sunshine off the Virgin's face made him think she had winked at him. He mused about his first "miracle" in San Miguel. Hector felt welcome.

A few rickety benches along the walls served the elderly. Parishioners must stand through services, he thought, the way their ancestors had. He'd keep his homilies short. The dark figures along the walls must represent the twelve stations of the cross although in the dim light, he couldn't be sure. Curiosity drew him to a doorway to the left of the altar.

Hector bent low to enter a short tunnel leading into a large, circular room. Its only light filtered from cracks around a door opposite. The walls rose about six feet before converging into a dome. It dawned on him that this giant beehive was the building described by Edwardo. It would be his home for the next six months—if he could resist other plans the bishop might make for him.

Hector felt a warm motherly protection emanating from the walls, but they then pressed in upon him. It could be his prison, he thought. No light pierced the domed top. At least, he'd stay dry—if it ever rained.

As his eyes adjusted to the darkness, Hector made out a candle stick on top of a chest of drawers. He found a lighter and a box of old fashioned matches, struck one to light a candle, and looked around. He gasped. A hugh crucifix hung from the stretch of wall nearest the church. Most of the cross occupied the vertical part of the wall, but the top swung out, nailed to the curve of the dome. Jesus hovered over him.

Hector felt the crucifix out of place, yet its location created an overwhelming presence in the room. He held the candle closer to the sculpture. The cross was of oak, the figure made from a material he couldn't identify, but it was almost white. It didn't appear to have been painted. The skill of the sculptor matched the best of any he had seen elsewhere in Mexico. Christ's anguish was so real that Hector fought back tears.

After a while realty set in. Hector lit a second candle to examine how the crucifix was held in place, fearing that Jesus might soar down on him one night while he slept. Railroad spikes had been hammered into the adobe walls. Iron ringlets held the cross to the spikes. Hector decided the crucifix was secure, but he moved the chest of drawers below the crucifix and located his cot to a far side.

He left by the exterior door to examine his backyard. Scrub forest, clear-cut long ago, and afterwards giving up so much firewood that trees never grew back, didn't surprise him. It was typical mountain landscape. A thick country aroma reached his nose. The church outhouse sat twenty yards away.

Hector turned around to study the dome. It looked to be built for defense, yet he saw no way for defenders to look out or to shoot down on attackers. Gun ports may have been filled in, Hector thought. He'd look for evidence of scaffolding inside when he had more candles.

He walked around the church and headed to his jeep. Two men stood beside it. The tall one chewed on a stalk of grass, half smiling at his friend who must have been talking as wildly as he gestured. The taller one stretched toward six feet while his companion failed to reach five. The short one was clean shaven, but hair sprouted from his nose and ears as if fertilized.

The two contrasted as sharply in their dress. The tall man's denim jacket was worn through at the elbows but clean. His blue jeans were held in place by a leather belt that looked as if it had seen years of saddle soap. The short one clutched at pants frayed to the knees, held in place by a rope. His shirt might have been blue at one time, but stains overlapped stains to conceal the original color.

The tall one had a presence about him that made Hector hope he was Alejandro. As he approached them, the tall one swept off a battered, wide-brimmed straw hat to reveal graying hair. A short beard matched it in color. He took the stalk from his mouth and flipped it away with a finger, a gesture reminiscent of Hector's father.

"We're sorry we weren't here to meet you, Father. We were in the fields when we saw you drive up."

"That's all right. You probably didn't know I was coming."

"Oh, we did." the short man said. "We've been so anxious for you to get here, we watched every morning. It's a miracle to have a priest live here. You will be full time like Father Edwardo promised? No?"

"For as long as I'm needed."

"Forever, then. We have no one to marry our young people. No one to say the right words over us in death." He glanced at the man beside him. "Well, we have Alejandro, of course. He knows so much! But it's not like having a real priest. One with years of education!"

"The bishop wasn't sure how long I'd be needed, but I hope it's a long time. Besides marrying and burying," Hector laughed, "I want to help you farm."

"Oh Father, we don't have any hoes with handles long enough for you." Gustavo's tone was serious, but the sparkle in his eyes betrayed his jest.

Hector laughed. Alejandro turned to his companion. "What he means, Gustavo, is that he'll tell us which plants will do best for us. Like strawberries or tomatoes."

"I've hoed a lot of corn, Alejandro. I expect to hoe a lot more. Cash crops aren't meant for everyone in Mexico."

Alejandro bowed his head to acknowledge his mistake. "So many people are getting old here that we can use your help."

"That, and all the young ones leave San Miguel." Words bubbled out of Gustavo. "You won't have many to marry, Father, but there are lots to bury."

"We saw you come from behind the church," Alejandro said. "Can we show you anything more?"

"We should carry Father's things to his room," Gustavo interrupted. "Shouldn't we?" He looked at Alejandro first before turning to Hector.

"They can wait," Hector said. "First, I'd like to hear more about the church."

"It was built by Jesuits, a long time ago," Alejandro said.

"Before my grandfather's time," Gustavo said, shrugging and throwing up his arms. "Maybe even before his grandfather's time."

"When the Spanish settled this part of Mexico, the Indians tried to drive them away. So the church served as a fort as well as a place of worship." Alejandro hesitated. "At least, that's what they say."

"It certainly looks like a fort," Hector said. "And the room behind it. Was it a fort?"

Gustavo laughed. "You mean the Womb? You think the Womb could be a fort?"

Alejandro cleared his throat. "It's built like a fort."

Gustavo tilted his head at Alejandro. "But there are no gun ports. Indians could come up to it and ram holes in it to attack. There would have to be gun ports."

"Perhaps the gun ports were filled in when peace came," Hector said.

Neither man spoke. Hector waited, knowing it to be a mistake to tell them about their own community. His patience rewarded him.

"They say," Alejandro rubbed his chin, his first nervous gesture. "They say that when the church was built a giant came to help. After all, there were only two Jesuits. How could they bring big trees from the mountains? How could they build such tall walls and lift up large roof beams?"

"But Indians have done that all over Mexico," Hector protested. "With a little guidance from missionaries."

Alejandro shrugged. Hector kicked himself for interrupting.

Gustavo couldn't contain himself. "They say no Spaniard could have built the dome atop the altar even with Indians to help them. How could they do that, Father?"

This time Hector held his tongue.

"The giant built a room for herself right beside the church," Gustavo gestured with his hands to match the flow of his words. "It used to have a big door for her to get in and out, but our ancestors filled it in. They said it had been like a womb for her, and they wanted to keep it that way to protect her memory. After the giant left, our ancestors connected it to the church with a tunnel." Alejandro shrugged to signal an end to his explanation. "It makes good quarters for a priest, no?"

Hector nodded his satisfaction with the room, but he took more interest in the giant. His mind raced to ask the right question. "Was the giant the first miracle that came to San Miguel?"

Alejandro and Gustavo stared at each perplexed. After hesitating, Alejandro said matter-of-factly, "We never thought of the giant as a miracle."

Hector bit at his lip. He wondered what they thought of his ignorance.

Gustavo rushed to explain. "Our giant wasn't the only one, Father. There were giants in other valleys, too."

"How long ago?" Hector asked.

Gustavo looked at Alejandro with a raised eyebrow.

"They say it was in the time of our grandfathers' grandfathers. Maybe longer ago."

Gustavo continued. "So our giant couldn't be a miracle. I guess it would be a miracle if the giants were as tall as some people claim. They say she had to bend down to build the dome." He scoffed. "My grandfather knew that the giant had to reach as high as she could to build the dome. Don't you think there might have been some people that tall?" He looked up at Hector as if pleading for agreement.

"There have been stranger things." Hector was at a loss for an answer. He clowned, "Some people claim I'm a giant." He laughed, but Alejandro and Gustavo managed only polite chuckles.

"It was a miracle that told the giant where to build her church," Gustavo said.

"But that's another story," Alejandro put a hand on his friend's shoulder and turned him away. "It's time we put Father's things in his room."

Between the three of them, it took only two trips to unload the jeep. Hector wondered what he had forgotten, but what troubled him most was that in his first discussion of miracles in San Miguel he had stumbled. How was he to explain miracles to people whose understanding of them differed radically from his own?

3

Hector bolted upright in his cot, sweating from a dream where a giant attacked him. He flailed at her knees, as high as he could reach, while her fingers strangled him. He shook his head, then struggled to free himself from Edwardo's sleeping bag.   The room remained warm, having held the heat of yesterday's sun. Hector slipped into jeans and a jean jacket to go to the outhouse. The seat held none of yesterday's warmth, and his bowels yielded little of theirs. He'd have to eat more than the energy bars he'd stocked. On his return, roosters cried their greetings to the sun.

He washed in a basin atop the chest of drawers, then went to Rosa's store. An old man, sitting at the entryway, squinted at him, and said the store was closed, as if it might never open. Hector explained that Rosa expected him and that he'd be a regular customer.

A smile replaced the suspicious frown, and the man opened the door. "Rosita keeps the accounts. You can pay her later. Just make a list of what you take."

Hector found three sticks of jerky and a bunch of wilted carrots. In a corner he discovered a hoe, thought about a shovel, but decided it could wait. He listed his purchases on a remnant of wrapping paper and handed it to the old man.

"I'm Father Hector." He extended a hand. "And what do they call you?"

"When they don't call me Rosa's father, they call me Pedro."

"I'll be back later, Pedro. Do you think Rosa would cook a hot meal for me tonight?"

"If she doesn't, I will," Pedro said. "You want to eat your beef sticks there?" He pointed to a homemade chair half hidden behind an empty display case.

Hector devoured half the carrots and a stick of jerky. He wondered if jerky ever petrified. The ones he purchased were close to it. The carrots were as limp as the jerky was stiff.

Considering his need for roughage, he gnawed at another carrot. A rustling noise from a corner caught his attention. A young man wielded a broom as if he were sanding the floor. Dust swirled up to his waist like a cloud of gnats. Hector glanced at Pedro with a raised eyebrow.

"That's my grandson, Pablo. His father went to the coast to look for work—when he wasn't looking for a bottle."

"Looks like you've got an eager worker to help you."

"He works hard with his hands to make up for what he lacks." Pedro tapped his forehead with a finger.

"We do the best with what God gives us." Hector gritted his teeth. Did he have anything more than platitudes to offer a grandfather with a slow witted grandson? He pocketed the last three carrots and nodded a goodbye to Pedro.

✝✝✝

Outside, the sun promised more warmth. Hector went behind the store to look over the fields. Men were filtering onto the land with hoes on their shoulders.

The land sloped down from a high ridge. The steep part was covered with scrub forest, but the valley widened out into nearly level fields. When first settled, the land must have been an Eden. Now the weeds along the edges of the fields begged for nourishment.

A herd of goats grazed on what was left of corn stalks. Their bleating suggested they needed to be milked. When one goat shook its head, a bell rang. Hector wondered how many goats might roam the highland forest. He walked farther into the fields and recognized Alejandro from his height. Gustavo's rotund figure contrasted with his friend. Up close his smile radiated a welcome.

Gustavo stared at Hector's hoe with skepticism, but he chuckled a greeting and bowed his head. "Is your handle long enough to reach the ground, Father?"

"I may work on my knees, my Son."

"We thought you'd need to rest, Father," Alejandro said, "so we didn't ring the bell for morning mass."

Hector took a deep breath. His conscience said he should have served mass this morning, but he used as excuse that the people didn't yet know of his presence which was unlikely, if gossip rushed even at half the speed in San Miguel as it had in El Hidalgo.

"I'll announce Sunday when we'll have morning mass, Alejandro. Will you and Gustavo help? Besides ringing the bell."

"Whatever you wish us to do." Alejandro said.

"Alejandro has done everything for years, Father, just like a regular priest. His father did the same."

"Gustavo and others do their share. But we'll be glad to have your example while you are here. We know we're a poor village and can't afford a priest for long."

"The government is the same," Gustavo rushed to say. "It thinks four years is enough schooling for farmers like us so we don't have a teacher. When a teacher is here, he does nothing more than show the children how to read and to add and subtract." He shrugged. "But what do we need of advanced mathematics like multiplication." Gustavo's tongue twisted getting out the word multiplication. "It doesn't help us hoe."

"But reading could help you understand such things as miracles," Hector said.

Alejandro fixed Hector with a stare. "The bishop has never shown any interest in our miracles. Will you teach us something about them while you are here?"

Before Hector could take advantage of Alejandro's question, Gustavo interrupted. "We hear about new fertilizer and pesticides all the time. But in the past they poisoned us. Maybe our children could read about safe chemicals."

"Or even better, methods that don't use fertilizer or pesticides. In his enthusiasm for agriculture, Hector forgot about miracles.

"You mean like growing tomatoes or strawberries?" Alejandro sounded skeptical.

"There are new ways to grow corn and beans," Hector said. "And chili. Tomatoes, too, but for our own use. Corn and beans give us nourishment. Chili and tomatoes add vitamins. The Mayans and Aztecs grew them long before Europeans invaded us. Potatoes, too, even if they are called Irish potatoes."

"But what about our ancestors, the Mayos and Yaquis?" Alejandro asked. "Didn't the missionaries teach them to farm?"

"No. Your ancestors were farming long before the Spanish came." Alejandro and Gustavo met Hector's words with blank stares, and he kicked himself for having lectured so soon after meeting them. "So our bodies are well accustomed to the hoe, even mine. How will we use them today? I want you to see that my handle reaches to the ground." He laughed but his two companions had to force their smiles.

"Everyone is clearing irrigation ditches. We're almost finished. Then a week or two to rest until we plant," Alejandro said.

"While we're resting, I'll make you a new hat, Father." Gustavo stared at Hector's tattered straw hat.

"What do your hats sell for?" Hector was curious what money might be earned in off season employment.

"Oh, I wouldn't think of charging you, Father. We know about your vows of poverty."

Hector shook his head. He lived in relative poverty to city dwellers, but these villagers would consider themselves rich if they had his allowance.

"And you, Alejandro, do you weave hats, too?"

"He carves wonderful figures." Gustavo gushed. "You can see them laughing or crying. The buyers call them 'enchanting', but they won't pay what they're worth. He takes two or three days to carve one."

"It's getting hard to find the wood," Alejandro said, obviously embarrassed by Gustavo's praise. "Anyway, it's time we cleared our ditches."

The three walked toward a small channel that led down from a spring. Hector noticed the underground source for the first time. "Does the spring flow year round?"

"It has to, Father," Gustavo said. "The last rain was never. No one knows where the water comes from. You'd think the nearest mountain would provide the water, but sometimes it fails to rain there and the spring gushes. Or it rains there and the spring dries up. Right now it gives only enough for drinking water. If we had to irrigate, I don't know what we'd do." Gustavo's shoulders drooped. "Some say it's a miracle it flows at all."

"He doesn't mean it's like the other miracles, Father." Alejandro shook his head. "He didn't mean a miracle from the finger of God."

"I understand." Hector was elated to have a second chance to discuss miracles. "It's often difficult to trace a spring's source. Scientists can do it, but it's costly."

"Then it would be a miracle for us to learn the source." Gustavo laughed harder at his joke than the other two.

"Miracles are events that cannot be explained by scientists. Take cures, for example. The body often cures itself, or a drug has a delayed reaction. It makes sense to scientists even if they couldn't predict what would happen." Hector realized his lecture was going no where. "We'll talk more about it later."

He turned to study the pattern of the irrigation ditches. A main ditch through the center carried water to branches that led to individual fields. It ended in a trickle flowing past a few houses. From there it wound its way to the plaza where it served as the village's water source.

Close to the spring, a wide feeder ditch provided abundant water to a field larger than the others. A woman with two young girls was supervising a laborer, tugging at debris that clogged a ditch. The woman pushed him aside to demonstrate what she wanted done. Hector heard her berating the worker with words more often used by men.

Gustavo said to Hector, "That's Inez Yepiz. Her husband bought the best land before he died. Now she holds on to it for her two daughters."

"I'm surprised the land can be sold. A lot of mountain villages redistribute land so everyone has enough."

"Her husband was a lowlander. He didn't understand our ways," Alejandro said. "He'd lend money to families in need. When they couldn't pay him back, he'd talk them out of their land. He didn't exactly buy it, and since he always put it to use, he could claim it. According to our ways."

"Looks like he acquired only the land closest to the spring," Hector concluded. Gustavo shook his head in agreement.

"He planted tomatoes and melons. They took more water." Alejandro said.

"Then fertilizer," Gustavo jumped in. "The chemical kind. Not like ours from chickens and goats. Then he sprayed the crops to keep the bugs off. They say the poison killed him. I don't think so. He had too many sons to be weak from poison."

"And two daughters?" Hector asked.

"Inez calls them her daughters, but they're her grandchildren," Gustavo added. "From one of her older sons."

The two girls chased each other down the ditch, the youngest laughing loudly. Her sister held a finger to her mouth to quiet her.

"How did the lowlander get his crops to market?" Hector asked. "I can't imagine buyers driving up here on that road."

"He'd rent a truck," Alejandro said.

"The family made a lot of money." Gustavo was nodding his head so fast it made Hector dizzy. "Señora Yepiz wanted us to grow tomatoes, too. One summer I raised a good crop, but the buyers said there was no market." Gustavo looked ready to cry. "They paid me less than I needed for my family's corn and beans. Maybe they cheated me. Who knows?"

A scream from Inez interrupted them. The two daughters had made their way to a field where a man had put down his machete while using his hoe. He was standing rigid with his mouth open. The youngest girl stood staring at the machete stained with blood. A gash spurted blood from her leg.

Alejandro and Gustavo froze in place as did the other farmers. Hector dashed toward the church, calling over his shoulder, "I've got a first aid kit in the jeep. Lay the girl on her back and raise the leg."

When Hector returned, Inez was sobbing over the girl, begging Alejandro to carry her daughter home. "Marta needs to be in bed. I can clean her wound."

"I have a canteen," Hector panted. "I'll clean it. Let's use some sulfa on the wound and give her a penicillin tablet."

Hector daubed at the cut with a moistened gauze pad. Blood was everywhere, but the bleeding stopped. He no longer feared an artery had been gashed, and it looked as if the wound wouldn't require stitches. He found another gauze pad, pressed it to the cut, and taped it in place. The girl was smiling at him and kept telling her mother it didn't hurt. The older sister held Marta's hand, wiping tears from her own eyes. Inez kept insisting that the men carry the girl home.

Hector showed Alejandro how to grasp their arms to make a seat. Gustavo lifted the girl onto it. She giggled as she put her arms around Hector's shoulders. Once they reached the Yepiz home, Inez opened the door and showed them a bed. Her older granddaughter pulled back the covers.

"Will you bless my wound, Father?" Marta said.

"We're Protestants, Marta. Priests don't bless us. Thank Mr.—what's your name, Sir?"

"Cardenas."

"Thank you, Mr. Cardenas."

"She'll be alright now," Inez said. "She has Maria to care for her as well as myself."

"And thank you, too, Alejandro," Marta called from her bed.

Maria took Alejandro's hand and walked with him. "Say a prayer for my sister," she whispered.

"We all will, Maria," Alejandro whispered back. "You can be sure God will watch over Marta."

Gustavo waited at the door. Inez smiled at the three men but offered no thanks. Her wave was curt. Neither Alejandro nor Gustavo commented on their dismissal.

"The house took much money to build," Alejandro said. "Her husband came from a rich family in Hermosillo, but he lived in the mountains for his health. He died some years ago."

Gustavo interrupted. "Inez went to the coast as a maid and met the son. It wasn't long before he married her. Not long after that, they received a remarkable inheritance."

"She's a remarkable woman," Hector said.

"Some say she's a witch," Gustavo said.

"Don't gossip," Alejandro said. "Father will think we're backward Indians."

"I was joking, Father. They said that because she had twelve sons. Now she's raising the two girls. Isn't that remarkable?" Gustavo was shaking his head as if attacked by bees.

"Indeed," Hector said. "Do any of the sons live with her."

"No, they've all left. Like most young men." Alejandro shrugged.

"Mateo and Marcos are in Culiacan," Gustavo said. "People say the two are drug runners. They always have money for their mother. They visit often. Just yesterday they were here."

"You must have passed them on the road," Alejandro said.

"Were they driving a large black van?"

"A Ford Explorer," Gustavo beamed. "Can you believe someone from San Miguel drives a Ford Explorer? It's like a miracle."

Alejandro frowned at Gustavo.

"I mean it's remarkable," Gustavo said.

"Two other sons left for Mexico City," Alejandro continued. "Lucas is a pimp, I've heard. Juan sells lottery tickets. They bring their mother money, too. She inspired loyalty."

Gustavo interrupted. "Juan must peddle drugs, too. The last time he was here, he had a black eye and a cut down his neck. Would selling lottery tickets be so dangerous?"

"Mexico City is a dangerous place," Alejandro said. "We shouldn't guess how he got into trouble."

"You're right, *Compadre*. I'm sorry. Don't listen to me, Father. My wife says my mouth runs ahead of my mind."

"What about Inez's other sons?"

"Simon Pedro and Jaime went to Los Mochis, the last we heard." Gustavo raised his hands to gesture his ignorance. "Two of their father's brothers have jobs on the Copper Canyon railroad. The nephews started out as guards, but the work was too dangerous." He lowered his voice, "But it's said they were caught sleeping on the job."

Alejandro added, "It's been more than a year since they've been home."

"The sons have spread all over Mexico?" Hector asked.

"Others went North. They seldom return, but they send money." Gustavo was wound up in his revelations to Hector.

"Were all of them named for disciples?"

"All of them! Isn't that," Gustavo searched for a word, "remarkable?" He obviously admired Señora Yepiz.

"Even Judas?" Hector meant to joke.

"She has a Judas, too!" Gustavo punctuated with a finger.

"Well, not exactly," Alejandro said. "The youngest boy never fit in with his brothers. They called him Judas but only behind his mother's back."

"But now his mother calls him that," Gustavo said. "He hasn't come back since he left for Mexico City, and he's never sent money. So his mother doesn't want to hear his real name."

"She refuses to believe what people say," Alejandro shook his head. "We can't be sure, but someone ran into him on the streets of Mexico. They say he's a Catholic Worker caring for people with HIV."

"And he went to college!" Gustavo burst out. "A few years anyway. He was his mother's favorite until he dropped out. Now she says he lives on welfare."

"Was it his father who sent Judas to college?" Hector asked.

"No. They say his brothers supported him," Alejandro said. "Until they found out he was homosexual."

"I see," Hector said.

"How did his mother take the news?"

"She said it couldn't be true," Gustavo said. "He was the youngest of her sons, and she was so proud of him."

"Was Inez's husband devout?"

"No. He loved money too much. Judas didn't like his father buying up land," Gustavo said. "Said it wasn't right. He and his father fought about it so much Inez didn't know which way to turn. Her husband or her little baby!"

A young rotund boy came toward them in a pigeon-toed walk.

"But Inez said she was Protestant," Hector said.

"Yes," Gustavo said. "She became Protestant after her husband died and that Protestant missionary came."

"Granpa," the youngster called to Gustavo. "Dinner's ready. Grandma said that if you didn't come right away, she'd give me everything to eat."

"Would you eat my supper, grandson?"

"If you don't come, I will," the boy smiled.

"We'll finish the ditches in the morning," Alejandro said. "After that, we can call on people to tell them you'll offer mass on Sunday."

"Thank you Alejandro. You too, Gustavo. I'll join you in the fields in the morning."

Maybe then I can find out about the Protestant missionary, Hector thought and ask about the miracle that caused San Miguel to be located where it is. And maybe think of a way to define a miracle and explain why they are rare.

His stomach rumbled. He hoped Rosa had fixed something hot to fill it. A full stomach might ease his doubts about resolving all the problems that faced him.

4

Hector's second night in the Womb passed without incident. if he dreamed, it didn't disturb him. He slipped into his clothes, lit a candle and prayed before the crucifix for help to improve life in San Miguel. When he finished his trip to the outhouse and washed, the eastern sky lightened. A cloudless sky meant another day without rain.

He took his hoe with him to Rosa's. Pedro greeted him at the door and told him Rosa had prepared a hot breakfast before going back to bed. Hector filled his stomach with warm corn mush that satisfied his stomach if not his tongue. Two left-over tortillas topped off his breakfast.

He took his time eating, hinting at the subject of miracles to Pablo, but the old man talked only of last year's poor crop and the dismal prospects for rain in the coming year.

As a dust cloud approached from Pablo's broom, Hector left to join Alejandro and Gustavo. Even fewer men than yesterday headed toward their fields. Half way to where they had worked yesterday, Hector saw Alejandro approaching carrying a shovel as well as a hoe.

"You should be using your time to prepare your sermons," Alejandro greeted Hector.

"I thought you might help me with what to say after we finish clearing the irrigation ditches."

"My sermons don't amount to much," Alejandro frowned. "I just tell people what's right and wrong. No one told me how to find the right Bible passages like you learned to do."

"I also spent a lot of time studying farming."

"Did you grow up on a farm?"

"My father had fields like these. He worked himself to an early death."

Alejandro nodded his understanding. "Gustavo will join us soon. We work our fields together." He sunk his shovel into a ditch to clear a side that had caved in.

Hector dug out debris below the stretch where Alejandro worked. He was warming from the work when Gustavo joined them. "Good morning, Father. Did you sleep well?" Gustavo's grin showed two missing teeth.

"Very well, thank you."

"No, no." Gustavo said. "You're supposed to say 'like a baby'." He laughed until a tear swelled in one eye.

Hector frowned his lack of understanding.

"Because your room is called the Womb," Alejandro smiled. "Is it comfortable enough for you?"

Hector forced a laugh. "The Womb is fine. I almost said like my mother's womb, but I can't remember what it felt like."

From their stares, Hector guessed neither man understood his attempt to joke.

Gustavo changed the subject. "I talked to Manuel on my way here. He's thinking about planting tomatoes this year. Maybe some others will, too. Inez promises that the missionary will spray the fields from a plane and find a truck to take the crop to market."

"What will the missionary charge?" Alejandro asked.

"He promised to do it at cost. We go to the market with him to bargain."

"I'm tempted to try tomatoes myself," Alejandro said. "Even when we have a good harvest of corn and beans, half goes to feeding the mice and birds."

"The mice eat better than we do, Father," Gustavo laughed. "And they don't hoe a single weed."

"Did you ever think about the village going together to build a storage bin? You know, a concrete base. Metal breathing strips. The cost is reasonable."

Alejandro raised an eyebrow.

"The last place I worked built such a bin," Hector said. "One man kept records of who put in how much of their harvest." Hector knew from their looks that he wasn't getting far with his idea, but it was time to plant a seed. He'd fertilize the idea later.

"We've been planting our own corn and beans ever since I can remember," Alejandro said. "Each family has always stored its own." He paused. "Where they can keep their eyes on it." He chortled, "With the birds and mice watching, too."

Hector nodded, then changed the subject. "I'd guess you grew your beans over there," he pointed. "And your corn here."

"That's right. You can see the stalks that the goats missed," Alejandro said. "We plant the corn nearer to the water. The beans hold up better in dry weather."

"Did you ever try planting the corns and beans together?" Hector asked.

Both men shook their heads. Gustavo said, "The corn begs for water before the beans."

"Are you suggesting that we plant corn and beans in the same row?" Alejandro asked.

"In rows next to each other, or beans in the same hole as the corn."

"Won't the beans take the corn's water in a drought?" Alejandro asked.

"Don't plant all your field that way. What about setting aside a patch of land to try it out?"

"I don't understand," Alejandro said. "Our ancestors always planted separately."

"The beans put nitrogen into the soil. Look." Hector went to a few bean stalks and pulled them out. He found a few nodules on the roots and showed them to Alejandro and Gustavo. "These are like little bits of nitrogen that the corn lives on. The fertilizer companies make nitrogen fertilizer and sell it for a fortune. The beans give it to you free!"

Alejandro wrinkled his nose, but Gustavo beamed when he heard 'free.' Gustavo said, "It's like a partnership."

"But what do the beans get out of it?" Alejandro said.

"There are pole beans that use the corn to climb. But you wouldn't have to plant them. Pintos fertilize the corn, too. The beans don't seem to mind that they get nothing from the corn."

"The beans are like Christians," Gustavo said. "Giving away and not worrying about receiving."

"When you eat them, too," Hector said. "Have you heard of protein?"

Both men nodded they had although Gustavo frowned as if uncertain.

"The corn has incomplete protein." Hector tried to remember the words his extension instructor had used to communicate with peasant farmers. "It lacks something called lysine. Beans are full of lysine. So when we eat corn and beans together we get all the protein the corn has as well as what the beans have."

"That's remarkable," Gustavo said. "I've eaten corn and beans as long as I can remember and didn't know they gave me protein."

"And your ancestors long before you."

"Did our ancestors know about this lysine?" Alejandro asked.

"I guess not. But they certainly gave us a wonderful inheritance. We couldn't live by corn alone, and we might never have enough calories if we depended solely on beans."

"Calories?" Alejandro raised an eyebrow.

Hector realized his enthusiasm had raced ahead of their vocabulary. He explained slowly what calories were and hoped he'd given a better understanding of protein, but he doubted his extension teacher would grade him Excellent for his explanation.

Both men seemed to give Hector's ideas some thought. Alejandro finally said, "I still worry about the corn needing water if we have a dry spell. Maybe our ancestors learned that the beans could take too much water."

Alejandro provided Hector with an opportunity to explain more. "Indians knew something about that, too." Hector couldn't remember who deserved credit for the innovation in mulching techniques he'd recently read about so he didn't feel too guilty in crediting early Indians.

Gustavo and Alejandro paid full attention.

"There's a technique called mulching. You gather up whatever is green, even if it's no longer green." Hector couldn't think of any other way to explain 'organic.' "Dried leaves, grass, just about anything that goats eat." Hector wondered if there was anything organic that the goats hadn't eaten. "We put it around the plants, and it holds moisture."

"Is black plastic sheeting mulching?" Alejandro asked. "Inez's husband put it around her tomatoes one year. It kept out the weeds. I don't know if it kept moisture in the ground."

"It's something like that," Hector said. "But plastic sheeting costs a lot. In your free time before planting, you could gather mulching material with no cost."

"But Alejandro won't be able to carve his figures," Gustavo said.

"Does it mean I won't get my new hat?" Hector said to Gustavo.

"Perhaps there will be a rainy day when I can work on it."

"Mulching shouldn't take much time away from your crafts. Especially the first year if you only plant an experimental plot."

Alejandro studied Hector out of the corner of his eye.

Hector tried further explanation. "If you use just a little land for corn and beans together with mulching it won't take much of your time."

"We could start now," Gustavo said. "Our ditches are in good shape."

"How about the day after tomorrow?," Hector asked. "Could we visit the other families and welcome them to mass on Sunday."

"We'll be glad to come with you," Alejandro said.

"My conscience is bothering me because I haven't let people know I'm here."

The two men laughed. Gustavo said, "Everyone has known you were here since you got out of your jeep."

Hector frowned. "How can that be?"

"It's San Miguel, Father," Gustavo said. "What else do we have to do but stick our nose in everyone's business?"

"Gustavo's right. We have nothing else to talk about except who's coming or going."

"Or who was sneaking out of someone else's house while the husband was away."

"Father doesn't want to hear about that, Gustavo."

"I'll hear about it in confession soon enough." Hector laughed with the two of them.

"Shall we go meet these people who will be coming to confession?" Alejandro said.

"As soon as we put our tools away," Hector said. "Let's meet in front of the church in an hour."

The two men left without replying. Hector knew an answer wasn't necessary.

✜ ✜ ✜

Hector gnawed at a beef stick, then washed and put on a clean collar. He dozed a few minutes on the cot. When he woke, he looked at his wrist before remembering he had abandoned his watch as unnecessary, just as in El Hidalgo.

Alejandro waited in front of the church and said they'd join Gustavo at his home. Along the way, Alejandro pointed out two empty houses, explaining the owners had worked elsewhere over the winter months and stayed on their jobs to earn enough money to pay off Rosa.

Hector let the two men select which homes to visit. Gustavo pointed out a small, mostly stone house with a well-kept yard as belonging to Alejandro. They knocked at the house next door where two widows lived. Between them the two were rearing five grandchildren. At the next home, a blind man invited them in and urged them to stay. Alejandro managed to keep the visit short. He later told Hector that a widow provided the man with one meal a day.

After visiting ten of about twenty homes, Hector made a mental census. Four families were headed by grandparents with one or more grandchildren—seven or eight children of school age. Two elderly widows were almost as helpless as the blind man. An elderly widower looked like he'd soon lose a leg to diabetes. Only four of the dozen families could be described as capable of working a farm field year round. At the last house a widow greeted them warmly, insisted they have coffee, and promised to attend mass. She offered to clean the sanctuary when her arthritis got better. Gustavo mentioned how men got together to whitewash the church.

Hector's hopes rose for a cooperative, and he asked what else they had done. Gustavo explained that he had been a boy when the church was painted so he didn't know.

Alejandro added that a miracle led the men to whitewash the church. That gave Hector a chance to ask about other miracles, mentioning that Alejandro had promised to tell him about the one that had determined where the church was to be built.

Alejandro protested that they didn't have much time before nightfall when people no longer visited, but he gave Hector a brief account.

In times before his grandfather, maybe his grandfathers' grandfather, the village was conducting the Christmas *posada*. A bright star lit the way for the procession. They'd almost finished their rounds when a star shot over their heads to lead their way. A bright light appeared on the ground and stayed for days, so the people decided to build a church there. After San Miguel was built, they erected a large crucifix behind the altar. It began to glow. The Madonna stands there now, and sometimes she glows like her Son did.

Hector was bursting to ask why the Madonna had replaced the crucifix, but Alejandro was not to be interrupted. He said he first thought the light around the Madonna was a clever trick of the priests who built the church. They were good at lighting parts of the church with their narrow openings, but there were times when the light could not possibly come from outside.

Hector took a deep breath. Alejandro's description coincided with what the Catholic Church frequently concluded was a miracle. Brilliant light forming a pattern on church walls was a common—well not uncommon—phenomenon in the urban world, documented time and time again. When Alejandro asked if he had ever heard of such a thing, Hector evaded an answer.

He looked at the sky and claimed it was light enough for one last visit. Without thinking, he mentioned Señora Yepiz. Gustavo squinted at Alejandro. "Her home is pretty far away."

"Yes, I know," Hector said. "But we could see how Marta is doing."

"Don't you remember she's Protestant?" Alejandro asked.

"Yes, but everyone is welcome in our church. Her family was Catholic for a long time, no?"

"Inez was, too," Gustavo said. "She switched a few years ago when the Protestant missionary held a revival."

Alejandro stopped and told the two to go ahead.

Once they were beyond Alejandro's hearing, Gustavo said, "Inez and Alejandro were widowed about the same time. Alejandro began courting her. She twisted his arm to move in with her. She said he looked like Don Quixote. Who's he, Father?"

"A man in a novel. Alejandro looks like what I imagine Don Quixote to look like. He was a real gentleman."

"So is Alejandro. Always thinking of others. Maria and Marta think of him as their grandfather."

"What happened then?"

"Alejandro kept waiting for Inez to come back to his church, and she kept waiting for him to become Protestant." Gustavo chuckled.

By this time he and Hector reached the Yepiz home. The two story frame house was out of place in San Miguel, freshly painted, and with metal furniture on the porch. Hector knocked. Minutes passed and he asked Gustavo where Inez might be. "She's in there. Where else could she be? She probably saw Alejandro holding back and is waiting for him to join us."

Hector wondered if Gustavo could be right. Alejandro remained behind on a trail that served on occasion as a road. Hector knocked again. If they waited much longer, they'd be struggling home in darkness.

"Who is it?" Inez asked curtly.

"As if she hasn't been watching us." Gustavo laughed.

"It's Father Hector and Gustavo, Inez. We wanted to see how Marta is and visit a minute."

She opened the door. "Marta is well, thanks. No sign of infection. I'm glad to be able to thank you again, Mr. Cardenas. Is that all?"

"I know you're Protestant, Inez. If you won't call me Father Hector, then please call me Hector. I hope you'll visit with me at the church. You wouldn't let it being Catholic interfere, would you?"

Inez hesitated. "I suppose not."

"Of course you're welcome at services, too. Come to visit old friends if nothing more."

"Then you'll be after my money, I suppose. As if the Vatican coffers weren't full of the world's gold."

"I'll not ask a peso of you, Inez. I promise."

"But you'll want me to testify that I've seen the miracles that San Miguel experienced. I'm tired of doing that!"

"I'm not qualified to investigate miracles. I don't even know if there will be an investigation."

Suddenly, Inez opened the door and stepped onto the porch. She wore what looked to be her Sunday best. Hector heard a footstep on the porch and knew it must be Alejandro. He turned to see Alejandro sweep off his hat, but the man said not a word.

"Good evening, Alejandro. I suppose you've come to invite me to your church."

"Good evening," Alejandro added 'Inez' in a whisper. "It's the Father's church, now."

It hurt Hector to think that Alejandro believed he had been dispossessed.

Before Hector could say anything, he found himself caught in a duel between Inez and Alejandro.

"But you'll be helping him look into the latest miracle, I know."

"What miracle would that be?" Alejandro wore an expression of innocence.

"You know perfectly well. Reverend Johanson cured that man on crutches. You Catholics had nothing to do with it, but you claimed you did. And for once your bishop listened to you. First that spy who stayed overnight. He should have learned that the San Miguel church had nothing to do with it. Then those two investigators taking hundreds of pictures. Only the Vatican could pay for so much film. But they failed to disprove the Protestant's miracle. So now the bishop's sent a priest to take however long is necessary to discredit the Reverend." Inez pushed back strands of hair that had worked loose. "Well, the Reverend will be back soon enough to work more miracles."

Inez turned to Hector. "You, sir, might as well pack your bags. I respect what you did for my daughter, but San Miguel has no further need of you."

Inez glared at Alejandro and slammed the door.

Hector's head spun. He felt as if he, and not Alejandro, had charged a windmill.

5

Alejandro touched Hector's arm as they left the porch. "I'm sorry," he said. "I should have come alone."

"I don't know why Inez should be mad at you," Hector said.

"She shouldn't be mad at any of us," Gustavo said. "She used to be pleasant, until . . ." He glanced up at Alejandro.

"Let's start back," Alejandro said. He turned to Gustavo. "It's in the past, *Compadre*, let's not talk about it." They took a few steps in silence before Alejandro said, "We can't know for sure if the Reverend is to blame."

"Who is this Reverend?" Hector threw up his hands in frustration. "And what did he have to do with the miraculous cure?"

"Reverend Olaf Johanson is a Protestant missionary from Minnesota," Alejandro explained. "Is that a state or a city?"

"A state, I think," Hector replied.

"He showed up a few years ago," Alejandro continued. "He visits other villages, too. He's in San Miguel a few weeks and then gone maybe two or three months."

"The last time he was here, a stranger came from another village," Gustavo couldn't hold back. "He'd crawled part of the way. His knees were bloody. Part of the time he used crutches."

"And what happened?"

Alejandro took a deep breath. "That stranger hobbled around the town until he was sure everyone had seen him. All the people followed him to those footings the Protestant calls his church. The man kneeled before Reverend Johanson. The Protestant prayed and prayed over him. I've never seen a man sweat so much."

"He ran his hands all over the man's legs. He acted like he didn't need God's help," Gustavo said.

"The man moaned and twisted and turned. Some people thought the

Reverend was driving out the devil. At one point the Reverend was speaking in tongues. Like they say in the Bible."

"Or he was speaking English real fast. Who would know?" Gustavo said.

"You sound as if you don't believe the Reverend cured him."

"Who knows," Gustavo shrugged. "We never found out where the man came from or if he had a bad leg."

"He didn't have chest muscles like I've seen on other people using crutches," Alejandro said. "We think Johanson paid him to act crippled, but who knows."

"Inez believed in the cure." Gustavo's words came in a rush. "Half the town came to hear Johanson preach the next Sunday. He carried on about how Jesus saves, but Jesus doesn't save Catholics because they worship the bishop and the Virgin. He called them 'false idols.' Are they idols, Father?"

"Of course not, my Son. I agree with Alejandro. There's cause to be suspicious about this so-called cure." Hector brushed back his hair. "I want to see the foundation for this church tomorrow. Did the Reverend construct it?"

"Mateo and Marco brought the cement and a mixer. They helped pour it," Alejandro said.

"They left half-way through, as soon as their mother went inside." Gustavo held his sides laughing. "At least, they mixed all the cement."

"Inez was over-doing herself pushing a wheel barrel so I took her place," Alejandro said. "The Reverend pays Pablo to help."

"The Protestant is a hard worker," Gustavo said. "He dug out the footings and nailed the forms, then hauled a lot of cement. He has muscles like he might have used crutches," Gustavo laughed at the thought.

"Isn't there more than a foundation?" Hector asked.

Alejandro shrugged. "Well, Inez' sons brought some lumber. Pablo and Johanson started a storage shed, but the Protestant didn't like its shape."

"Are the crutches there? Or leg braces?" Hector tried to remember what the journalists had told him.

"The man left his crutches. Johanson paid Pablo off with the lumber in the storage shed. Pablo thought the crutches were included," Alejandro explained.

"How did you know about the crutches, Father?" Gustavo asked.

Hector told of his encounter with the two journalists.

Alejandro laughed, looked at Gustavo. "I told you not to jump to conclusions."

Gustavo reddened. "I was sure the young one was a prostitute, Father, the way she dressed. I believed the older woman must be a madam. I said to Alejandro that they were foolish to think they could make any money here."

"At least you didn't tell them that," Alejandro chuckled.

"I didn't tell them anything. You did all the talking."

"There wasn't much to say. They'd ask a question and then they'd answer it themselves. I guess they were satisfied with their pictures."

"You may be on the front page," Gustavo looked at Alejandro. "What do you think, Father? Is San Miguel going to be famous?"

"It's already famous for its miracles. Why do you think San Miguel has witnessed so many miracles?"

Gustavo tilted his head at Hector. "San Miguel has had no more miracles than other churches around here. Wouldn't you say, *Compadre?*"

"We might need more miracles because we're so poor." Alejandro reasoned. "But the other villages are just as poor."

"Maybe it's that San Miguel has reported more miracles to the bishop," Hector said.

"We had a committee to write letters about them," Alejandro said. "Inez is good with the pen. She wrote long, beautiful letters until she became a Protestant."

"The other villages don't have anyone like her," Gustavo said.

Hector chuckled to himself. He could assure the bishop he'd completed his assignment. Yet, it didn't seem that simple. There had been miracles long before Inez was old enough to write. Besides, the planting season was weeks off, and Hector wanted to see his innovations in place before he left.

"It's almost dark. I must be back in my Womb before I turn into a vampire." Hector bared his teeth.

Alejandro responded with a blank stare.

By the time Hector explained the European myth, the three were at the church. He asked if they would introduce him to the rest of the village in the morning.

✝✝✝

The next day Hector found the remaining households similar to the first—a few single women with children, planning to join their husbands when their men found steady work, grandparents raising grandchildren, and two more widows who promised to clean the church. The last visit was to a widower so hard of hearing, Hector found himself hoarse after the visit.

Hector invited Alejandro and Gustavo to Rosa's to see if she had anything for a late lunch. Apparently, she'd made a trip to town as well as a pot of coffee. The brew filled the store with its aroma. Hector and his guests gnawed at fresh beef sticks and a bag of potato chips, followed by a can of peaches.

"I haven't had canned peaches in years." Alejandro wiped at his chin with a shirtsleeve.

"I haven't had such a treat since Christmas," Gustavo said. "So many months ago!"

"Hardly four," Alejandro said.

Hector cupped his chin in a hand. "Help me, my friends, with names." He went through a roster in his head, having memorized half the people they had visited.

Gustavo was quick to add the names Hector didn't recall. Hector's face reddened when he realized he didn't know either family name of his friends.

"It's not important," Alejandro assured him. "Gustavo's family is Martinez."

"And his name is Guichoca," Gustavo said.

"I've read that name somewhere," Hector exclaimed.

"I don't know any other Guichocas," Alejandro said. "I can't imagine the name in a book."

"I remember," Hector exclaimed. "Guichoca led the Yaqui against Federal troops."

"You think he could be Alejandro's grandfather?" Gustavo said.

"Or his grandfather's grandfather," Hector said. "Your ancestors probably fled to the mountains after the Yaqui wars."

"That's when we mixed up and lost our Indian languages," Alejandro said.

"My grandparents talked about Mayo ways," Gustavo said. "My father regretted that he didn't learn any Mayo words from his father, but he was proud to be Mayo. I guess that makes me Mayo, but I think of myself as Mexican. Who knows?" Gustavo shrugged.

"It's true," Alejandro said. "Up here we think we're Mexicans, but in town the people look at us like we're dumb Indians. That's when we think we're Indians."

"You should never be ashamed to be Indian," Hector said. "People in Mexico City take pride in being Indian."

Alejandro looked at Hector with narrowed eyes as if doubting his words.

"How can we be proud when many of us can barely read or write?" Gustavo said. "And our children aren't learning anymore than we did."

"Perhaps I could teach the children." Hector regretted his words as soon as he spoke. He knew nothing of how to teach reading and writing. He did not even have paper and pencils.

"The village would be grateful," Alejandro's eyes shone. "The last government teacher left some books, maybe pencils and paper."

"It would be remarkable if our children learned to read and write!" Gustavo beamed at the thought. "Alejandro could help. He studied hard whenever we had a teacher. And Inez helped."

Alejandro blushed while he explained. "Her husband's family sent her to school when their son insisted on marrying her. She completed secondary school."

"That's where she learned to get her own way, too," Gustavo said.

Alejandro clicked his tongue in protest but didn't say anything.

Gustavo changed the subject. "We stored the teacher's things in the Womb when he left. Would you like to see them, Father?"

"Well, I don't know anything about teaching children." I'm here to teach their parents agriculture—and something about miracles, he thought. How do I get out of this?

Before he could think of a way to refuse, the three reached the Womb. Gustavo rummaged in a drawer of the chest and retrieved three candles. Each lit one and perused the four shelves lining the lower part of the wall. The upper shelves were filled with volumes buried in dust, probably church records. The lower shelf held a dozen or so primers, a box of pencils, writing pads, chalk and a chalk board. A wad of papers proved to be government forms, a few half filled out, the others blank.

✞✞✞

Gustavo claimed Hector must be eager to prepare for class so he and Alejandro left. Hector glanced through the school books, bewildered about how or what to teach. He put aside his misgivings to look at what looked to be church records.

The cache did indeed record San Miguel history. A cursory examination showed an assortment of ledgers, some of high quality, others so brittle Hector dared not leaf through them. It looked as if the Jesuits had kept a careful record of their experience.

The earliest volume Hector found was dated 1741. Hector marveled at how the ink and paper had withstood more than two centuries. The flourishes, misspelled words, and water spotted pages made difficult reading, but Hector learned that two Jesuits had been assigned to serve Indians who fled the massacres following the Yaqui and Mayo rebellion of 1740. Remnants of the two tribes had fled to the mountains when Spanish forces occupied their river valleys.

The two Jesuits came from a church farther south named San Miguel. They recorded the ordeal of their journey north and a stay in Alamos whose residents welcomed them until learning they intended to serve Indians. Then, their ensuing hostility made it difficult for the priests to obtain sufficient provisions to settle the new San Miguel.

Hector guessed from their writings that they'd erected a temporary chapel on the ridge above the present fields. The site would have had a commanding view of the valley. In addition to their work on the chapel, they instructed the boys in reading and writing along with the catechism. The two reported introducing wheat and peaches that grew well at the last mission. They'd brought six young trees as well as wheat seeds. The similarity of the early mission's goal to his own bemused Hector. He sneezed when he blew dust from another volume.

It included reports on aboriginal beliefs. Yaqui and Mayo believed in a powerful Male Force and an equally powerful Female Force. The priests described how they equated God and the Virgin with the native cosmos. A powerful snake god also figured in local legend, usually acting as a source of Good. Another legend about floods justified manufacturing wine from cactus. Drinking to the point of oblivion followed. The priests confessed their participation in the ritual and related how they awoke the next day soaked to the skin from an overnight downpour.

In 1744 or 1745 the two scribes nearly lost everything when Chichimecs raided San Miguel after the first ears of corn matured. The raid changed the minds of the two priests about preliminary plans for a church laid out in the usual form of a cross. San Miguel became a rectangle with reenforced corners, thick walls, light entering from high up, and a beamed ceiling covered with earth. Hector searched for further description of plans for light-wells to direct beams toward the altar, but he found nothing.

A later entry showed plans for a round building adjoining the church. A notation said it would serve visitors. Surely, it was the origin of the Womb, but Hector found no hint of its construction.

As his candles burned low, Hector skipped to the last volume, written in 1764, two years before the Jesuit expulsion from Mexico. The handwriting was poor, but Hector became engrossed. The entry indicated that the Indian parishioners were unhappy with the location of the chapel, claiming it disturbed the domicile of Serpent God. The priest readily agreed since it gave him the opportunity to build the fortress-like San Miguel.

When his parishioners made plans to celebrate the winter solstice, the priest convinced them to adapt enough Christian traits that he could call their procession—despite its numerous dances—a *posada*. In parenthesis, the priest admitted giving up on convincing his charges that Mary and Joseph had been refused a place to stay. According to Indian custom, such inhospitality was unimaginable.

A water stain marred the next page, and Hector strained to read. The posada started as the priest anticipated, but half way along the file of dancers veered from where they were to end. The priest rushed to the head of the line, trying to redirect the dancers, but the Indian leaders responded that they had no choice. They were following the light of Jesu Cristo. They had seen Him shining on a rock beyond the fields, just as the star had guided the three wise chiefs.

When they reached a stone the light illuminated, the villagers circled in a vigorous dance. The priest had no choice about locating San Miguel. In a note he wrote the luminescence of the stone had come from insects or he had heard of fungi or moss that on occasion glowed. He guessed one or the other must be the source of the light.

Hector sat breathless, his candles nearly burned out. He'd pursue the records in better light. Surely, at least one priest serving San Miguel had seen giants.

6

Sunday morning dawned as bright and clear as most mornings in San Miguel. Hector waited until eight o'clock before going to the bell tower where Alejandro and Gustavo awaited him.

"Good morning, Father. Did you sleep well? We wondered if we'd have to ring the bell for the Womb to give you birth." Gustavo's smile radiated his good humor.

"I slept well, my Son. And you?"

Gustavo shook his head so hard, he had to grab his hat. Hector noted that his clothes had been brushed if not washed. Alejandro somehow made his old clothes look new.

Alejandro took the bell rope. Hector stepped forward to help, but Gustavo reached ahead of him. "Allow me, Father. My *Compadre* and I are a team."

The bell rang loud and long enough to call villagers from neighboring valleys. Hector waited to greet people at the entrance, but Alejandro took his arm and led him inside. The church was already full.

"You've helped me reach everyone," Hector smiled at Alejandro and Gustavo.

"They are anxious to hear your sermon," Alejandro said. "And to hear how you plan to teach the children."

Hector bit his lip. He'd forgotten his promise to teach.

"Some young people have never seen a real priest," Gustavo added.

Hector had prepared a message about the poor inheriting the earth, but their special place in God's eyes didn't mean He showered them with miracles. He limited what he had planned to say about the nature of miracles because he saw Alejandro turning the pages of an imaginary book. So he announced plans to teach the children four mornings a week until planting time. Timid applause followed murmurs of approval. When he mentioned that he'd also advise farmers, he heard nothing.

Afterwards, Hector looked forward to reading church records and reviewing teaching methods, but villagers kept him on the church steps advising him on what education their children needed. When he assured people he would not charge tuition, the grandmothers promised to attend to make sure their offspring behaved, and young mothers gushed with gratitude. No one mentioned his comments about miracles.

✝ ✝ ✝

The sun was bright as ever Monday morning when Hector finished praying and heard the bell calling the children to school. He hastened to prepare lessons only to find the children already there. The benches were in rows near the entrance where daylight from the open doors provided sufficient light. Someone had built a small desk and chair for him and painted 'teacher" on the front of the desk.

Hector stood behind the desk. "Good morning," he said in the most pleasant voice he could muster, hoping to hide a gnawing fright at the uncertainty he faced.

The children ranged in age from kindergarten to high school. Standing along the walls were grandmothers and two young mothers who were chatting, but no one took their eyes off Hector. He felt Gustavo and Alejandro must be observing him from some dark corner.

When he sat behind the desk, silence flooded the air. He swallowed hard and said, "Who knows the alphabet?" As soon as he asked, he regretted the question, recalling how El Hidalgo children hesitated to stand out or to compete.

"I can say it." The voice was perky and eager, but Hector failed to connect it with a face.

"Who is that?"

A little girl of kindergarten age half hidden by a teenager, raised her hand. Hector didn't have to ask her to say it. The letters rolled off her tongue in a continuous flow.

"That's wonderful, my child. Who taught you the alphabet?"

"My sister, Adela. She knows so much she doesn't have to be here." Adela covered her face with both hands.

"And what's your name?"

"Rachel. And this is Gatita." Rachel held up a striped kitten that she had been holding in her lap. An older woman darted from the side to take the kitten. "Please hold her, Grandma," Rachel pleaded. "Or she'll run away."

"Has Adela taught you your numbers, Rachel?"

Rachel dashed through one to twenty as if the sounds made up a single word.

"Hold up six fingers for me, Rachel," Hector said.

Rachel glanced back at Adela who shrugged.

"Adela hasn't taught me that," Rachel said. "I count to twenty when we play hide and seek."

"How old are you?"

Rachel held up four fingers. Hector smiled. Numbers didn't yet add up for Rachel. He wondered if letters did and asked what words she could spell. She spelled out cat and dog.

When Hector asked if she could spell Rachel, she screwed up her lips and glanced back of Adela. Her sister whispered the letters to her, but instead of repeating them Rachel said, "I want to learn to print the letters, Father. And to write them."

"I'm sure you'll learn quickly, Rachel. Adela is a fine teacher, and she can teach you while she learns from me."

Hector saw hope for the first time. He'd make use of the older students' knowledge by assigning them to help the younger ones while he worked with other older ones. His ideas of lecturing flew out the window.

✠ ✠ ✠

Hector spent the morning matching teams of students. Several older children read well, and one or two could add and subtract. Alejandro appeared out of nowhere and offered to tutor.

Half way through the morning, the women vacated their positions along the walls, but instead of going home they found dust cloths and brooms in a church closet. Hector appreciated how little noise they made while they swept and dusted the sanctuary.

Rachel managed to be by Hector's side most of the morning. She pestered her sister, who wasn't as eager to learn as Rachel. Adela kept suggesting Rachel use Hector's blackboard to learn spelling.

After Hector finished encouraging one team to work on numbers, he turned to Adela and Rachel. Rachel's eyes twinkled even though Hector addressed Adela.

"How old are you, Adela?"

"I'm fourteen."

"What would you like to be?"

"A maid. I could work with my mother in Culiacan. Life is exciting there."

"What if you had your own maid service?"

"What do you mean, Father?"

"You could employ maids and arrange for them to work all over the city. They'd pay you part of what they earned for helping them find work. We call that a percentage."

"I don't know if that would be right," Adela said. "To get paid for doing no work."

"It takes much work, Adela. You'd have to keep records, work out what percentage you earned because of how you work with your head." Hector wasn't sure he reached Adela, but Rachel couldn't contain herself.

"You can help other women from the mountains, Adela. Remember how hard mother's life was until she found that nice woman she works for now."

Adela bit at her tongue. "Would you show me what a percentage is, Father?"

Adela chewed at her lip while Hector illustrated multiplication with percentages of wages. He found that she had memorized much of what she called the times tables. Rachel stood in awe. A few older students drew close when they heard Hector speak of multiplication. They, too, began to revive memories of their times tables. Hector didn't work long with them before they began helping each other.

A rumbling of thunder drew Hector's attention to the door. He smiled when he saw Maria and Marta, took his kerchief from his neck to wipe at sweat, then used the red cloth like a *bandero* to lure a bull. Marta charged at him with fingers on her head to imitate horns. Maria stayed at the door.

"Come in, Maria. You're always welcome."

Maria hissed something at Marta under her breath.

"Does your mother know you're here?" Hector asked.

"She said we could play with the other children," Marta chirped.

"But she doesn't want us coming inside the Catholic Church," Maria said.

"It's not a church, now," Hector said. "It's a school."

Marta dashed to Rachel. "Are you doing the alphabet? Have you learned to spell words?"

Rachel looked up at Adela.

Adela glanced toward the wall to see what her grandmother might say, but the woman had joined the other grandmothers cleaning the church. "I guess it's all right, if it's all right with Father Hector."

Hector reassured her she was welcome.

"I want to learn multiplication, too," Marta said.

"Do you know what multiplication is?" Rachel said.

"It's like if I had four friends and each one of them gave me five goats, I could multiply five times four and get twenty."

Rachel used her fingers trying to add five goats from four friends but had a difficult time.

"How do you do it?" Rachel asked.

"My grandmother is teaching me the times tables."

"Our mother." Maria hadn't let her sister out of her hearing.

"Mama has me memorize two times two is four, two times three is six, two times four is eight."

Marta was about to continue, but Rachel interrupted to repeat after her. "Two times two is four, two times three is six. Then what?"

Marta slowed down and repeated the twos for Rachel.

While she did that, the older sisters spoke in hushed tones. Hector approached them and asked what they would like to learn. They had been asking each other where their relatives were living.

Hector recalled a map of Mexico he had in the jeep and told the girls where to find it. He asked which of the older boys knew how to read a map. A tall lanky youth volunteered. When Adela and Maria returned, Hector spread the map on the floor. Soon the boy and the two girls were engrossed in Mexican geography.

Hector stood in the middle of the room for a moment watching the process he had initiated. He knew he'd have a hard time sustaining the interests of such a diverse group, but for the moment he felt a surge of pride. Certainly the approach worked far better than lecturing.

Another burst of thunder reverberated in the valley. Hector went to the door expecting to see approaching clouds but was disappointed. Gray masses swarmed over mountain ranges in distant horizons hurling lightning bolts in an electrifying display. However, nothing but blue sky covered San Miguel. Hector wiped sweat from his forehead, hoping the humidity foretold a shower. He clasped his hands for a brief petition to God for rain.

A keening wail interrupted his prayer. His mouth dropped open. The sound was too powerful to be made by the children. It came from the depths of the church, and he dashed toward the altar.

Two woman were hugging the Virgin, vying with each other to see who could wail the loudest. The other women gathered around them.

"Her tears were blood," one woman embracing the Virgin called.

"No, she was crying real tears." The other woman screeched even louder.

"I tasted her blood when I licked the tears." The first woman's tone was adamant.

"You're wrong. The tears were salty. I ought to know what tears taste like after all the crying I've done for my children."

"My children have been just as sick as yours. I've done my share of crying. The Virgin's tears this time were blood."

The two gave way to the other women as they crowded around the Virgin to examine her. Soon, all the women were licking at the Virgin's eyes. Her nose, forehead, and cheeks got equal attention from a dozen tongues. Hector's stomach churned. He'd have to report the miracle to the bishop. He imagined the man's disappointment with him.

He turned to find Alejandro by his side. "Has the Virgin been crying?"

"Apparently," Hector sighed. "But there's disagreement on whether the tears were salty or bloody."

"Blood, no doubt." Alejandro's sigh was audible.

"What makes you say that?"

"When she cries blood, it means drought. When she cries tears, it means rain." Alejandro's tone was so matter of fact, Hector had to ask him if the crying wasn't miraculous.

Alejandro raised an eyebrow. "She's just telling us what the weather will be like. Why would anyone think that's a miracle? When she cries blood, it means drought. When she cries tears, it means rain."

As the women became aware of Hector's presence, they backed away from the statue. He and Alejandro stepped forward to examine it. The Virgin's face was covered in saliva. If there had been blood, it had been licked away.

Hector rubbed his fingers over the back of the Virgin's head and examined them. He thought he felt moisture, but when he examined his fingertips, he couldn't see any. He was sure the statue was colder than the air but not cold enough to condense even humid air.

"They were blood." The anger in the assertion hung in the air.

"They were tears." The tone was equally angry. The two women renewed their argument. This time they faced off inches from each other. It wasn't long before one pushed the other.

"You dumb Indian. How would you know?"

"You fat witch. You were lucky you weren't struck dead kissing the Virgin."

Hector's jaw dropped. The last thing he expected was a fight among grandmothers, but two groups of supporters formed behind the two antagonists, shouting epithets seldom heard in church.

The shoving got worse. When Rachel's grandmother bent over to retrieve a broom, Gatita leaped from her pocket. The woman didn't notice as she poked another woman with the broomstick. However, Rachel raced from the makeshift classroom in pursuit, screeching the kitten's name. Adela darted to one side to head off the kitten. The young man who had been teaching her to read a map dashed to the opposite side. Both were calling to the kitten, but their voices could hardly be heard above the din of the women's bickering.

Hector and Alejandro edged between the warring factions of women.

"Ladies," Hector called. "You're in the presence of God."

"They can't hear you. Half are deaf, the other half are too busy settling old scores." Alejandro stood holding his sides, half in disgust, half in amusement.

Hector screamed. "This is the Lord's house! God is watching us."

His admonition worked. An appropriate silence smothered everyone.

Hector breathed a sigh of relief until a shrill voice called from the doorway. "Maria. Marta. What are you doing in this house of idols? How many times have I warned you never to enter the Pope's den?"

Hector called to Inez. "I invited them to school Mrs. Yepiz. It wasn't serving as a church. Then they wanted to see a miracle."

"Humph," Inez retorted. "They'll see miracles enough, soon. Reverend Johanson is on his way. Too bad he couldn't witness the pandemonium you call a church service. He'd say a prayer for you."

7

Hector watched farmers readying ground for planting. He visited several of them suggesting they talk with Alejandro about experimental mulching. Then he joined his two friends to chop the leaves and grass they had collected. He crumbled a handful of dirt and studied it, shaking his head in despair at its sterility. He couldn't believe it sustained a crop year after year.

"I grew only corn here last year," Alejandro said.

"It took a lot out of the soil year after year," Hector nodded.

"Inez gave me a little of the fertilizer she uses. I waited till it rained before I used it. Sometimes the chemicals do more harm than good when there's no water."

"Has Inez said when the Protestant missionary is coming?" Hector had looked at the mountain trail daily since his run-in with Inez at school, but time had passed with no visitors.

"He called yesterday saying he'd come today," Alejandro said.

Alejandro and Gustavo shaded their eyes to stare at the road. "Looks like dust high up," Gustavo said.

"What does Johanson drive?" Hector asked.

"A pickup truck. The last time he was here, the tires didn't have any treads. Are the Protestants too poor to pay him much?"

"There are different kinds of Protestants. Some have more money than others." Hector crumbled another lump of soil searching for signs of life. A small earthworm gave him hope. He worked more leaves into the ground while Gustavo chattered and watched the road.

"It's Inez' oldest sons," Gustavo said. "Mateo and Marco in their Ford Explorer."

"Have they come to help their mother with her field?" Hector asked.

Alejandro shook his head. "The boys are always in a rush. She employs Pedro and Pablo to do her farming."

"With their suits and shiny shoes, her boys won't come near the fields." Gustavo laughed. "No callouses on those hands. Only cocaine."

"We don't know, *Compadre*." Alejandro shook his finger at Gustavo. "Maybe only marijuana."

Gustavo shrugged. "Everybody says so. Where else would they get so much money?"

"We'll go help them unload, Father. If that's all right with you?" Alejandro slung his hoe onto a shoulder.

"I'll go with you. Maybe they'll have news from Culiacan. You did say they're from Culiacan, didn't you?"

For once, Gustavo seemed satisfied with Alejandro's nodding yes.

The three arrived at the Explorer just as Mateo and Marcos opened a side door. The cargo space was filled with a dozen bags of cement.

"How are you, *Compadres*?" The tallest one half smiled. He looked at Hector through slitted eyes. "Who's your friend?"

"This is Father Hector," Alejandro said. "Mateo," he gestured toward the tall one, "And Marco."

Both men shook Hector's hand. "I understand you're living here," Mateo said.

"That's right," Hector said. "I don't know for how long."

"How can you serve such a small town when there's a shortage of priests?" Mateo studied Hector's face while he replied.

"I'm an agricultural missionary. Learning what I can here and carrying the results elsewhere."

"Must be an exciting life." Marco didn't try to hide his sarcasm.

"San Miguel has an interesting history. From the church records and what people tell me, it's an exciting place."

"Whatever," Marco muttered.

"What's new in Culiacan?" Hector asked.

"Much the same," Mateo said. "All sorts of rumors about people being shot. The violence is exaggerated."

"Just like the rumors about the city being a drug center," Mateo said. "What nonsense."

Before Hector could ask anything else, Inez waved and called. "How are my little boys?"

"We've brought the cement for your friend, Mama. We're waiting for Pablo to unload."

"I've started supper for you two." Inez descended from her porch and hugged the two men. "It's been a long time since we ate together."

"Mama, I told you on the phone that we couldn't stay." Marco had a whine in his voice.

"I know how busy you are. But you can't let those pharmaceutical companies run all over you. Surely you can find time for your mother."

"The next time, Mama," Mateo said.

"You say that every time." Inez's eyes flashed.

"We're way behind, Mama. Where's Pablo?"

"He's hurt his back. I ordered him to rest. You'll just have to stay."

"What about you, señores?" Mateo looked at Alejandro and Gustavo. They looked at Hector. He gestured it was up to them.

"I'll give you 100 pesos each. How's that?"

The two men hesitated.

"How about you, padre?" Mateo nodded to Hector. "Will that violate your vows of poverty?" His tone was cynical.

"Why can't you boys unload the cement?" Inez waved a finger at her sons.

"Mama, we've had to dress for business. We can't show up at a pharmacy or a doctor's office covered in cement dust."

"If I help out, will you pay Alejandro and Gustavo 200 pesos each but nothing for me." Hector guessed Mateo was anxious to leave. "That way I can keep my vow of poverty." His tone answered Mateo's cynicism.

"Whatever," Mateo grumbled. "We've got to be in Hermosillo before dark. A lot of people to call on in the morning."

"Oh, you two work so hard," Inez whined. "Can't you take some vacation time and visit me? The Reverend will be coming soon. He'll need help pouring the footing. You did so much for him the last time."

"You best hire help, Mama," Marco said. "We'll send money."

Mateo took his mother's hands. "Business is stacked up right now. We've got competition you wouldn't believe. Drug companies from the south are crowding Culiacan."

"All right," Inez sighed. "Put the sacks where they won't get wet."

"Mama, it hasn't rained in weeks. Why can't we unload them right here?" Marco shook his head in impatience.

"Stack them so I can cover them with a tarp if it should rain. After all, it is the beginning of the rainy season."

Mateo glanced at his watch. It looked as expensive as the clothes the two men wore. He turned to Alejandro. "I'll give the two of you five hundred each if you'll unload the damn stacks and then put 'em where Mama wants them."

"You watch your language, Mateo. What if Reverend Johanson were here?"

"Okay, Mama. I'm sorry." He turned to Alejandro. "Drop the sacks here. We'll get the van out of your way, and then carry them where she wants them." He turned to Hector and said under his breath. "You going to hold services in the new church, padre?" He chuckled and Hector laughed with him. Mateo didn't look like anyone to offend.

Hector reached into the van and tugged at a bag of cement. He dragged it to the edge of the Explorer floor, then grabbed both ends, and lowered it to the ground. It was heavier than he anticipated, and he wondered how long his back would hold up.

"Pardon me, Father." Gustavo was hauling out a second sack. Hector turned back to do his share.

"What if I pulled out the bags and passed them to Gustavo," Alejandro said. "You could stack them to make it easier to lift again, Father."

"Good idea, my Son." Hector smiled. It was the first time Alejandro addressed him as father.

While they were unloading, Mateo and Marco talked with their mother about all their customers and how relentless their pharmaceutical company was about keeping appointments. When Hector stacked the last bag of cement, he joined Alejandro to shut the van's doors.

Alejandro pointed to the space beneath the front seat. "What kind of rifle is that?"

Hector gasped. "It's a sawed-off shotgun."

Mateo peeled off five, one hundred peso notes from a roll of bills and handed them to Alejandro. Inez insisted on embracing her sons before they left. She stood waving to the back of the van until it was out of sight.

"I'll have to throw out the supper I prepared for those two if you gentlemen won't join me," Inez said. She was quick to add, "After you finish stacking those bags so I can cover them."

"Thank you," Gustavo said. "But my wife is expecting me."

"I'd never turn down a meal of yours," Alejandro said.

"And you, Señor Cardenas? Will you join us?" Hector hesitated. He wondered if Gustavo had declined to allow Alejandro to dine alone with Inez.

"Please join us." Alejandro could not have been more sincere. "Come over to my house after you've rested."

"I'd be happy to. I haven't had a home cooked meal in a long time."

"We'll wash up and come back before it gets dark," Alejandro said to Inez. "If that's all right with you?" He looked at Hector.

"That's fine."

Inez nodded to Hector. She smiled at Alejandro and wiggled her fingers in an intimate wave.

✞✞✞

Hector laid on his cot to rest his back a few minutes before scrubbing his face and hands. Dust from the cement had worked into his hair. He decided the streaks of gray added ten years of dignity and didn't bother to brush his hair, substituting his fingers for a comb.

He walked over to Alejandro's and knocked. Alejandro called for him to enter. The front of the house was divided into a kitchen area and living room by a rough wooden table with four chairs. A bedroom stretched across the back.

Hector sat on a dining table chair. "Is Inez a good cook?"

"One of the best. If she feels like cooking," Alejandro called from the bedroom. "She learned while a maid in Culiacan. They say the son of the house couldn't resist her soups."

"How long have you known her?" Hector asked.

"We played together as kids. Went to school the few years government sent a teacher. She was the star pupil."

"She impresses me. Except I wonder why she has let the Protestant missionary influence her so much?"

"He's a good talker and knows what she wants to hear. Preaches a lot about men and women being equal. Inez believed no one here listened to her because she's a woman."

"What did she want you to do?"

"She thought we should all plant cash crops even though her husband died from the chemicals."

"But you seem to trust her judgement."

"Not on tomatoes." Alejandro shook his head. "Then the Protestant showed up and promised to spray them from an airplane so no one would be poisoned. But we had to promise to join his church."

"You've kept people in the church despite the promises." Hector put an arm on Alejandro's shoulder.

Alejandro shrugged. "I do my best."

The two walked to Inez's in silence. Hector realized it signified acceptance.

At Inez's house, Hector noticed details he'd missed the first time he saw it. A tiled patio, bounded by a wall, extended beyond the porch. Half a dozen large pottery jars held a variety of flowers. A few garish ornaments nailed to the wall suggested they might be gifts from her sons.

Alejandro knocked once. Inez opened the door before he could knock a second time. Her hair was pinned in a bun atop her head. She wore a floral patterned dress that looked freshly ironed. "Come in." Her smile radiated at Alejandro, but Hector felt welcome, too. Inez exuded warmth.

Maria and Marta ran to Alejandro. Marta grabbed his leg and smiled at Hector.

Maria took Alejandro's hand and curtsied to Hector. "Good evening, Mr. Cardenas."

"You both look lovely this evening," Hector said. Before he could add more, Inez shooed the girls upstairs.

"Your cooking smells as good as ever," Alejandro said.

A hint of roast beef caught Hector's nose. Unidentified spices mixed with the aroma.

"It's just my beef stew. Rosa didn't have any better piece of beef, and stew's a favorite of Mateo's." She gestured to a sofa and invited the two to sit. A matching easy chair sat at right angles to the sofa. An expensive, well polished dining table with eight chairs occupied the other end of the room.

Alejandro sat at one end of the sofa. Hector studied a wall filled with framed photographs. He recognized Mateo and Marco as youths. Their picture was in black and white with hand colored features added.

He was studying one of a tall man with fine, almost feminine features that made him look like a movie star, when Inez startled him. "That's my Lucas. He's an agent in Mexico city. He doesn't have any movie stars under contract yet, but he makes contacts for dozens of artists."

Hector suppressed a smile as he recalled Gustavo telling him that Lucas was a pimp.

He looked at another picture. The man was short, pox marked, going bald at a young age. He wore a cockeyed grin.

"Juan is a brilliant mathematician. But he's unlucky. He has a part-time job as a university professor and tutors private students. You wouldn't believe how many parents fail to pay him. But when a parent is honest, he sends me money."

Juan must be the gambler selling lottery tickets, Hector guessed.

Hector was about to turn away when a small photo caught his eyes. The young man's eyes had an ardent quality even in a photo.

"That one's her Judas," Alejandro pointed.

Hector did not know what to make of the comment.

"Oh, Alejandro," Inez hissed at him."You know I don't mean it." She turned to Hector. "Jesus hasn't come home since he left because of a blowup with his brothers. He writes me at Christmas, but he hasn't visited. So I joke about him betraying me, but he'll always be my baby."

"I'm sure he'll return some day." Hector touched her arm.

"When I despair about him, I think of the prodigal son."

"Good for you, Inez." Hector said. Alejandro put a hand on her shoulder.

Hector studied another grouping. "They look ambitious. You must be proud of them."

"They've gone north to farm in the United States." Inez bit at her lower lip. "They send money, but they can't come back because of the bureaucracy." She took a breath. "Don't think they're illegals. I insisted they get the proper papers. I won't have the Yepiz name shamed."

"That's good of you to honor your husband's name." Hector could think of nothing else to say.

"Not just my husband. His parents were good to me. When they found out their son was going to marry me, they never again thought of me as their maid. I suspect they came from humble backgrounds, but they became part of high society in Culiacan, I can tell you that."

"What did your father-in-law do for a living?" Hector asked.

"He had a degree in agronomy, I want you to know. Bought his own farm. One of the first to ship cash crops to the United States—you know, tomatoes, cucumbers, strawberries. The Americans couldn't get enough of them."

"His father must have been a farmer, too," Alejandro said.

"Possibly inspired by a teacher like you." Inez looked at Hector. "He farmed when Lazaro Cardenas was president."

"Our hero," Alejandro said. "I heard stories when I was a child about how Cardenas fought corruption in the government and redistributed land."

"He must be your hero, too, Mr Cardenas?" Inez asked.

"Yes, because of his name even if we're not related. But most important he stressed honesty and equality. He made things better for workers as well as farmers."

"An unusual politician," Inez said.

"Well, he used the organizations he created to make his political party more powerful. It's one reason we've never had much of a two party democracy."

"But, there's democracy within the party," Inez countered.

Hector shrugged. He didn't want to go into all the arguments he'd had in the university about what kind of democracy was good or bad for Mexico.

Inez must have guessed Hector wanted to change the subject. "Won't you gentlemen come to the table while I look at my stew?" She smiled at Alejandro. "Would you open the wine, Ando? There's a bottle in the kitchen."

Hector heard giggling from the kitchen until a cork popped. Inez came into the living room with a serving bowl of salad and another of stew. Alejandro followed with three glasses and a bottle. He poured the wine while Inez served slices of jicama.

"I apologize for the wine. It's all Rosa could find. I wanted to surprise my sons, but I'm happy to have two such handsome gentlemen as you." She gazed at Alejandro.

"To your health." Hector raised his glass. The three clinked glasses and sipped the wine.

"It's good," Hector said. "But I'm no connoisseur. The only difference I recognize is between red and white."

Inez giggled. "Ando is the same." She batted her eyes at Alejandro. "Aren't you?"

"Is there a difference between red and white?" Alejandro joked.

The three laughed. Inez took a long sip. Hector did no more than taste his. Alejandro drank little more than Hector.

"You set a fine table, señora. The stew smells very rich." Hector's mouth watered.

"Help yourselves," Inez downed her wine waiting for the two men to serve themselves. Alejandro refilled her glass.

"Do you remember how we played as children?" Inez looked at Alejandro. "Why don't the children play the way we did? My daughters are alone so much."

"None of the children play the way we did. Maybe it's because their fathers are away," Alejandro said. He poured a little wine for himself, more for Inez. Hector covered his nearly full glass with his hand when Alejandro gestured with the bottle.

Inez's eyes misted. "It's because people don't like me, isn't it? It's wrong for them to take it out on my girls."

"No, no," Alejandro protested. "Everyone likes you."

"They hate me because of my big house." Inez downed the rest of her wine. "I wouldn't live here, but my sons insist. Besides, my daughters are used to it."

Alejandro poured her the last of the wine. "People don't hate you." He put a hand on hers. "You're one of us."

"You've always been so kind." Inez gazed at him.

The three finished their jicama and the stew in silence.

"I have a plain pastry for dessert," Inez said.

Alejandro rose when Inez did, and the two cleared the table.
"It's Marco's favorite," Inez said. "I hope it's passable." Inez mumbled on her way to the kitchen. She returned carrying a tray with three servings.

Alejandro praised the pastry and Inez's coffee while they finished. Inez was about to stand when a thunderclap rattled the windows. She stifled a shriek.

The three went to the living room window. A dozen large drops hit the panes, but the rain stopped as quickly as it began. In the distance, a lightening display played over the mountain tops. Alejandro edged toward Inez until their arms touched. She dropped her head to his shoulder as they watched.

Maria and Marta came half way down the stairs. "Is it going to pour down? Will it end the drought?" Maria voiced hope. "Can we watch with you?" Marta said.

"It stopped before it started," Inez said to them. "But don't worry. Reverend Johanson will bring rain when he comes."

"When will that be, Mama?" Maria asked.

"He phoned me this morning. He said he'd be coming any day now to lead us in prayers for rain."

Just what I need, Hector thought. If he ends the drought, it will be another miracle for the Protestant. What do I report to the bishop?

8

After another week without rain, Hector stepped outside to study the sky. He had introduced long division to the older students and their interest in it impressed him. Other students were teaching times tables to their younger charges. He glanced at the Yepiz home and wondered what Inez was teaching Maria and Marta.

Half a dozen lightning strikes in the mountains distracted him. He mumbled a prayer for rain thinking of Alejandro and Gustavo who had mulched parts of their fields. Their demonstration plots could use rainfall as much as the other fields.

Two of the highest mountains bathed in a downpour as gray clouds turned black and touched the peaks. Hector wondered if either mountain supplied the flow of San Miguel's spring. At least, some villages in the area would benefit from the bounty.

Before he turned back, a dust cloud rising above the road drew his attention. He wondered if Rosa was returning from a trip to town or if Mateo and Marco were paying another visit. He could taste the dust in the air even as the cloud hung a mile from the village.

He felt a burst of pride when Adela asked how to divide a smaller number by a larger one. It was the first time she had shown any interest beyond memorizing what he taught. He explained how one could have numbers less than one by reviewing fractions before introducing percentages.

✝✝✝

Hector became so absorbed with the students' interest that he forgot the dust cloud. When school ended, he stepped outside to see a pickup truck with a camper rumble over the cobblestones in front. A stranger headed toward Inez' home, stopping at the site of the yet to be built Protestant church.

Hector munched an energy bar before going to meet the driver he assumed was the Protestant missionary. He rehearsed in his mind what to say, wanting to appear friendly. Above all, he didn't want to offend Inez.

The stranger was unloading rolls of plastic sheeting. He glanced at Hector but did not interrupt his work. Hector decided to out-wait him, took a deep breath, crossed his arms, and stood still watching. The man removed Inez' tarp and covered the sacks of cement with plastic sheets.

When he finished, he turned to Hector. "Well, Padre, what can I do for you? Beside pray for your soul."

Hector hadn't expected sarcasm. "Thank you. I welcome any prayer I can get. I'm Hector Cardenas. You must be Reverend Olaf Johanson."

"I am indeed, Padre." Johanson slurred the word, Padre. "Inez told me you had invaded my territory."

"All territory is God's territory, my Son." Hector hesitated to call Johanson, my son, but since the man called him Padre, Hector reciprocated, injecting an equal dose of sarcasm into son.

The man turned his back on Hector while he tidied the rolls of plastic. The man's long, square chin raced a jaw to the ground. It reminded Hector of a bulldozer blade. A sparse moustache of dirty blond hair did little to divert attention from the over-sized jaw. Hector couldn't help thinking—the jaw bone of an ass—not the four legged kind.

When Johanson turned to Hector, he took off a wide brimmed straw hat which shaded a pink skin that refused to tan. Liquid blue eyes snared Hector's in a hypnotic trap. Hector shook his head to evade the stare and studied a blazing red scar stretching from Johanson's forehead to his left cheek. Hector wondered how the man had managed to keep his eye.

"God watches over drunks and children," Johanson said.

"I beg your pardon." Hector could not phantom Johanson's comment.

"My father was a Lutheran missionary in Minnesota. Served the Ojibwa heathens—though he converted very few. I was a devout son. Until my teens." He paused for dramatic effect. "I ran off to a circus." He paused to laugh. "An aerial circus. Soon I was flying biplanes in crazy stunts. Wowed the ladies. The devil won my soul with whisky and wild women." He studied Hector to gage his reaction. "I suppose you don't know anything about wild women, Padre."

"Not much on whisky either." Hector was tempted to share some of his own upbringing with Johanson, but his adolescence was so tame in comparison that he held his tongue. When Johanson said nothing more, Hector asked. "And the scar? A fight over women?"

Johanson laughed. "No, although that would have been better." He looked lost in thought for a moment. "I'd just finished stunts that few others would try. Can you believe it? I hadn't studied the field on take-off. Missed seeing a telephone line on landing. Course, I'd had a nip from the devil's bottle." Johanson gazed into nothingness.

"And," Hector prompted.

"And my wheels tangled in the line. Flipped the plane upside down, and I landed wheels up." He roared with laughter. "Not a good practice in an open cockpit."

"You were lucky to survive."

"I realized Jesus was leading me to God. Not that meaningless Lutheran doctrine of my father but by personal witness. In no time I found Jesus, and I haven't strayed from his path since."

"An intriguing story."

"I've saved more souls than I can remember. I confess," he snickered. "I may be sinful vain counting the number of saved souls."

"God forgives you, I'm sure," Hector mumbled not knowing what else to say.

"How about you, Padre. Aren't you proud of the souls you've saved?"

"I think it's the Lord who saves souls. I just try to direct people toward Him."

"Well put." Johanson sneered. "But be truthful now. Recall all the truth I laid on you." His eyes enveloped Hector. "The Pope sent you here to drive me out of the highlands. Isn't that right?"

"Not at all," Hector said, considering how to explain his mission to Johanson.

"Why else would the Church pay you to live here except to keep reins on the people?"

"The people here have been without missionaries for two centuries. They developed a need for frequent miracles to prove their faith. I'm here to show them that faith comes from integrity, devotion, and conscience. They don't need constant miracles."

"Are you saying you won't be here long?"

"I'm also here to teach new methods in agriculture. To make them independent in their livelihood."

"And to keep me from making converts." Johanson's voice glared defiance as much as his eyes.

Hector saw little hope for compromise so he changed the subject. "Looks like you've got a lot of work cut out for you as well as soul saving." He gestured to the bags of cement.

"Yes. San Miguel is central to a half dozen villages I serve. Since I can't build a church in each one, the Lord picked San Miguel." He sneered. "Would you like to help?"

"Sorry, I'm helping to plant."

"If it ever rains." Johanson looked at the sky. "It will take a miracle for rain to fall on San Miguel." His chuckle was sinister.

Hector felt such discomfort with Johanson that he excused himself while Johanson rolled up his sleeves.

✟✟✟

A day later, Hector jointed Alejandro in his field. The two hoed under leaves and brush the goats had overlooked. Alejandro took off his hat and waved it in front of his face. "It's warm enough to plant. If only it would rain."

"Can you save the seeds until next year?" Hector was familiar with how seed fertility rates dropped after a year.

"It's all we can do." Alejandro sighed. "Do you think in such drought, it's a good idea to plant beans and corn together? What if the corn sucks the water away from the beans?"

Hector sympathized with Alejandro. Innovation in a stressful situation took courage. "You could plant less than you intended to in your experimental plot."

"Gustavo was thinking he might do that. We'll discuss it when he gets over his stomach troubles."

"You might cut back a little on the fertilizer that we planned. It will burn if there's not enough water."

"I planned for less fertilizer." Alejandro's brow furrowed. He looked at the sky. "If only it would rain."

Before Hector could say anything, Alejandro turned to the road leading into San Miguel. Swirling dust announced another visitor.

"I suppose Mateo and Marcos are coming to help the Protestant," Hector said.

77

"They're early then. The missionary has more work to do." He laughed. "Mateo and Marcos time their arrival to get here after work is finished."

"How does their mother like that?"

"Inez can give a tongue lashing, but she always forgives her sons."

"What kind of mood has she been in?" Hector asked.

"She feeds the Protestant when he's here so I haven't seen her. I can't stand that man's eyes. In the old days they'd call him a witch. Besides he's always after me about seeking the Holy Ghost. He says you can't be saved without experiencing the Holy Ghost." Alejandro squeezed his temples as if he had a headache.

The two turned to watch the dust. The sight parched Hector's throat. A sedan, not meant for mountain roads, parked before the church, and a figure mounted the steps.

"I'd best go find out who it is," Hector said. "I'll see you tomorrow."

As Hector drew near the church, he was surprised to see Edwardo.

"It's a miracle my car made it up this road," Edwardo called. "I forgot what an obstacle course it is."

"You're too early to help plant. You'll have to stay a few days."

Edwardo grimaced. "Good thing I brought an air mattress. I'd hate to drive that road twice in one day."

Hector reached out a hand. They shook before grasping each other in a hug. Hector almost reached to grip Edwardo by the head but thought better of it when he saw two women watching.

"It's good to see you," Hector said. "But if you're not here to plant, what brings you?"

"The bishop insisted you must be out of toilet paper. He sent me with a carton and a prayer for your hemorrhoids."

Hector laughed. "I am down to my last. My last roll, not my last hemorrhoid. If you hadn't come, I'd be wrestling goats for tree leaves."

Edwardo pretended to gag. "The trunk is filled with energy bars and jerky. But the real reason the bishop sent me is to find out how you're doing. He hasn't received word of a single miracle since he sent you."

"I haven't been here that long," Hector protested. He worried that the bishop might cut short his assignment.

The two carried boxes from Edwardo's trunk to the Womb. Edwardo made a second trip to retrieve two jugs of wine meant for communion. He got a transistor radio from his glove compartment.

"I can't believe this sky. I don't see blue like this in the city. A few days off from cultivating rich widows is a blessing."

"Before you come next time, cultivate some nuns who teach, and scrounge school supplies for me. You wouldn't believe how eager the children are to learn."

"I don't recall the bishop directing you to teach."

"Of course teaching is part of my mission. I have to introduce science to better understand miracles."

Edwardo shrugged. "If you say so. I'll scrounge school supplies behind the bishop's back, but a nun is out of the question." He handed Hector the radio. "I thought you might want to keep in touch with the world. I meant to bring a cell phone, too."

"Thanks for the radio. I didn't have a cell phone in El Hidalgo and enjoyed being out of touch. Señora Yepiz has one if there's an emergency."

"Imagine Indians up here using cell phones." Edwardo shook his head.

"She's educated and has sons in the city who brought it."

"Anything else you could use? The bishop's truly interested in your work."

"You could ask him to pray for rain. We've had good rainfall in the surrounding mountains but none here."

"You expect a miracle from the bishop?" Edwardo gave a half cocked grin. "Seriously," he said. "How are you discouraging your congregation from experiencing miracles."

Hector motioned Edwardo to sit on the cot. He sat on the floor. "You don't need to tell the bishop this. You've seen what a miraculous place it is up here—the sky, the air. It affects the people who live here."

Edwardo frowned incomprehension.

Hector continued. "Centuries ago a miraculous light showed the people where to build the San Miguel church. The two Jesuits who were here weren't convinced the light was a miracle, but they saw it and their attempts to explain it as natural are laughable."

Edwardo nodded his head, but a cocked eyebrow showed skepticism.

"Alejandro and Gustavo are convinced a giant helped build the church.

You know there's often truth behind oral history."

Edwardo wrinkled his nose, then his face paled. "I recall reading about giants up here in a history of highland missions. Sixteenth century I think, farther south. Half a dozen Jesuits independently reported giants roaming the land. A psychology professor referred me to an article on mass hysteria. It could have been an epidemic of hallucinations."

"A miraculous place inspiring miracles," Hector said.

"You mean illusions of miracles, don't you?," Edwardo countered.

Hector shrugged in reply.

"But what about the recent miracle cure. A man on crutches, wasn't it?" Edwardo squirmed on the cot to get comfortable.

"Yes. A Protestant missionary probably faked a cure."

Hector told Edwardo about his meeting with Olaf Johanson.

"Hmm," Edwardo frowned. "I wasn't going to tell you this, but the bishop thinks you'd be perfect for a vacancy that's coming up next month."

"No." Hector's face flushed. "I've got work to do here. Five months minimum."

"Well, the bishop is impressed with what you've done. If you don't encounter anymore miracles, I might be able to convince him to let you stay."

"You've got to. I'm needed here," Hector pleaded.

Edwardo chewed on his tongue. "No more Dutch Rubs, promise?"

The two laughed.

Edwardo stroked his chin. "Perhaps this Protestant can help the cause. The bishop won't want to retreat before a Protestant." The prospect of competition didn't appeal to Hector, but it did look like an opportunity. "Johanson has made inroads by converting Inez Yepiz. She's influential if not always liked."

"Let me be sure of what I can tell the bishop. A Protestant missionary is proselytizing San Miguel. He looks to be a threat. Also, since you've started an education program, there have been no miracles."

"Well, there may have been one," Hector hesitated. "Or not."

"Oh great. I can report there have been no miracles or maybe there have. Will you please explain."

"The first day I was teaching, all the grandmothers came to watch. When they got tired of supervising, they started cleaning the church. After a while I heard, 'It's blood, no, it's tears'."

"You had a Virgin crying," Edwardo sighed. "It's in the category of miracles. How'd you check it out?"

"By the time I got to the statue the women had kissed her so much she looked to have stepped out of a shower. I did touch the back of the statue. It was cold and the air humid, but I didn't feel any moisture."

"So was it blood or tears?" Edwardo chortled.

"It was a battle. Alejandro told me it set off old grudges between the women. I did get everyone calmed down before blows were exchanged."

Edwardo chuckled. "Any chance someone will tell the outside world? Otherwise, I don't see any need to inform the bishop."

Hector nodded agreement. "It's weird. Alejandro witnessed everything. He saw nothing out of the ordinary. The Virgin simply predicts the weather, nothing miraculous about that." Hector shrugged.

"What does it take to make a miracle?" Edwardo said.

"I'm far from sure. But one reason so many miracles occurred here is that Inez Yepiz used to report them. She's good with a pen."

"What's holding her back, now? Your education program?"

"No," Hector sighed. "She's the woman who turned Protestant. Any miracles henceforth are likely to be Protestant miracles."

"Has this Protestant made many converts?"

"Only Inez. But if Olaf comes up with an honest-to-goodness miracle, like a good downpour, he'll convert a lot more."

"Is Johanson sponsored by one of the denominations or does he free lance?" Edwardo asked.

Hector shrugged. "I didn't ask. He's very independent. Maybe even unstable. How you'd like to meet him?"

"I wouldn't, but I guess I should if I'm going to make him out to be a major threat. Where's he live?"

"While he's here, he sleeps in a camper on his pickup. Inez feeds him at her place."

"That's ominous. At least it will be when I report it to the bishop."

✝✝✝

When the two priests reached the camper, they heard a radio and assumed Johanson was listening to it.

"Hate to wake him if he's sleeping," Hector said. "He's put in a hard day's work judging from those footing frames."

Just then, Johanson tuned his radio. Through the static they heard a weather forecast, announcing a good chance of rain later in the week. Hector clapped Edwardo on the back. "You may have brought us rain."

Johanson must have heard the two priests. He opened the door to his camper and stepped to the ground.

"Well, if it isn't Hector the Rector." He looked at Edwardo, then back to Hector. "I see the Pope has sent reinforcements."

The confrontation tensed Hector's shoulders. Edwardo stepped forward to shake hands and introduce himself. His suave manners disarmed Olaf, and Edwardo learned that Olaf financed himself, in small part by what supporters contributed, and in large part by aerial crop dusting. Edwardo steered the conversation to probe Johanson's attitudes on a variety of other matters until Inez called him to dinner. Johanson excused himself with a brief nod to Hector.

"What was that interrogation all about?" Hector asked his friend.

"A few questions from a pop psychology survey on mental health."

"And the results?"

"Your friend is mad as a hatter," Edwardo said. "But then, the bishop didn't do much better so I wouldn't rely too much on the test."

9

Alejandro and Gustavo had scoured the hills to gather leaves and grass. Hector was helping them work the organic matter into their demonstration plots when a flash of lightening interrupted. Menacing clouds skirted San Miguel. Darker ones spewed the foothills and neighboring valleys with steady rain.

"Our prayers have not been devout enough," Gustavo said.

"If God answered every prayer for rain, we'd be building another ark." Alejandro wiped his brow.

"God could be testing our faith. It's remarkable to see all this rain around us and not a drop falls here." Gustavo glanced at Hector.

"Remember the patience of Job," Hector said. "The source of the spring must be in one of those mountains that is getting rain. At least, we'll have its water."

"It's a mysterious source, Father," Gustavo said. "A couple of times the weather was like this, and the spring dried up."

"What did you do?"

"More men left," Alejandro said.

"Many families went hungry." Gustavo rubbed his stomach and sighed.

Hector bowed his head. He wished Edwardo had stayed longer. He'd have a more satisfactory reply for his friends.

"Perhaps Reverend Johanson can bring rain," Gustavo said. "What do we have to lose if he fails?"

"What's he planning?" Hector swallowed hard. He started to tell them about Johanson listening to weather forecasts but decided against it.

"Tomorrow he's going to have a revival. Inez told everyone she'll feed them her beef stew. The whole village will turn out." Alejandro looked at Hector. "She's expecting you, too."

Thoughts of China's rice Christians raced through Hector's mind. He couldn't believe missionaries still spread their faith through people's stomachs. Yet, in a way that's what I'm hoping to do, Hector thought. He changed the subject. "How many more days before the rainy season ends?" he asked.

Alejandro squinted, obviously thinking Hector must know, but he replied, "Two weeks at most. The corn won't have much time before frost."

"I think you should plant," Hector said. As soon as he spoke, he reconsidered. "But it really is up to you."

His two friends shrugged. They'd been making such decisions their whole lives.

✝✝✝

The next morning, Hector woke to a crash of thunder. He rushed to his door to discover the sky covered by ominous, blackening clouds. A lightening flash made him blink. The time it took for the thunder to reach him suggested the lightening had been on the mountains. He finished dressing, washed, then recalled it was the day of Inez' feast. He wondered if rain would force her to postpone it and how Johanson could take credit if it arrived before his revival.

Since there was little to do and the possibility of rain, Hector wrote to a friend and pondered over how many might convert if Johanson brought rain. He tuned his radio to a news station. A meteorologist forecast a ninety percent chance of rain in the highlands. Hector's heart sank. God was siding with Johanson. Still, Hector muttered a prayer of thanks for the clouds and the prospect of rain.

The clouds spit out sparse drops at noon. Hector made his way to the Yepiz home, one eye on the sky another searching for Alejandro or Gustavo. He saw Alejandro helping Inez cover a table with an oil cloth. As he got close, he realized all the villagers had turned out. The elderly men stood around the least able who sat on a bench. The grandmothers were divided into two groups, and Hector wondered if they were the factions who had battled over the tears being blood or water. Young women either watched children or stirred pots.

Inez waved a greeting to Hector when he reached the table and gestured for him to sit.

"Where is your plate, Father?" Gustavo asked. "And your spoon?"

Hector stammered that he didn't realize he should furnish utensils. Gustavo looked baffled. His wife slipped away.

"I'll go back to the church and get them," Hector said.

Before he could get up, however, Gustavo's wife reappeared with a chipped plate, a tin cup, and a serving spoon. She handed them to Hector.

Alejandro came to tell Hector that Inez expected him to be the first to serve himself. Puzzled, Hector asked why the honor wasn't reserved for Johanson.

"He's fasting," Alejandro said.

Hector froze. He guessed Olaf was playing on an Indian custom. He'd be feasting while Johanson was sacrificing himself for the village. What more can I do wrong? he thought.

Alejandro nudged Hector to start. Inez had decorated the serving table with twisted crepe paper in swirls of red, white, and green. The first item was a mountain of tortillas, their aroma mixing with that of beef stew. Hector's mouth watered as he reached for a tortilla.

"Take two or three," Alejandro advised. "Inez provides the flour, but all the women made tortillas the whole morning."

"Did you help with the stew?" Hector said.

"Johanson's not eating so I stayed overnight, and we started the stew before daybreak."

"What's in it?" Hector asked.

"It would be easier to answer, what isn't in it." Alejandro guffawed. He insisted on serving Hector, piling on stew with a ladle until gravy edged over the side of the plate. A pot of the inevitable strong, black coffee occupied its own table at the end of the serving line. Hector half filled his tin cup. Alejandro ushered him toward the old men. The infirm insisted Hector take their place while they weaved to the table to fill their plates.

Hector had seldom felt so uncomfortable with such preferential treatment. Before Alejandro could return to serve himself, Inez appeared with an overflowing plate and a handful of tortillas.

"Ando, you keep Mr. Cardenas company. See to it that our guest doesn't leave hungry."

"I have enough for the rest of the week," Hector protested.

"You eat everything on that plate. I've seen how you've worked in the fields. And that church school saps your energy, too." Inez wagged a finger at Hector.

Alejandro and Hector were stili eating when the first of the infirm men returned. Hector scooted close to Alejandro to make room. The men ate in silence except for jokes about who would eat the most or who had searched for the largest chunks of beef.

Hector wondered how all the women and children could be fed, but Inez managed to appear with a cauldron of stew whenever the serving bowl emptied.

The last of the villagers had finished eating when an ear splitting boom reverberated in the air. Hector wondered why he hadn't seen the lightening when a second boom sounded. He looked at Alejandro.

"It's Pablo beating a drum. It's meant to bring rain."

The villagers walked to the footings where Pablo provided an irregular rhythm on a large bass drum. Johanson had built a two foot high platform to serve as his pulpit. Dark clouds rose to provide a backdrop.

Gustavo held out his hand to test for rain as his wife joined him. "I wouldn't mind getting soaking wet." He patted his wife's hand. "Angelita would warm me up when we got home."

The wife hissed something at Gustavo. Hector guessed she admonished him not to talk like that before a priest.

"Surely you don't expect her to cook you a hot meal after all you ate here," Hector said. Gustavo and his wife giggled.

Hector looked for Johanson. He'd heard that revivals could last for hours, and judging from the murmurs the villagers were ready for this one to begin.

Inez walked to what would be the front of the church and stepped onto the platform. The crowd quieted. She began a hymn that Hector didn't recognize. He couldn't catch all the lyrics, but the words Jesus and saved made up close to half. The melody was catchy, and Hector heard people humming along. When Inez ended, Johanson strode to her side to praise her voice and then her cooking. He asked for a show of hands from those who had enjoyed the meal. Everyone waved both arms. Then he asked if it wasn't the best meal they'd ever had. Children jumped up and waved their arms to make sure Inez and Johanson would see their hands. Next,Johanson invited everyone to join him in a song. He sang a few lines, then villagers echoed them. The next verse called for snapping fingers. Soon people were tapping their toes, turning in place, and cheering on Jesus. Hector found himself caught up in the experience.

Johanson switched to a prayer to bless the ill. Gustavo whispered to Hector that Inez must have prompted him with their names. The prayer rose in intensity when the subject turned to the need for rain. Johanson worked in a few lines on how people didn't need government help nor did they need aid from Rome, neither of which helped anyway. The people had the power within themselves—with reliance on Jesus and a subtle hint that Johanson could put in a good word for them—to bring rain and prosperity.

The Protestant was dripping sweat when he turned to Inez, "Now sister, please sing the praises of Jesus. Hallelujah."

Inez stepped to the center of the platform praising Jesus in words and song. She used her voice the way Johanson used his eyes.

When Inez sang the last note, Johanson took her place. "Brothers and sisters, how many of you want rain?" he shouted. Every one's arms shot into the air. "How many believe Jesus can send rain?" The arms danced again. Out of the corner of his eye, Hector saw Gustavo and his wife waving their arms. "Who has it in their power to call out Jesus' name?" Arms waved. "Who will call out Jesus' name?" A few of the older women shouted, Jesus. "I can't hear you. How can Jesus hear you?" The rest of the women and many men bellowed out, Jesus.

Just then the wind swept through the crowd and rustled the ends of plastic sheeting. "You hear the name of Jesus in the wind?" Johanson shouted. A dozen arms shot up. Lightning flashed overhead, and a clap of thunder followed.

"Send us rain, Jesus!" Johanson bellowed. "Please, Lord, send us rain!" He paused a moment, a moment of absolute silence. Then he screamed. "Who will send us rain?"

"Jesus," the people shouted. Inez yelled. "Jesus will send us rain." The crowd echoed her refrain.

"I can feel myself in Jesus' arms," Johanson exclaimed. "He wants to send us rain." He paused a long time, staring at Hector. "Unless some Evil works its power against Jesus."

Hector felt a dozen nearby eyes stare at him. If it rained, Johanson would get credit. If it didn't rain, Johanson could blame the Vatican. Particularly Hector.

10

Hector listened to his radio every morning the next week. The weather was so unfair. Northern Mexico received above average rainfall, abundant water fell in the mountains, but the chances of rain dropped to almost nothing for the remainder of the rainy season. His feelings were mixed. Johanson's revival had failed, but Hector suspected that more than one family blamed him for the drought. He sighed at his inability to do anything about the situation and wondered how much worse it could get. He washed and dressed, ate an energy bar, and headed toward the fields, not knowing what work was needed, given the drought.

When he didn't see any farmers in their fields, he headed toward Alejandro's home. His friend was sitting outside his house on a straight back chair propped against the wall. Gustavo sat on a bench, the two in an animated conversation. When Hector approached, Alejandro put down a piece of wood he had been carving.

"Good day, Father," Gustavo called. He patted to a place on the bench for Hector to sit.

Hector returned the greeting. "I don't see any one in the fields. Is the soil too dry to plant?"

"Tomorrow," both said.

"Why tomorrow?"

Gustavo looked at Alejandro. Neither spoke.

"You're carving one of your figures," Hector said. "May I see it?"

Alejandro handed the wood to him. The figure of a man astride a burro showed only in roughed out form, but Hector saw that the rider wore an oversized sombrero, so large to be comical. Hector smiled as he returned the carving.

"Already you can see how the sombrero is too big, no?" Gustavo beamed. "Some tourist will pay much for it. Especially after the poncho is painted bright colors. My compadre both sculpts and paints."

"The painting is nothing," Alejandro said. "And amateurs are turning out dozens like this with machines."

"But not so life-like, not so detailed," Gustavo protested. "It's unique."

"And why aren't you working on your hats?" Hector asked.

"I have to go to the coast for palm leaves."

"Well, if you're planting tomorrow, you don't have time to weave hats." Hector revived his question of why they had decided to plant.

"Remember, Father, I've promised you a hat." Gustavo talked about people who wore his hats, and Hector realized the two were not ready to tell him their reason for planting the next day. He asked Alejandro where he got his paints and where he would market his carvings.

Alejandro answered in detail. After that, the three men sat in silence.

Finally Hector spoke. "The weather report this morning was not favorable."

Alejandro put down his wooden figure and looked at Hector for a long time before speaking. "A long time ago we went through another drought as bad as this one."

"I was afraid because my children got so little to eat," Gustavo said. "We asked the government for help, but their promises did nothing to fill our bellies."

"We had a procession—with the old ways. I didn't know if it violated the Faith or not. We were desperate." Alejandro evaded looking at Hector.

"When your heart is with God, it's hard to violate the Faith," Hector said. "I know you meant right."

"We prayed and prayed, Father." Gustavo took off his hat in respect for the memory.

"It wasn't long after the procession when the rains came," Alejandro said. "Good steady rains."

Hector realized that the two planned a procession with or without his permission. "Will you lead another procession?" He looked at Alejandro.

"No, but he would." Alejandro nodded at Gustavo.

"Why not both of you?"

"Gustavo has been fasting for four days. We want you to say Mass before we start."

"I'd be glad to do that," Hector said.

Alejandro nodded. "There's more, Father."

Alejandro's use of father warned Hector to expect something unusual.

"We carry the Virgin in the procession," Alejandro said.

"That strikes me as appropriate," Hector said.

"She blessed us so much the last time, we gave her special attention." Gustavo wiped at sweat on his forehead. His eyes darted between Alejandro and his carving.

Hector searched for a neutral response, finally offering a meaningless shrug.

Gustavo looked at Alejandro. Alejandro studied Hector. "We all agreed afterwards." He paused. "We agreed that the Holy Mother deserved the place behind the altar. That's when we moved the crucifix into the Womb."

Hector took a deep breath. Some of his fellow priests would consider the change an act of blasphemy. It didn't matter to him, but if the Virgin failed to bring rain this time, he'd suggest they switch the crucifix to its original place.

"You did what you thought was right," Hector said. "What more can I do to help." He regretted his words as soon as he spoke, recalling that some Indians drank to the point of drunkenness in order to bring rain. No doubt, someone had seen the wine intended for Communion that Edwardo had brought. Hector wiped away sweat on his own brow.

"Will you bless Gustavo for fasting? So he can lead the procession," Alejandro said. "And bless the men who carry the Virgin?"

Hector hastened to agree.

"That's why we want to plant tomorrow. In the dust. The next day we carry the Virgin through the village." Alejandro looked into Hector's eyes as if sealing a contract. "Then the Virgin will soak the seeds."

It dawned on Hector that the day after tomorrow would be a Sunday, a fortunate coincidence—if the bishop didn't learn of it.

Hector was surprised Saturday morning when he went to help Alejandro and Gustavo plant. Every villager bent over digging sticks or hoes. He joined his two friends in Alejandro's field. Hector and Gustavo ran ditches for corn seeds while Alejandro planted. When they finished, Hector turned to Alejandro's demonstration plot.

"Let's not plant the mulched area yet, Father." Alejandro's tone made the words a command.

On their way to Gustavo's field, Gustavo said, "Father, we've been thinking about the way you described planting corn and beans like our ancestors did. I believe it best to plant four corn seeds in a hill with a few beans. What do you think of that?"

Hector had seen farmers in his youth planting four corn seeds in order to get one strong stalk, never questioning why they choose four. He still didn't have an answer. "Why not? We know not all the seeds will sprout." Indeed, when Hector examined the seed corn, his hopes sank because of its poor quality. "Five or six would be all right."

Gustavo's mouth dropped open, and he sucked in a breath. "The old ways call for four, Father. Four."

"Four is a good number," Alejandro added, his jaw set.

Hector didn't argue. He recalled four was an auspicious number among many Indians.

When the men finished their work, Alejandro reminded Hector of the special Mass he had promised and the blessings he was to give the next day. "Perhaps we should start earlier tomorrow?"

"That would be fine, Alejandro. I'm looking forward to your procession."

The tolling of the church bell woke Hector. He shook his head in the darkness, rushed to the door to check on the sunlight, and found it dark. He wondered if anyone besides Gustavo and Alejandro would be in church. He dressed quickly, forgot breakfast, and strolled around the Womb to enter the church from the front.

When his eyes adjusted to the dim interior, he saw that every villager must be present. A group of older men huddled at the back. Other men of various ages stood near the front. Women and children shuffled in their places. A baby was crying.

While Hector walked to the altar, Alejandro lit half a dozen candles, then half a dozen incense sticks. When Alejandro finished, he lifted his arms. The people responded in turn, joining Alejandro in what must have been a prayer but with words that Hector guessed to be Indian. When Alejandro finished, he signaled to Hector to proceed with his ritual.

Hector stifled a sneeze, his nose reacting to the incense, then uttered a short prayer blessing the Creator. He recalled his promise to bless Gustavo, stepped down, and stood before him. Gustavo dropped to his knees.

Hector didn't know what to say. He put his hand on Gustavo's shoulder and muttered a short prayer in Latin, ending with an admonition of blessing in Spanish.

Gustavo rose with a stream of thanks and signaled the ten men nearby. They came forward and kneeled. Hector was at a total loss for an appropriate blessing. He touched each man on the shoulder and mumbled the Lord's prayer in Latin. From their smiles, his recital proved satisfactory.

He rushed an abbreviated mass, anxious to find out what Alejandro and Gustavo intended. When he concluded, Alejandro raised his arms and spoke briefly. While he talked, two of the men Hector had blessed went out the front door and returned with a litter. Brightly colored crepe paper flowers covered a box, centered on the litter.

Gustavo turned to the altar, dropped to his knees, crossed himself, and muttered words under his breath. He rose and went to the Virgin, lifted her with all the care he would have given a baby, and carried her to the box. Two of the men strapped her to the litter as Gustavo assumed his place before her.

Ten men, five to a side, lifted the litter onto their shoulders and followed Gustavo from the church. Hector hustled to join the people who followed.

Outside, Gustavo halted at the top of the stairs, and Hector looked onto the plaza. The older men who had been at the back of the church, had left earlier. They had wrapped their legs in strings of cocoon shells that covered their calves. The shells rattled as the men danced to the rhythm of the drum that Pablo used at the Protestant revival. Four men propped up the drum with their knees, their drumsticks decorated with red, white, and green ribbons. The drummers sang in an unknown language. Hector recognized a few words he had heard at El Hidalgo. The dancers shuffled counter clockwise, their torsos as well as their feet keeping time to the drum. The beat had a hypnotic effect. The buzzing rattle of the cocoons imitated rainfall.

At the thought of rain, Hector looked up. Clouds had gathered on the mountains. A few made their way overhead but looked anemic. Hector uttered a prayer for rain, despite misgivings raised by the weather report.

He jumped when Alejandro touched his arm. "It's just tradition," he said. "We're not doing anything that's pagan."

"It's good to keep up traditions," Hector replied, pondering how many European traditions were woven into Christianity over its two thousand year history.

When the dancers stopped, Gustavo led the procession down the steps and into the plaza. Alejandro stayed with Hector behind the Virgin. The dancers followed the women and children. The procession circled the plaza stopping before each house. Home owners had pounded a small cross into the ground before their house. Gustavo sprinkled something on each cross as he invoked a mysterious power. Hector recognized the smell of pine and realized Gustavo was scattering pine needles. The dancers executed a short dance before each cross without the benefit of a drum. Gustavo called out what must have been a blessing on the inhabitants of each house.

Hector assumed the procession would return to the church after circling the plaza, but Gustavo surprised him by leading every one toward houses beyond the plaza. As they paused before the first home, a lightening flash interrupted the dancers. The distant thunder sounded benign. The dancers increased their pace. Gustavo shouted a blessing and began a song, everyone joining in on a refrain that became a chant.

Gustavo led the procession along the ditch carrying the town's water supply. Young mothers dipped their hands into the water and sprinkled their children's heads. At the next house, the dancers' intensity made Hector think he could hear their hearts beat. He was certain Gustavo would be hoarse for a week from the way he shouted.

Hector felt rain drops. When he looked up, rain peppered his face. Clouds from the mountains joined ones forming above. The cluster turned a deep gray. Hector prayed under his breath for a downpour.

The promise of rain did nothing to change the pace of the dancing and Gustavo's shouts. If anything the incantations and dance increased in intensity. When the procession stopped at a distant house, Hector realized that only Inez' home was left. He squinted to look at it. Maria and Marta stood on the porch. Hector wondered if Inez knew they were watching.

When Gustavo moved on, Hector pondered talking with Inez. At least he'd talk with Maria and Marta. But Gustavo headed back to the church. He deliberately bypassed the Yepiz household.

Hector thought to urge Gustavo to return to Inez'. How would Maria and Marta feel to be passed over? Wasn't it Hector's priestly duty to counter Gustavo's decision? What if Alejandro had made the decision? As Hector reflected on the turn of events, he regretted what he had blessed. Would he ever find a proper role in San Miguel? He became so engrossed in the quandary that he failed to realize a downpour had drenched him.

11

Hector fidgeted in bed sneezing and blowing his nose. He hoped it would be a mild cold. The Sunday downpour caught the procession in the open. Gustavo had refused to change its pace. Everyone ended up drenched. The storm threatened to wash away fields until a steady rain followed the initial deluge.

The weather report on Monday failed to mention rain in the northern mountains. Hector blew his nose a second time, remembered his school didn't meet, and laid back down. The fields would be too muddy to work, and little remained to be done beyond planting Gustavo's and Alejandro's demonstration plots.

Enough light seeped into his room that Hector saw Jesus looking down on him, could feel his eyes admonishing him. He recalled failing to direct Gustavo to the Yepiz home, and in the aftermath of the storm he had failed to say anything about the slight. Hector pondered what to do, realized he knew, and rose to do it. He sneezed, decided to skip breakfast, and went in search of his two friends.

He found Gustavo propped in a chair leaning against the wall of his home, trimming a hat. He chatted to a toddler playing with a strand of palm. When Gustavo saw Hector coming, he rushed inside to return with a chair.

"Good morning, Father. Did you ever dry out?" he chuckled.

"Dried out but not warmed up," Hector covered his nose with a hand as he sneezed.

"I'm sorry. Alejandro hasn't warmed up either. He's in bed with his cold."

"I'm sorry to hear that. I see you're working on a hat. Looks like you've got a good helper." Hector held out a hand to the toddler who took a step back. His nose was running more than Hector's.

"He'll be in the fields helping me, soon," Gustavo beamed, but then grimaced. "Until he leaves San Miguel like all the other young men."

"We'll see," Hector said. "There must be a better future for Mexico than migration north."

Gustavo wove a few loose strands into the hat's brim. "I started this for you, Father, but the palm leaves are too brittle for a first rate hat."

Hector concentrated on a way to admonish Gustavo for leading the procession past Inez and her two girls.

Gustavo must have guessed what was on Hector's mind. "You think I did wrong to pass up Señora Yepiz the day of the procession, no?"

"Yes, I do, my Son. I felt you were wrong, and I was wrong not to tell you at the time."

"Did you know Alejandro has spent his nights with Inez since Reverend Johanson left?"

"No. That's not my concern. But my heart sank when we passed those two girls expecting us to visit their home. Anyone could see the anticipation on Maria's and Marta's faces. They must have cried half the night. I'm disappointed with Alejandro that he didn't tell you to stop there."

"You know Alejandro should have led the procession, Father? Everyone feared it wouldn't bring rain without him leading it."

"Well, no one could have done a better job than you did," Hector said. "But it was wrong to ignore those two children."

"Alejandro could not have bypassed the girls, even if Inez didn't set out a cross." Gustavo put down his weaving. "That's why he asked me to lead."

"I don't understand." Hector was baffled. The puzzle was more annoying than his cold.

"When Alejandro told Inez we were going to ask the Virgin for rain, she told him she didn't want any pagan blessings on her home. She warned him that he'd better not come anywhere close to it."

Hector was shocked to learn that Inez considered the procession pagan. "Didn't she report it as a miracle earlier when the Virgin brought rain?"

"Oh no, Father. No one believed that. We know the Virgin helps us in a drought. It's not a miracle because we have asked for her help."

Hector chewed at a fingernail, reconsidering what he thought about miracles. "I'd think Alejandro would have been angry enough at Inez that he could have bypassed her home. After all, she didn't set out a cross."

"Alejandro respects Inez' opinion even when she is wrong. After all, a few old timers still cling in their old gods. I mean their old ways. No matter how much Alejandro talks to them they maintain tradition. They're sure the customs don't contradict Catholic faith so we include them." He chuckled. "Besides, some of them are our best dancers."

The two sat in silence while Hector absorbed what Gustavo had told him. Finally, he asked if Inez had accepted Alejandro's decision to let Gustavo lead.

"I guess she did. But Alejandro was so upset to exclude anyone, especially Maria and Marta, that he left her and moved back to his house." Gustavo fingered the hat a while longer. "You know the two girls are like grandchildren to him. His only grandchildren, unless you count some in the Indian way."

Hector had been introduced to the intricacies of native peoples' kinship in an anthropology class and decided not to pursue the complexities of Alejandro's relationships. Besides, his concern focused on his friend's welfare.

"I'm sorry he left Inez. Is there anything I can do to get them back together?"

Gustavo laughed. "Those two argue about everything, but they always get back together." He smiled an after-thought. "Their make-ups must be something remarkable."

"So there's nothing for me to do?" Hector asked.

Gustavo laughed. "Inez probably guessed that Alejandro's sick. First thing this morning, I saw her coming back from his house, carrying a big pot. It must have been her chicken and green chili soup. You'd never worry about them separating if you heard Alejandro rave about her soup."

Gustavo related other anecdotes about Alejandro and Inez before the conversation turned to farming and how the crops would prosper with the rainfall. Gustavo reported that the mountain for San Miguel's water supply had been equally blessed. The spring was flowing at record heights.

"And your demonstration plot?" Hector asked. "The one you mulched so carefully. It should do well with corn and beans even without rainfall later."

Gustavo nodded. The gesture didn't radiate enthusiasm, but he added, "As soon as the field dries out, I'll plant it."

"I'd like to help you. Shall we plant Alejandro's plot for him since he's sick? We could surprise him."

Gustavo motioned to the toddler as if ignoring Hector's offer of help. He took the boy on his lap when the child came to him. "It's the custom, Father, that we don't decide things for other people. It wouldn't be right to plant for Alejandro unless he asked us to."

Hector kicked himself. The same custom at El Hidalgo had taken him a while to learn. He should have realized the people at San Miguel might have a similar respect for other people's actions. He made small talk with Gustavo, acknowledging that he understood the people's respect for each other, and he would try to refrain from deciding for others.

Then, excusing himself Hector said he'd go talk with Alejandro to ask what he wanted done with the land he'd set aside for experimentation.

He knocked at Alejandro's door and was greeted by a weak invitation. He found his friend propped up in bed. A large crock on the floor gave forth a tantalizing aroma of chicken and green chili. Hector's mouth watered as his eyes fixed on the crock.

"Would you get a bowl from the kitchen?" Alejandro asked. "You've never tasted soup like this." He pointed to the crock with his chin.

Hector retrieved a bowl and chair from the kitchen. The soup had cooled, but the taste was beyond measure. A blend of tomato and spices with chicken and chili delighted his tongue. He made a mental note to ask Inez for the recipe.

"There are some tortilla bits, if you want to add them. But I think they detract from the soup."

"The soup is perfect the way it is." Hector smacked his lips recalling the custom at El Hidalgo. "I didn't know you were such a terrific cook. I should say chef." Hector pretended not to know the soup came from Inez. "I've never tasted better. But, you shouldn't be cooking with such a cold."

Hector's attempt to bring up Inez failed. Alejandro didn't acknowledge her hand in it, but he didn't claim credit for the soup either.

The two sat in silence until Hector grew uncomfortable. "I just saw Gustavo," he said. "He's thinking of planting the land we mulched. Even if we don't get rain later, I think corn and beans will do well."

"I'm sure they will," Alejandro said. "Even without rain later."

"Would you lead another procession if it doesn't rain later?" Hector asked.

"No. It's only when we're desperate that we parade the Virgin. We deserve only so much from her."

"I noticed all the people put crosses in front of their houses." Hector felt a little guilty trying to trick Alejandro into saying that Inez had not set out a cross.

"They used to set out three crosses when I was a child," Alejandro said. "I don't remember when the custom changed. If my father were alive, he'd know."

"What does the cross represent?" Hector recalled his anthropology professor discussing how important it is to elicit the meanings of symbols.

"It reminds us that Jesus Christ died for all of us. The whole community. Everyone must be included."

"Was Gustavo able to include everyone when he led the procession?" Hector felt he had succeeded in bringing the conversation back to Inez.

"It's the custom to include everyone. The cross reminds us that we are all related."

Hector realized Alejandro did not want to talk about Inez and decided to drop the matter. "What do the pine needles stand for? I saw Gustavo sprinkle pine needles around the crosses."

"It's the custom." Alejandro's tone and his accompanying nod said that his answer was the most Hector could expect.

"Well, it's interesting. Everyone must have been sincere. There could not have been a more abundant rainfall."

"The rain in the mountains also helped. Gustavo told me the spring is as high as ever. We can irrigate if there's no more rainfall. It will be a good season."

Alejandro stretched and slid down a little in his bed. Hector realized he should leave. He told Alejandro he'd look in on him tomorrow. He returned to the Womb to write Edwardo saying he had witnessed a miracle, but villagers would not be reporting it since they regarded it as normal.

✟✟✟

The next morning was a day for classes. Hector's older students were excited about the success of the procession, laughing about how soaked they had been. The younger ones talked about how their grandfathers had danced to bring rain. Hector got a few older ones interested in percentages and directed their teaching of division to the youngsters, but the excitement of the procession took precedence.

After Hector sent the students home, he went to see how Alejandro felt. His friend was sitting up, reading his Bible. Hector smelled tomatoes and guessed Inez had refreshed her soup, but Alejandro must have finished it. The crock was empty.

Hector's enthusiasm led him to bring up the subject of planting. "You look like you'll be able to get into the fields soon."

"I was up a while before you came. I may look over my fields tomorrow."

"I guess you'll be planting the experimental plot soon?" Hector bit his tongue. He was close to making a decision for Alejandro.

"I don't see any rush to do that. The ground is soaked."

Hector had enough sense not to pursue the matter. The seeding could wait. He was too eager to have Alejandro serve as an example to the community. In the meantime he'd help Gustavo.

✞✞✞

The next day he joined Gustavo. His friend had two bags each of corn and bean seeds. The corn bags had chicken feet attached to the string that tied the mouth of the bags.

Hector couldn't contain his curiosity. "What are the feet? They look like chicken feet."

Gustavo nodded that they were.

"I suppose it's the custom," Hector said, assuming he'd get no more of an answer.

"It is the custom," Gustavo answered. "The claws of the chicken show the roots of the corn how to hold on to the ground."

Hector recognized the magical reasoning involved in the corn roots imitating the chicken feet. "I wonder why the beans don't need chicken feet?"

Gustavo's eyebrows squeezed together. "Father, the wind doesn't blow down the beans the way it does the corn."

Hector regretted his lack of reasoning.

Gustavo hoed soil into hills, then used a digging stick to drill holes for the seeds. Hector dropped four corn seeds into the hills along with a few bean seeds. While they planted, the two men joked about the downpour soaking them on Sunday. Shortly after noon, Gustavo announced they were finished although ample space remained.

Hector couldn't refrain from asking, "Don't you want to use this space?" He pointed to the unused land with his chin. "It's well mulched. I'm sure it would do well."

"I can plant onions and chilies in it. Maybe a few tomatoes." He rubbed his chin in thought. "Garlic grows well up here, too. I've always said that's what makes Inez' soup so good, the right amount of garlic."

"Of course," Hector struck his forehead with his open hand. "I should have guessed you'd plant garden crops. The variety makes for good nutrition. Your family will thrive." Then a question struck Hector. "Have you started the plants someplace I don't know about?"

"Inez promised she'd supply the garden plants at a fair price. She's done that a couple of times."

"You mean Mateo and Marcos bring them in their van? Where do they buy them?" Hector thought of all the outlets he knew that prepared healthy garden plants. He could have advised Inez.

"They bring them, but Reverend Johanson knows all about farming. His contacts supply him with seedlings at cost, and he pays for them. He'll come with Mateo and Marcos to distribute his selections."

Hector's stomach churned. Would the Protestant always be one step ahead of him?

12

A week later Hector and Gustavo compared corn and bean sprouts between the mulched and unmulched parts of his field. "Quite a few beans have sprouted here," Gustavo pointed. His brows knitted. "But not many where we mulched."

"With all that rain, we won't see any difference right away," Hector said. He had recorded the plantings but didn't recall the dates. "Didn't we plant the beans in your regular field about a week before the mulched area?"

"I don't remember," Gustavo answered. "Look, here's a corn sprout breaking through. I hope the bugs aren't worse where we mulched. We hoed under a lot of weeds that could have had eggs on them."

"It's possible," Hector said. "That's why we use demonstration plots. It'll be interesting to see how Alejandro's plot does compared to yours since he's planting later." Hector stared at Alejandro's fields where a few weeds were breaking ground. All his extension courses emphasized the importance of persuading leading farmers to accept innovations first. "He has been up and about, hasn't he? I saw him walking over to Inez' yesterday."

"He wasn't home last night when I stopped to see him. I'd guess he and Inez got back together. Their quarrels never separate them long."

"I guess he'll plant soon." It was not like Alejandro to procrastinate, Hector thought.

"He'll be home as soon as the Protestant shows up," Gustavo said. "I'm surprised Johanson's not here already."

"I didn't think he'd return," Hector said. "His prayers for rain failed. It was the Virgin's procession that brought rain."

"That won't stop the man. He's talked failure into success before."

"His revival showed me how persuasive he can be. Those eyes—I don't know what it is about them—but they are more powerful than his words."

"If he looked a snake in its eyes, he could talk it out of his skin," Gustavo laughed. "I wonder if he'll be able to talk his way into heaven. Do you think he can fool St. Peter, Father?"

Hector laughed. "I don't know. Perhaps the devil will invite him first."

Gustavo nodded. "Let me invite you to coffee, Father, since we don't have much to do in the fields today."

Gustavo related other incidents about Johanson's visits on their way to his home. There, Gustavo gestured to two chairs near the door. His wife appeared in moments with black, sweetened coffee. At El Hidalgo Hector had learned to drink coffee with more sugar than coffee.

Hector declined a second cup when he saw an SUV turning the last hairpin on the road into San Miguel. "Looks like Mateo and Marcos in that black car of theirs," he said.

"At least the top half is black," Gustavo chuckled. "I can't see any color on the bottom with all that mud."

"How many stream crossings do you think they maneuvered on their way here."

"I've never seen their car so dirty. What do you think their shoes look like?"

"I wonder if they've had to put up with Johanson the whole way. He'll be preaching salvation to them if he sees that sawed-off shot gun they carry."

"Do you think they have drugs in the Ford, now? In one of those hidden compartments you hear about? Or in the gas tank?"

"Maybe it's hidden in the bags of fertilizer they bring. You best be careful, or you'll end up with a field full of marijuana."

Gustavo chuckled, then sighed. "I'd be a rich man. I'd retire to Mazatlan and sell my hats to the tourists myself."

"Is it all right if we go over to see what they're bringing?" Hector asked.

"The whole village will go. Everyone can't wait to see what they bring."

Hector studied the fields of other farmers as they made their way to the Yepiz household. The fields were less than half planted. A few showed no sign of being worked.

Before Hector could ask Gustavo about them, they reached the van. The brothers were on the porch talking with their mother and Alejandro.

Hector could not hear what was said, but hands flashed through the air. When Johanson struggled from the back of the van where he had been riding on a foot stool, Alejandro greeted him but avoided looking him in the face. Inez called something to Alejandro, but he did nothing except shrug.

When Hector reached the SUV, he saw the back seats had been removed. Pallets of plants were stacked floor to ceiling. Bags of fertilizer filled the rest of the rear end. Hector couldn't guess where Johanson had found space to sit. Johanson's face was flushed, and he did nothing but stretch his legs and twist at the waist.

Hector nodded to Alejandro and Inez, then shook hands with the brothers. When he offered his hand to Johanson, the Protestant brushed his hands together in a gesture of cleansing dust. "Too dirty to shake." He glanced at Gustavo and nodded, looked around, then said, "Well, Rector, I don't see your backup today. Has the Pope assigned him elsewhere since you reported how my revival failed."

"No. Edwardo . . ."

Before Hector could say more, Johanson interrupted. "You must have heard the latest weather reports when you staged your procession." He wrinkled his nose. "You don't really think an idol can bring rain, do you?"

"Only God sends rain," Hector spoke with such force that Johanson couldn't interrupt. "Faith and prayer assures God that rain is needed. The Virgin symbolizes that faith."

"Well, we Protestants don't confuse idols with symbols. Jesus looks after us and answers our prayers. We don't need middle men." He scoffed in his laugh, "Nor middle women."

The faces of Alejandro and Gustavo were frozen masks. Inez bit at her lip. Hector realized that Johanson was trying to provoke him into a fight. He took a deep breath to remain calm. Soon, most of the villagers gathered around the SUV. The children jumped up and down to glance inside. Adults pretended to restrain their curiosity, but young men peered into the windows.

Johanson had his audience and mounted a stool from the SUV. "It's so good to see all of you again," he shouted. "I know you've all shown Señora Yepiz your gratitude for the feast she provided at our revival. I hope you've all thought about taking Jesus Christ as your Savior. Jesus doesn't listen to you through a priest or a saint. Jesus listens to you directly. Any time. Any place." Johanson's eyes darted from individual to individual among the villagers who stood before him. "Some times he doesn't seem to answer our prayers. It may take days. Even weeks. Like it did after the revival. We were all praying for rain with such faith that we were rewarded. We reached Jesus with our prayers."

Johanson fixed his gaze on Hector, his eyes flashing. "Because of our prayers, Jesus brought rain, not some statue."

Hector realized the man knew the value of his eyes in capturing an audience, but he wondered if Johanson would have any luck preaching now when the people were so curious about the contents of the SUV.

"Again, it's time to pray to Jesus for help. Help that will bring money to San Miguel. Money to buy the food you need, the clothes you need. Money to send your children to a proper school, one with qualified teachers!" He sneered at Hector. "How many of you could use some money?"

Everyone raised their hands. The children, ensnared in the excitement, jumped up and down waving their hands and arms, yipping me, me, me.

"How many of you would like to be paid handsomely for tomatoes the Americans can't get enough of? Who would like that?"

The children danced and waved wildly, but the older men and women showed restraint.

Johanson sensed the change of heart. "Señora Yepiz and I have brought tomato plants for anyone who wants to plant them. You know how much the Yankees pay for tomatoes. She wants to share that wealth with you."

"But how do we get the tomatoes to market?" one of the older farmers asked.

"Her sons and I will come with a truck if enough of you plant. Otherwise, Mateo and Marcos will use their SUV."

Gustavo had peered into the van but returned to join Hector. Alejandro kept his distance, standing beside Inez. Hector's shoulders sagged. He pondered if Johanson could make tomato Christians out of his San Miguel congregation.

"Who will be the first to plant a red fortune?" Johanson screeched. "You know corn and beans are cheap because the Yankees ship so many of them to Mexico. But they pay dearly for the tomatoes you grow before theirs ripen. When their winters cripple their production."

Alejandro stepped forward and motioned to Mateo that he'd take ten cartons of the plants. Mateo congratulated him on his choice, but it was

Johanson who lifted the cartons out of the SUV and promised to carry them to Alejandro's field.

Hector's shoulders sagged as he realized that Alejandro intended to use his demonstration plot for tomatoes—after all the work they had done mulching. He turned to Gustavo. "Did you know Alejandro intended to plant tomatoes?"

"He told me Inez urged him to try them. He's doing it to satisfy her." Gustavo shrugged. "But, he won't plant all his land in tomatoes. Much is already in corn and beans."

Two more men stepped forward and took many more plants than Alejandro had.

"Did Inez pester them into planting?" Hector asked. "I don't recognize the dark complexioned one."

"Roberto's my cousin. He told his wife he's been too sick to plant, but the truth is he's lazy. I think he just put off planting. Now he's got an empty field and a head filled with dreams of money."

"What about the other man? I can't remember his name."

"He's my wife's cousin, Manuel." Gustavo sighed. "He told me that Mateo promised him five hundred pesos if he'd be the first to plant tomatoes. He was supposed to talk his brother into planting them, too, but I don't see him. Mateo knew that if one person stepped forward others would follow."

"Do people look up to your cousin?" Hector asked.

Gustavo shrugged. "No more than other men in the village. We're all equal here, Father."

"Don't you think people look up to Alejandro?"

"Oh, sure. But he's different."

Hector didn't have to ask how Alejandro differed. Everyone in the village looked to him for guidance while at the same time regarding him as an equal. His decision to plant a cash crop could affect San Miguel in years to come. Most likely forever, Hector thought. His fingers cramped and anxiety gnawed at his spirit.

"Father, is your priest-friend coming back?" Gustavo asked, pointing toward the road.

Hector did not recognize the car and nodded his ignorance.

"Maybe I can sell the driver one of my hats." Gustavo scurried toward his home.

Hector considered talking to Alejandro but didn't know what to say. The decision to plant tomatoes was Alejandro's. Hector had Gustavo's plot to demonstrate the value of mulching—except a successful tomato crop for Alejandro would make much more of an impression on villagers.

Hector's mind was still on corn and beans when the car parked behind the SUV. Then Hector recognized it. It belonged to the two women journalists he had helped with their flat tire. His fingers tingled again. Journalists were the last people Hector wanted around when he and Johanson verged on confrontation.

The young woman, who was driving, seemed reluctant to leave the car, but when her mother climbed out, the daughter followed. Hector was relieved to see both were modestly dressed. The mother wore a loose fitting tan suit with a white blouse. Her reddish hair was recently dyed, but her makeup was restrained. The daughter wore a denim jacket and pants as if to fit in with farmers, but her mascara ran and her green nails clashed with the blue denim. As she approached, an overpowering aroma of perfume proceeded her.

"Father Hernandez?" the daughter said when she saw Hector.

"Hector," Hector corrected.

"Hector," she repeated. "I'm Yolanda." She motioned to her mother. "And this is my mother, Isabela Mendoza."

Inez and Johanson stepped close, and Hector introduced them.

"We have an editor interested in our story about the miracles here at San Miguel. But he couldn't get a confirmation from the bishop's office."

"Not yet," the mother added, "but the bishop didn't deny the possibility that a miracle had occurred, and he admitted that in the past the village had reported other miracles."

"What kind of miracle are you talking about?" Johanson asked.

"A miraculous cure. We saw the crutches. Right here, in the chapel of the new Catholic church."

"You shouldn't be asking the bishop about that cure," Inez chimed in. "Reverend Olaf Johanson is responsible. He cured the cripple, and he's building a Protestant church." She emphasized Protestant.

"Jesus is the miracle worker." Johanson stepped closer to the women in order to block Hector from the conversation. "But he chose to do his work through me. Praise the Lord!"

"Did you see the cure?" Isabela turned to Alejandro.

"I didn't know the man. He came on crutches. Reverend Johanson touched him all over, and the man put away the crutches."

"How far away is the nearest village?" Isabela asked.

Gustavo shook his head while he thought. "Twelve or fifteen miles. But I have relatives there, and no one knew him."

"So he had to come from more than fifteen miles away. On crutches." Yolanda stared at Johanson and Inez.

"The word about Reverend Johanson's powers has spread throughout the mountains." Inez crossed her arms over her chest and glared at the two women.

"I don't mean to dispute you," Isabela said, "but our editor wants verification.

"What about you, Father Hector?" Yolanda stepped forward in order to look at Hector. "Were you sent here to investigate the miracle?"

"I know little about miracles. You should understand that the footing here is for a Protestant church." Hector was desperate to change the subject. "It's not part of San Miguel."

"Oh," Isabela exclaimed, looking at Johanson. "So you're building a new church, and it would be constructed right on the site of a miracle you performed."

"You make it sound as if that was his only miracle." Inez' voice rose on the last three words.

"What do you mean?" Isabela asked.

"Just a few weeks ago, Reverend Johanson held a revival right here. The whole village attended." She fixed her gaze on Alejandro. "Isn't that right, Alejandro?"

"Yes, everyone was here. No one would miss a fies . . ."

Inez interrupted. "No one misses one of our revivals. Everyone was present when Olaf Johanson led us in prayers for rain. Prayers that brought steady rain. Rain that revived our oasis." Inez laid a hand on Johanson's arm. "We'll be forever grateful."

"But what about the procession?" Alejandro exclaimed before Inez could stop him. "It was the Virgin who brought rain." His voice matched Inez' in intensity. "Isn't that right, Father?"

"We all agree that the rain was God's work." Hector looked at the two women. "The Protestant prayed for rain a few weeks before the storm came. The day of the rain, the villagers held a procession carrying a statue of the Virgin from the church." Hector rushed his explanation. "Before Gustavo—the man leading the procession—could return to the church, we were all caught in a beautiful rainfall that soaked us all and replenished the village spring."

"So it was a Catholic miracle." Isabela emphasized Catholic.

"We can always count on the Virgin!" Alejandro said.

"There's no proof of that," Johanson exclaimed. "It was coincidence."

Everyone looked at Hector.

He swallowed hard, certain the journalists were skeptical of a miraculous cure, but wondering if the sudden rainfall qualified as a Catholic miracle—and a sensational story for them. The timing of the deluge was convincing evidence for Hector. However, newspaper coverage of a San Miguel miracle would be bad news for the bishop.

"We have to wait and see how San Miguel prospers from God's gift of rain," Hector answered. His answer didn't satisfy himself anymore than it did the mother and daughter, but it might postpone their story.

13

"Will the newspaper print five pictures of me in one paper, Father, or will it print a picture on five different days?" Gustavo hitched up his pants.

"It's hard to say." Hector had evaded the question earlier when he met Gustavo to help him finish planting.

"Señorita Mendoza took so many pictures. How did that camera hold so much film? She must have much money, no?"

"It's a new kind of camera, Gustavo. It uses a disk." Hector took a deep breath. It was hard to explain a phenomenon he didn't comprehend himself.

"Does a disk have chemicals?"

"No. It's electronic. The light is recorded in electric impulses." Hector fingered his jaw. "I don't really understand it." He started to explain that a picture could be looked at, and if unsatisfactory, discarded, and the disk reused. Gustavo's puzzled expression decided Hector against further explanation. "I'd guess one picture of you would be used one time, my Son." Hector smiled. "Were you grinning when she took it?"

"I tried to grin in all of them, but one time I wasn't ready. I must have looked like a wild Indian. That's the one those newspapers will use. To show how backward Indians are."

"More and more people know that Indians aren't backward. I think we convinced the Mendozas that we rely on hard work and not miracles. I believe we made them understand the importance of sustainable agriculture, and how you're helping to achieve it. That's the story I hope to see in print."

"I hope so, too. The Mendozas seemed nice. I can't believe I thought they were a prostitute and a madam that first time they came here." Gustavo shook his head. "Instead, they're important newspaper people."

"Possibly not too important. They have to sell their stories and photos to any newspaper that will buy them."

"So maybe my picture won't be in any paper?"

"We'll have to wait and see."

"How will we know?"

"Señora Mendoza promised she'd send us whatever stories or photos are published."

Gustavo sniffed, wrinkled his nose. "It doesn't mean anything, anyway. What matters are the crops, no?"

"That's right," Hector said. "Even the tomatoes. It was good of Mateo to give out all those plants. He surprised me with the chili and onion sets. Everyone got some for their gardens."

"Inez had her sons do that before. When they brought her tomatoes, they'd bring chilies and onions. Then she'd urge us to plant more tomatoes. But most of us stuck to the old ways. Corn and beans. Beans and corn."

"Sometimes the old ways are best." Hector took his hoe off his shoulder at Gustavo's field. He swatted at a cloud of gnats curious about his smell.

Gustavo showed him the places in his field he'd left vacant, anticipating the chili and onion plants. He prepared holes with a digging stick. Hector placed seedlings and patted earth around them to keep them in place.

"The ground is getting dry." Hector crumpled a second clump of dirt with his hand. "When will you irrigate?" he asked.

"Inez waters first. That's our way of returning her gifts."

"Who gets water after that?" Hector wasn't anxious to hear. At El Hidalgo complex mores regulated water rights. In a dry year, innumerable disputes arose over water usage. He'd heard of more than one case when people resorted to violence.

"Alejandro and the elders decide." Gustavo straightened. Only a few onion sets remained. He looked toward Inez's land, shaking his head. "Alejandro will have more work than he can handle."

"What do you mean?" Hector asked.

"Pablo was supposed to plant Inez' field, but he went to town with Mateo and Marcos. He was supposed to come back yesterday with Rosa. She looked all over town but couldn't find him."

"What could have happened to him?"

"He loves the bottle, like his father. Marcos promised to keep him away from the cantina, but who knows. It isn't the first time he's missed a planting, and Alejandro had to do the work. Or he tries to. Look how he's holding his back." Gustavo gestured to Inez' field.

"We're about finished, Gustavo. Shall we help Alejandro?"

"I'm glad to hear you say that, Father. I thought you might be angry with him for planting tomatoes."

Hector nodded his head. "Priests shouldn't get angry," he chuckled. "But we do. I confess I was angry with Alejandro. Then disappointed."

Gustavo shook his head. "It's up to him what he plants."

"I know. I should leave it to him, but people from the city think they know what's best for others."

When the two joined Alejandro, his greeting was polite but reserved. He kept his head down when he addressed Hector.

Gustavo said, "We don't have anything more to do, *Compadre*, so we came to help you."

Alejandro stood upright to stretch his back and rubbed at his waist. "I can use help!"

A light breeze cooled Hector's brow. He welcomed it as an omen. A few hours later, the three finished planting, and Alejandro asked if they'd join him for coffee.

"You don't make the best coffee, *Compadre*," Gustavo laughed. "Why don't we start planting the tomatoes in Inez' field?"

"Thanks for the compliment, *Compadre*." Alejandro used both hands on his back while breathing deep. "But do you mind if I rest? My back is troubling me. We can plant Inez' field tomorrow." He looked at Hector. "Is that all right with you?"

"Fine. Since school adjourned for the summer, I have time on my hands."

"There's been no one yet to marry or bury," Gustavo guffawed. "I guess you'll have to wait until Alejandro and Inez tie the knot."

Alejandro gave Gustavo a friendly poke. "I don't know if I could live full time with that tongue of hers. It's nice to get home and be alone once in a while."

"Until you get hungry for her chicken and green chili soup." Gustavo returned the poke.

The three men ended up at Alejandro's with Gustavo making fun of the too weak coffee although Hector couldn't tell if it was strong or weak, given all the sugar Alejandro added.

✝✝✝

The next morning Gustavo stopped at the church just as Hector was leaving the Womb. Hector wondered how poor Mexicans were ever stereotyped as being lazy. His friends kept the hours that priests do but worked far harder.

"Good morning, Father," Gustavo said. "Did you sleep well in your Womb?" It wasn't the first time Gustavo had cracked the joke, but he laughed as hard as ever.

"I dreamed of giants. Can you imagine the size of their hoes?" Hector was about to run out of giant possessions, but it made little difference. Gustavo laughed at any response Hector made.

"I dreamed I harvested a crop of marijuana." Gustavo's grin foretold a joke. "Would you report me to the authorities, Father, if I raised marijuana?"

"Would you give all the money you earned to the poor?"

"Of course, Father." Gustavo laughed. "Of course, I am first among the poor."

The two traded more barbs as they made their way to Inez' to find Alejandro.

He was coming from behind her home when Hector and Gustavo arrived. He carried a digging stick and a hoe. "You two are up early," Alejandro called. "You must want some of Inez' coffee after tasting mine?"

The aroma of freshly brewed coffee stirred Hector's nose, but his tongue twitched as it recalled yesterday's sweet brew. He felt relieved when the two decided against coffee and started toward the fields instead.

"Granpa," Marta called from the porch. "You forgot your hat." She dashed toward him with a tattered sombrero. When she reached him, he knelt to grab her sides and swing her high. Something between a groan and a screech bellowed from Alejandro's lips. Marta looked terrified. He put her down but was unable to straighten up. She held his sombrero up for him, but he didn't notice the gesture. He clutched his waist with both hands while uttering a low groan.

"Oh, no, *Compadre*. Not your back." Concern flashed across Gustavo's face.

"How can we help?" Hector said.

Gustavo went to Alejandro's left side, Hector to his right. They put

113

their arms around his chest to half carry him to Inez' home. Alejandro grimaced with each step, stopped every other step to gasp. Sweat broke out on his brow. Gustavo anticipated whatever Alejandro did, dabbing a kerchief at Alejandro's forehead.

Marta had dashed back to the house, carrying Alejandro's sombrero. Inez appeared on the porch moments before the three men reached it.

"I'll bring a chair. He can't manage the steps." Inez fought to hold back tears. "What'd he do this time?"

"He was bending down and . . ." Gustavo said.

"I dropped something and stooped to get it. My back won't be out long." Alejandro grasped his back with both hands, his lips a straight line. Sweat ran down his cheeks.

"I have some pain medication," Hector volunteered. "I'll get it once we get you settled."

Inez rushed into the house and returned with a straight back chair. Alejandro lowered himself onto it with Gustavo's help. Hector and Gustavo lifted the chair by its rungs and carried Alejandro inside.

"I'll open the sofa. You'd never make it upstairs, and the sofa bed is just as comfortable."

Hector helped Inez pull out the mattress and springs. She pounded the mattress with her fist a few times, dashed upstairs and returned with a pillow. She fluffed it half a dozen times.

"It's ready," she said to Gustavo. Inez half frowned at Alejandro. "When are you going to learn? You're not a young man anymore, you old coot."

Alejandro bit at his lips as he adjusted himself to the bed. His face blanched, and a trace of saliva trickled onto his chin. Inez retrieved another pillow to prop him up, then wiped around his mouth.

"I'll get aspirin," Inez said.

Hector thought he could wait to return later with his pain medication since it wasn't much stronger.

Inez thanked Hector and Gustavo, claimed she didn't know what she would have done without their help, and dismissed them with a wave.

✿✿✿

"Do we dare plant her field without Alejandro to supervise?" Hector drew his fingers through hair that was getting far too long.

"Oh, we must, Father. The last time he threw out his back, it was weeks before he recovered. The time before that was even longer. The tomato plants have to get into the ground, or they'll dry up."

"Well, we can start today. How about your own back? Will it last?"

"I have a wife to rub it after a hard day in the field." Gustavo smiled. "I wish she cooked as well as she rubs."

When the two men reached Inez' field, Hector examined the tomato plants. The potting soil around their roots felt dry. He selected two trays with plants that showed signs of wilting. Gustavo found three others needing attention.

Hector let Gustavo determine the space between plants and show him how to loosen plants from their trays. Gustavo chattered as he judged various methods of planting and cultivating tomatoes. In the end he declared the outcome was determined more by weeds, insects, and plant diseases than by anything humans did.

Gustavo stood to stretch and rubbed at his back. "I bet the Yankees in California have machines to plant their tomatoes."

"They have machines that help." Hector hadn't kept up on the latest developments in agricultural technology.

"But they have to pick them by hand, no?" Gustavo nodded affirmation to his question. "No one will ever invent a machine to pick tomatoes."

Hector sighed. "In California they harvest by machine."

Gustavo's mouth dropped open. "How can that be?"

"I've only seen pictures of the machine. It looks like a corn picker."

"I saw a cornpicker once when I went to the lowlands. I never saw it working. I guess they lose corn that isn't ripe. But with tomatoes how can a machine tell red tomatoes from green ones?"

"Well," Hector sighed. "An airplane sprays the tomatoes with a chemical that forces the green tomatoes to ripen. That way, all the fruit is harvested at one time."

"A chemical ripens the tomato?" Gustavo's eyes opened wide.

"Not good enough to eat, but all the tomatoes are used in catsup and salsa." Hector shook his head as he contemplated the waste.

Then he smiled a moment. "You'll be pleased to know that more tomatoes are now used to produce salsa than catsup."

"I can't believe they'd do that to tomatoes." Gustavo's eyes remained wide open. "I mean ripen them with chemicals."

Hector frowned. "After the spraying, the machine scoops up the plants. It spits out most of the roots and dirt, but it takes in a lot of dirt since the tomatoes are spread on the ground."

"You mean the tomatoes aren't tied up on a stake?"

"No, they're not staked. They spread all over the fields."

"How do they get out the dirt when that machine scoops them up?"

"Everything passes over a giant sieve with holes the size of tomatoes. The tomatoes drop through the holes and are conveyed by a belt to a truck."

"Aren't some tomatoes too large?"

"Workers on the machine pick out whatever large tomatoes they can. But many go to waste."

Gustavo fingered his chin, considering what Hector had told him. Then he chuckled, obviously making a joke. "Do any clods of dirt the size of tomatoes make it through the holes?"

"There are clods like that. The workers are supposed to sort them out."

"You sound like the workers don't get all the dirt. What happens then?" Gustavo was frowning.

"In small print on the catsup or salsa bottle, it says 'less than one percent foreign matter'."

"I don't understand." Gustavo shook his head. "How did any of the tomatoes become foreign?"

"Not the tomatoes. The foreign matter is dirt," Hector said.

Gustavo screwed up his face as if about to gag. "I guess I'll stick with the salsa my wife makes."

"You won't go wrong. It tastes far better without foreign matter."

Gustavo said little the rest of the morning. Hector wondered if he was thinking about the consequences of modern technology or his wife's salsa.

When the sun peaked, Maria came to the field with a pottery jug. "Mama didn't know you were planting her tomatoes. She sent me with water, and told me to apologize for not bringing it earlier."

"It's all right, Maria." Hector took the jar and held it for Gustavo. "We brought bottles with us, but our water has warmed up."

"I never tasted colder water, Maria," Gustavo said."A thousand thanks."

"You're welcome," Maria said.

Hector took a long draw from the jug before putting it down and thanked Maria profusely.

"Mama says to come for lunch. She'll need another hour to cook, but you can come now. She says it looks like you've got a good start, and she says for your next meal she'll serve Pablo's head on a platter. But I don't think she means that."

"I don't want to eat Pablo's brain," Gustavo laughed. "It might be contagious. I'll stick with goat brains."

☩☩☩

Hector and Gustavo finished half the field when they decided Inez had time to prepare a meal.

"We could do a few more rows this afternoon and finish tomorrow. What do you think, Gustavo?"

"Or we could wait for Pablo," Gustavo chuckled. He took off his hat and wiped his brow. "You're right, Father. A few more rows on a full stomach, then we finish tomorrow."

The two shouldered their tools and made their way to Inez'. She had put two basins of water on the porch so they could wash. Gustavo took off his shoes. "She nagged me once for tracking in dirt," he said. "She won't expect you to take off your shoes."

"It's an opportunity to cool my feet." Hector untied his shoes and slipped them off. "If you don't mind the smell."

"You mean the feet of priests smell?"

Hector wasn't sure Gustavo kidded since he covered his lower face with a hand, but when Gustavo wrinkled his nose in exaggerated disgust Hector laughed.

Inside, Inez greeted them warmly but frowned when she saw Hector without shoes.

"I can never thank you enough Gustavo," Inez said. "You too, Mr. Cardenas. You've worked so hard I can't imagine how I'll ever repay you."

"Why can't you call him Father Hector like everyone else?" Alejandro's voice was more gruff than usual. "You and your, Mr. Cardenas. It hurts my ears."

"Now, Ando. I know you're hurting, but let's be civil. Your friends don't want to hear us squabble."

"I'm ready for my chili," Alejandro said, ignoring Inez' admonition.

Gustavo and Hector went to his bedside. The aroma of chili and tomatoes made Hector's stomach rumble. He hadn't realized how hungry he was.

Gustavo took Alejandro's plate to him. "If this chili doesn't straighten out your back, my wife's will." Gustavo turned to Hector. "Her chili cures any ache I have."

Hector stepped closer and put a hand on Alejandro's. "How are you feeling, my friend?"

"I'm okay. The back will fix itself. I just don't know how long it will take."

"It needs lots of rest," Inez called from the kitchen.

"And a little peace and quiet." Alejandro grumbled to Hector in a loud whisper.

"You can come to the table, gentlemen," Inez called.

In the dining room, a tablecloth graced the table. Forks and spoons guarded sparkling white plates. A few stains on the tablecloth were partly hidden by a large serving bowl of beans and a smaller one with gravy and bits of meat that turned out to be goat.

Hector surprised Inez by pulling out her chair for her. "Thank you," she murmured. "Will you say grace, Fa . . . Mr. Cardenas?"

Alejandro grumbled something from the other room that Hector couldn't comprehend and that Inez ignored.

Gustavo helped himself to beans as soon as the three of them muttered an "Amen." Inez passed the gravy to Hector. "My mouth can't stop watering," he said.

"In a few months I'll be cooking with fresh tomatoes. You must come back for dinner then."

"Just don't use tomatoes from California," Gustavo said. He went on to describe the process Hector had explained to him. Hector was impressed with the details Gustavo remembered.

"Their technology is miraculous," Inez exclaimed.

"It's a miracle they all don't get sick from foreign matter." Gustavo laughed so hard that gravy started down his chin.

"I'm proud that my tomatoes are all hand picked," Inez said. "Ripe from the vine. Of course, they're staked. They never touch the ground."

"When did you start growing tomatoes?" Hector asked.

"My husband and I returned to San Miguel for his health. He showed everyone how to grow tomatoes with a variety that does well in the mountains. He got good prices."

"Did many people grow them?" Hector asked.

"The third year my husband got terrible boils and a rash everywhere. Well," she blushed, "almost everywhere."

"It was punishment for turning against our corn," Alejandro called from bed. "We've planted corn from the time of Creation."

"It was not against God's will." Inez tried to include Hector in her declaration, but she spoke for Alejandro's benefit.

In a softer voice she said to Hector, "The Virgin cured my husband's boils. Would she have performed such a miracle if planting tomatoes was sacrilegious? I want you to know I crawled from here to the church to beg her help. And she cried tears for me. That's her way of telling you, she'll answer your prayers."

"Your husband changed the type of insecticide he used." Alejandro shouted from the other room.

"That's nonsense," Inez raised her voice. "Insecticides are insecticides. It killed the worms just like the first one did."

Inez laid a hand on Hector's arm. "I wrote the bishop and explained what a miracle it was. I begged him to appoint someone to investigate. Instead, he sent a letter that didn't say anything," she snorted. "I'm surprised he didn't ask me for money."

"How often did you write?" Hector asked.

"Whenever there were miracles." Her tone was indignant. "Until I got so disgusted with his answers—or more often no answer—that I quit."

"It was when you turned Protestant," Alejandro called.

Inez looked Hector in the eyes. "What would you have done? I wrote dozens of letters to the bishop. Never did he take any interest in San Miguel's miracles."

"I'm sorry," Hector said. "But the bishop is very busy. I understand many remote churches experience miracles. They can't all be investigated."

"The church didn't send anyone to examine any of the miracles." Inez stomped her foot.

"That was long ago," Alejandro mumbled from his bed.

"Your grandfather reported miracles that no one investigated. I'd think you'd stick up for him." Inez scowled in Alejandro's direction.

"She means the miracle about the snake," Gustavo said to Hector. "In those days, I guess everyone saw it. My grandparents talked about the snake all the time. Of course," he laughed, "what else did they have to talk about?"

"I suppose they talked about each other. Just like people are gossiping these days. I'm sure they must have had someone to talk about the way they talk about me." Inez sucked at her lower lip.

"Maybe it was our grandparents' grandparents who saw the snake." Alejandro seemed bent on changing the subject. "I guess it must have been in the times when our ancestors fled the Mexican army."

"It's too bad they couldn't have trained that snake to attack the soldiers," Gustavo said.

Hector joined Gustavo's attempt to joke. "It could have eaten the mules that the soldiers used to pack their supplies up here. Maybe even their artillery."

His comments didn't produce any more laughter than Gustavo's.

"Whatever the time was," Gustavo said. "No one has ever experienced a drought like the one they had to live through. I guess not all of them lived through it."

Hector wished he had paper and pencil to record the conversation. The story of this miracle promised to be an important part of San Miguel folklore.

Before either Gustavo or Inez could say more, Alejandro cried out in pain. The three rushed to his side. He had been trying to get out of bed.

"What are you doing?" Inez screeched. "You're supposed to lie there and get well."

"I need to use the outhouse, woman. How can I lie here all day?"

Gustavo and Hector took him by his arms and helped him outside. By the time they got him back in bed, Inez was excusing herself to put her daughters to bed and to prepare Alejandro an herbal brew to help him sleep.

Hector would have to wait to learn details about the giant snake.

14

Hector awoke in a sweat. In his nightmare, he had jabbed his hoe at a monstrous snake threatening to suck dry the village spring. Wherever he slashed the beast, water gushed forth to heal the wound. Hector felt exhausted from his endless battle, guessing he had confused the snake with the Protestant missionary. He shucked off a soaked nightshirt, longed for a shower, but made do with a basin half full of water.

His mind focused on leftovers Inez had insisted he take. He welcomed the rice and beans as an alternative to his breakfast bars. He was running low on his supply since Rosa seldom found them—or refused to believe anyone would eat them regularly.

By the time Hector reached Inez' field, Gustavo was half way down a row preparing holes with his digging stick. The morning was sticky but cool. Hector loosened tomato plants from their cartons and dropped one in each hole. He caught up with Gustavo who rested at a row's end. His friend was whistling a familiar tune, 'It's off to Work We Go' from a Walt Disney movie.

He welcomed Hector with a grin. "I'd rather be digging up diamonds and rubies," he said to Hector. "Like those seven dwarfs." He guffawed. "Why didn't they live in a bigger home and each have his own bedroom?"

"Where did you see Snow White?" Hector asked.

"Alejandro and I went to Culiacan a couple of times to visit Inez. She took us to the movie."

"Did you like the city?"

"It's exciting. So many cars. But you pay for everything. We spent all our money by the second day even though Inez' in-laws let us stay with them and fed us breakfast and dinner."

"When did her husband die?"

"A long time ago. I think from all those poisons he used on his crops. But Inez says he was too educated to buy the wrong chemicals." Gustavo shrugged. "Who knows?"

"What did the doctors say?"

"They said he died from cancer. He didn't live long after they told him. He wouldn't go back to the doctor."

Hector nodded his sympathy. "I hope Inez doesn't expect Alejandro to use sprays."

"Reverend Johanson promised to rent an airplane and spray for the weeds. I don't know if he will spray for bugs."

Hector's jaw dropped. He didn't know of any herbicide that could be used on tomato plants without serious harm. He hesitated to share his thoughts with Gustavo who might suspect him of jealousy.

"He works part-time crop dusting, doesn't he?" Hector muttered a reply.

"Do airplanes spray the poisons in California? Like that chemical to ripen tomatoes."

"They use herbicides but before planting. They try to avoid insecticides, but they use some."

"How can we ever compete with them, Father?"

"Well, Mexico doesn't compete with California for tomatoes. We grow ours to be eaten fresh, not canned. Staking keeps them healthy and customers want them good looking."

"But I remember times when the Yankee tomatoes drove down prices so much we lost money." Gustavo raised an eyebrow.

"They grow staked tomatoes in Florida. Mexican and Florida tomatoes ripen about the same time. So when Florida has a good season, Mexico suffers."

Gustavo bit his lip. "I heard that when Uncle Sam sneezes, Mexico catches cold. I guess Florida tomatoes cause pneumonia."

"I'm afraid so." Hector laughed.

Gustavo sighed and used his digging stick to prepare half a dozen holes. He stopped to look at Hector. "But do machines in Florida stake tomatoes and pick them?"

"The Florida growers hire migrant workers, mostly Mexicans and Central Americans. Since their fields are close to markets like New York City, they have lower shipping costs."

"I guess we're making a mistake to plant tomatoes. What do you think, Father?"

"It's a gamble more than a mistake." Hector shrugged. "Farmers always gamble when they depend on exports. If Florida has a hurricane, then Inez' gamble will pay off." And my efforts with corn and beans won't count for anything, Hector mused. His mind still juggled thoughts of tomatoes and herbicides. Johanson must know herbicides would kill tomatoes, didn't he?

Gustavo looked at Hector puzzled. Hector realized he had been lost in thought.

When the two finished their row, Hector broke apart a clump of dirt. An earthworm looked undernourished. He and Gustavo worked without talking until the sun passed overhead.

They almost finished when Maria and Marta came to the field, bringing sandwiches, a small cake, and a canteen. "Mother sends a thousand thanks," Maria said.

"Granpa Alejandro, too," Marta added. "Well, he didn't tell me to say thanks, but I heard him tell Mother what great friends you are."

"And you're good friends to bring us food," Hector said.

"I'd let you pick me up," Maria said. "But look what happened to Uncle Ando when he did that."

"It wasn't your fault," Hector said, picking Marta up and twirling her in the air. She shrieked her pleasure. "His back just wasn't ready. It's not as young as mine."

"Oh, Father, that was fun. Thank you. Would you spin me again?"

"Remember what Mother told us," Maria scolded. "Besides, Mr. Cardenas might have an accident with his back, too."

"But everyone else calls him Father." Marta's lower lip set in a pout.

"Will you girls share my sandwich with me? It's more than I can eat."

"Thank you, Mr. Cardenas, but we've eaten," Maria said.

"How about some of my cake?" Hector offered half of his to Marta. Before Maria could say anything, Marta took a large bite and proclaimed it the best sweet she'd ever tasted.

With help from Gustavo, Hector soon had Maria as well as Marta engaged in joking about Alejandro.

"Mother wants him to go to Culiacan to see a chiropractor," Maria turned serious.

"That's a doctor who straightens out your bones," Marta added. "He'd make Ando's back straight, and the pain would go away."

"What did Alejandro say?" Hector asked.

"He asked if he wouldn't have to walk all the way to Culiacan?" Maria giggled. "Mama pretended to get mad at him. She told him Mateo had called and was coming today with a load of tomato stakes that Reverend Johanson had found real cheap."

"Will Reverend Johanson be coming, too?" Gustavo said.

"No. He has more business in Culiacan." Maria watched Gustavo take a long drink from the canteen. "If you're finished, we should be going back. Do you want us to bring more water?"

"We'll be fine," Hector said. "It won't be long until we've finished."

✞✞✞

Hector and Gustavo had planted the last of the tomatoes when they saw Mateo's SUV coming down the road into San Miguel.

"Shall we go meet them?" Hector said.

Gustavo shrugged. "I'll come with you. If I go home now, my wife will find work for me to do."

The Ford had pulled up before Inez' home. Before Hector and Gustavo reached it, Mateo and Marcos had gotten out. Pablo was struggling out the back.

"Start unloading," Mateo shouted at Pablo. "We haven't got all day."

"I need a drink of water," Pablo whined.

"You'll get a foot up your ass, if you don't get to work." Marcos drew back his leg to add to his threat.

Gustavo hastened to Pablo and handed him his water bottle. "There's not much left."

"The damn drunk has been drinking since we took him to town. It'd teach him a lesson to go without water. We don't need . . ." Marcos stopped whatever he was going to say when he saw Hector.

"Pablo, my Son, how are you?" Hector put an arm on Pablo's shoulder as the young man finished Gustavo's water. Hector handed him his own quarter-filled bottle, pretending he hadn't heard Marcos' threat.

Pablo's sheepish grin crawled across a reddened face. He glanced at Marcos before finishing the water. "I've sinned, Father. Forgive me."

"We'll talk about it later, Pablo. There are ways of getting help when you have a drinking problem."

"One way is to keep him away from cantinas and bottles." Marcos jerked a bottle from under the front seat of the van. "He was hoping to sneak this one home." Marcos sneered, then broke the wine jug against a decorative rock in Inez' front yard. "When you finish unloading the van Pablo, you'll damn well clean up this glass. You know what Mama will do to you if you miss a single piece."

Pablo looked at the broken glass, then the van, as if confused about where to start.

"Start unloading! We haven't got all day."

"Where do you want them stacked?" Pablo asked.

"We don't have time to watch you stack tomato stakes, you idiot. Dump them out so we can leave. Then you can stack them wherever Mama wants them."

"Are you saying you don't have time for dinner with me?" Inez shouted her question. She had come from behind the house to stand in her front yard with arms crossed. "Well, at least give your mother a kiss."

Mateo strode over and pecked Inez on the cheek. Marcos planted a dutiful kiss on her lips. "We've been busier than ever, Mama. Pharmacies all over are ordering from our company. We even have a customer in the United States."

"Perhaps I should invest in your company, Marcos. Could you help me with that?"

"Eh, not right now, Mama. The stock market is in an uproar. It's no place to invest your money." Marcos walked back to the SUV to find Hector and Gustavo helping Pablo. "You two don't need to do that! Let him sweat out all the booze he's put away."

"We're almost finished," Gustavo said. "What do you want done with those pallets on the bottom?"

"We don't need them, but Johanson thought they might be useful." Marcos glanced around for a place to put them, shook his head in disgust. "Stow them with the stakes, I guess. We've got to leave."

Mateo came to the van and thanked Hector for his help, nodded at Gustavo, and told Pablo to stay away from the booze. He opened the glove compartment to retrieve a bottle of wine for his mother.

"I couldn't get your favorite, Mama, but here's something for you and Alejandro to enjoy with one of your special meals. I hope you like it."

"You're a good son." Inez held his arm and kissed him on the cheek. "Next time, you come, we'll have dinner. Promise?"

"Next time for sure, Mama. If they aren't working us to death."

Marcos kissed his mother's cheek, then threatened Pablo who was slinking away. He handed Gustavo fifty pesos. He thrust a hundred peso note into Hector's hand. "Put it in the collection plate for me, will you?"

Hector thanked Marcos. As he shut the driver side door, he noticed two bullet holes not quite seat high. He couldn't resist poking a finger in one of the holes and whistling in amazement.

"You wouldn't believe how rough it's getting on the frontier," Marcos growled. "Juvenile delinquents bringing guns in from the states. You'd think those gringos could do something to control guns. Those kids shoot at anything that moves."

"So put your trust in the Lord, my Son." Hector regretted his words as soon as he said them. He'd spoken without thinking, but he recognized that Marcos might read sarcasm into his words.

Marcos gave Hector the finger without turning around as the SUV's tires threw dust into his and Gustavo's faces.

Inez had walked up on her porch, apparently witnessing nothing of her sons' departure. She called to Gustavo and Hector to offer them the last of her cake but showed little enthusiasm in her offer. The two declined and returned to the field.

"My Little Angel asked me to invite you to dinner some time, Father," Gustavo said. "How about tonight?"

"Won't it surprise her?" Hector's brow wrinkled.

Gustavo shrugged. "Last night she prepared beans and tortillas," he laughed. "I'm sure she'll be ready with tortillas and beans tonight."

"Tortillas and beans are always a treat," Hector said.

When they reached Gustavo's, Angelita was waiting at the door and greeted Hector warmly, as if expecting him. She took him inside by the arm and seated him on a padded, rickety chair near the end of a long room. At the other end two homemade wooden chairs accompanied a table set with two plates. Angelita hustled into the kitchen to return with another plate and glass. Gustavo retrieved a third chair for the table.

The toddler appeared half chewing, half sucking at a piece of tortilla. He stood a few paces from Hector staring at him. Hector motioned to his lap, the infant took a step farther, but then stopped, glancing toward Gustavo.

"He won't eat you, *chacho*. Not even your tortilla."

The child turned toward Hector but didn't move.

"Would you like to wash up?" Angelita asked Hector. "Gustavo will get some water."

The two men went outside to clean off the dirt. When they returned, the table held a stack of tortillas and a large bowl of beans. Angelita motioned to a chair. She asked Hector to say grace before offering him the bowl of beans and a serving spoon. She motioned for the infant to come sit on her lap.

"Pepe is our grandson," she said. "Our son married a girl from the next village. They work on a farm in the lowlands. We share Pepe with his other grandparents."

"He looks like a good boy," Hector touched Pepe's nose with a finger, then his ribs. Pepe giggled.

"Have a tortilla, Father." Gustavo passed a stack of them. "They taste best while they're warm."

The three scooped beans with their tortillas, then Angelita asked if they had planted all the tomatoes. Gustavo told her they had finished and then related the incident with Pablo.

"More beans, Father?" Angelita asked.

"No thanks, but I can't resist another tortilla."

Gustavo handed him the platter.

"Your tortillas are very good, my Daughter. Very rich."

"It's the water from the spring, Father," Gustavo said.

"Pepe's other grandparents seldom have enough water," Angelita said. "They haul water or else watch their corn stalks wither."

"We have always been blessed with enough water," Gustavo bragged.

"Except that time long ago," Angelita said.

"That doesn't count. The serpent was too young to know what it was doing."

"What serpent is that?" Hector asked.

"The Plumed Serpent." Angelita spoke with hesitation as if she couldn't believe Hector didn't know about it.

"A Plumed Serpent?" Hector's question was full of doubt. He couldn't believe the Aztec deity had reached this far north.

"It's not plumed." Gustavo said. "I told you that Inez read about the Aztec God being a plumed serpent, and she started telling everyone our snake had feathers. It's not true."

"I think it's plumed," Angelita said.

"It's my ancestor who saw it. He never said anything about feathers."

"He could have missed the feathers," Angelita said.

"Alejandro's ancestor saw it, too."

"What made the snake unusual?" Hector recalled the importance of snakes in Mayo and Yaqui legends.

"It was as big as that cottonwood tree trunk by the spring." Gustavo's eyes flashed. "Ten feet in length, maybe more." He held his arms in an arch. "Two feet around. It's been known to swallow goats."

"Anyone who loses a goat blames it on the Plumed Serpent," Angelita whispered to Hector.

"Just remember, woman, that my ancestor saw it."

"And no one's seen it since," Angelita countered.

"Everyone knows there's a giant snake," Gustavo shook a finger at his wife.

Angelita didn't respond.

"And it guards the oasis?" Hector asked.

Gustavo nodded as if uncertain.

"Maybe it guards the oasis from itself," Angelita giggled. "They say that a long time ago the snake got scared or angry—who knows—and thrashed around underground. It caused the earth to turn and toss and that shut off the spring."

"What did people do?" Hector was breathless.

"Our ancestors," Gustavo said. "They did it."

"They had a procession, just like we did not long after you came," Angelita said.

"But our ancestors carried the crucifix. In those days, it hung behind the altar."

"And that brought rain?" Hector's heart beat faster as he awaited the answer.

"No." Angelita sucked in her lips. "They waited weeks after the procession, but the oasis remained dry. Since they couldn't haul water in those days, they were about to move to other villages. But there wasn't farm land for them."

"In their desperation, they organized another procession. This time they carried the Virgin," Gustavo exclaimed.

"And?" Hector felt he knew the answer but was anxious to hear it.

"It poured and poured," Angelita said.

"Some say it was just a good rain," Gustavo gave his wife an annoyed look. "But what mattered was the spring. It started flowing again, and the serpent hasn't thrashed around in his hole since then."

Hector didn't ask what they knew about earthquakes. He was more interested in what had happened to the crucifix and the statue of the Virgin. "And what did your ancestors do next?"

Angelita and Gustavo looked at each other in shock. They obviously hadn't thought about where their story might lead. Angelita pointed her chin at Gustavo to suggest he continue.

Gustavo waved his hands as he spoke. "That was when they built a special niche for the Virgin."

"Behind the altar." Angelita couldn't leave the whole burden of explanation to her husband.

"And they moved the crucifix to the Womb," Hector muttered under his breath.

15

For weeks Hector searched for holes in the Womb large enough for ordinary snakes while a giant serpent slithered in and out of his consciousness. He had to find out more about the snake guarding the oasis.

Hector used the morning to write Edwardo reminding him of San Miguel's need for school supplies. He also told Edwardo to assure the bishop that no miracles had occurred. Progress was being made in understanding miracles, but more time was needed. He added the legend of the serpent to demonstrate persistence of Indian beliefs showing continued need for a priest.

When Hector left the Womb, it was mid-morning and thunderclouds mounted over the mountains. Rain had sputtered sporadically since the tomatoes were planted, and all the crops were well established. The tomatoes fared well after a week of warm nights. The weeds also prospered.

Hector guessed villagers might be relying on Johanson's promise to spray for weeds. It had dawned on him that the man might use some harmless concoction in order to ingratiate himself, but what if the Protestant didn't understand the dangers of herbicides? Hector had to do something, but he didn't know what that was.

He watched some farmers stake plants beginning to flower. Others attacked the weed crop with hoes. Most farmers were too distant for Hector to see if they cultivated corn and beans or tomatoes. None of the figures resembled Gustavo or Alejandro.

Just as Hector turned back toward the Womb, he heard an engine backfire. He looked to the road leading into the village but saw nothing. Another backfire followed, then a flatbed truck appeared around a hairpin. Hector retrieved a hat and came back to watch the truck inch down the road. It was coated with mud, but a tarp protected its cargo. The lumps and bulges beneath the canvas gave no clue as to its contents.

When the truck reached the front of the church, Hector saw that

Johanson drove. He looked at Hector long enough for his eyes to underline the smirk on his mouth. He said something Hector could not hear, but guessed the lips pursed to pronounce, Hector the Rector.

Hector smiled and waved but kept his own mouth shut.

He thought to avoid Johanson until he saw Pablo leave Rosa's and head toward Inez'. Hector was curious to know how Johanson treated Pablo so he decided to join them. He reached the cement footing as Johanson parked. Inez and Alejandro stood on the porch, Maria and Marta by their side.

"Good morning, Reverend Johanson," Inez waved. "You surprised us. I'm afraid I won't have a proper meal for you."

"I didn't have time to call," Johanson said as he climbed out of the cab. "The Lord has had so much work for me. He sent these building supplies from heaven yesterday, and I've got to return the truck tomorrow." Johanson rolled back the canvas to reveal a jumble of building materials.

"The Lord has sent you enough to build two churches," Inez chuckled as she left the porch to examine the cargo. "How are you going to use these banners? They look like flags."

"They are flags. When I spray the crops, I'll need someone on the ground to show me where to spray. It would be so much easier if everyone had planted tomatoes."

"Well, you know how Indians are," Alejandro said from the porch. "We never agree on anything."

"Ando, you sound like you want to pick a fight. You remember that Reverend Johanson is going to make us rich." Inez turned to Johanson. "Alejandro may not be able to handle the flags, Reverend. He's hurt his back."

"I'll wave the flags for you, Reverend Johanson." Marta darted from the porch to the truck to look over its contents. Maria followed, holding Marta back from climbing onto the flatbed.

"You're a wonderful girl, Marta, with a wonderful mother. In a few more years you'll be a superb helper, I'm sure. You can wave the flags then."

"Pablo can handle the flags, I guess." Inez bit her lower lip in doubt.

"I was counting on Alejandro," Johanson said. "But I'm sure someone else can manage. The spraying won't take long."

"Do you think I could do it?" Maria said.

131

"Yes, yes, let her do it. And I can help." Marta went on tip toes to reach a flag and began to wave it.

"Put the flag down," Johanson glowered a moment before he forced a smile. "Two others have planted their fields with tomatoes. I'll need to spray their crops." He took the flag from Marta. "I adore you for wanting to be so helpful. In another year or two you'll be able. It won't be long before you're flying the plane."

"Do you mean it? Will you teach me to fly? I've always wanted to fly." Marta raised her arms and ran in circles, zooming over Inez' flower bed.

When Hector walked up, Marta ran to him and grabbed his legs. "Will you spin me around, Father? Fly me like an airplane."

Hector lifted her above his head and twirled her twice.

"Oh, that's so much fun! I wish I could fly by myself. An airplane is the next best thing, isn't it."

"You need to know all about arithmetic in order to navigate," Hector said. "So study your numbers."

"I will." Marta gazed into Hector's eyes.

He took her by the hand and joined Alejandro on the porch.

"Pablo should be here soon. He must have seen your truck," Inez said. "You'd think some other villagers would have come by now." Inez looked toward the other houses.

"Maybe they guessed that Reverend Johanson didn't bring anything to give them," Alejandro said.

"He always gives them the Lord's word, Ando. You know that." Inez scowled at him.

"I thought I saw Pablo heading this way," Hector said. "In the meantime, perhaps I can help." And get a chance to ask about herbicides, he thought.

Hector stepped down from the porch to join Johanson. A smell of freshly cut wood greeted him. He whistled when he saw a number of oak panels bound by metal-like bands. "I don't know much about construction, but those look like quality panels to me."

"They certainly are. Solid wood." He rapped his knuckles on them. "Took a fork lift to get them on the truck. We'll have to cut the straps and lift them out one at a time." Johanson's chest filled with pride as he studied the bundles of paneling.

"We could start with those two by fours," Hector said. "They'll work up a sweat."

"Why are you so eager to help the competition, Rector?" Johanson looked at Hector through slitted eyes. "Do you have permission from your bishop?"

"He's a good man, Reverend." Inez interrupted. "He's helped Ando, and he helped plant my tomatoes."

"What's the old saying, Olaf?" Hector grinned. "Don't look a gift priest in the mouth. After all, we're both eager to save souls aren't we?" Hector reached out a hand. "What if we start over?"

Johanson took Hector's hand but only for a moment.

"We need to unload those pine panels at the back of the truck. They'll do for the flooring. Set them over the footing, for now. I want to use the nail kegs to support the oak paneling to keep them dry. They're going to be the backdrop for my altar, erh, the Lord's altar. I'm short of roof panels, but there's enough to get a start." He rubbed his forehead. "Whenever I get the time."

Alejandro stepped down from the porch and started toward the truck.

"Don't you lift a thing!" Inez folded her arms and stepped in front of Alejandro.

"I can carry a two by four," Alejandro grumbled.

"We can manage, Ando," Johanson said.

Alejandro glared at Johanson. Hector made a mental note never to use Alejandro's nickname.

By the time the two unloaded the 4 x 8's for the flooring, Hector was sweating. He had to admire Johanson who worked as hard as anyone Hector had ever seen.

"Let's stack the two by fours separately," Johanson said. "Lay them on their wide side about two inches apart with the next layer running at right angles. That way we'll keep them dry."

Johanson picked up four of the boards when he saw Hector lift only three.

Hector grinned inwardly. He guessed Johanson could never overcome his competitive drive.

When they'd stacked the last of the 2 x 4s, Inez called to Johanson and Hector. "You two have to rest. Coffee's ready."

"I was ready for a break when I smelled the coffee," Hector said.

"If you could wait a moment, Inez," Johanson said. "Until I snip the strapping around my oak panels. I've got my clippers out."

"Take your time, Reverend. Just so long as you rest." Inez went back into the house.

Hector had never seen such strapping as that which held the oak. "I can't tell if it's metal or plastic."

"Something new those gringos came up with," Johanson growled as he struggled to cut the material. "I was warned it was elastic so I guess it can't be metal." When he snipped through the first strap, it popped and contracted into coils. Both men laughed at the reaction. Whatever the material was, the strap appeared to be alive.

While Johanson snipped the remainder, Hector pulled the first strap free and examined it. It wasn't metal but must have been as strong. He couldn't stretch it much, but when he released it, its coils resembled a centipede. He pitched it under the truck to get it out of the way.

"I'm finished, Inez," Johanson called. "If you're ready for us."

"She says to come into the living room," Alejandro replied. "The coffee's ready. She's just setting out the cups."

"I haven't seen Gustavo, today," Hector said to Alejandro as he mounted the porch steps.

"I haven't either," Alejandro said. He ushered Hector into the living room. Maria and Marta were sitting on the floor beside a doll's table, helping their dolls serve tea.

Hector asked the dolls' names, but the girls were so caught up in their play they gave only cursory answers.

Moments later, someone on the porch coughed.

"Maybe that's Gustavo," Hector said. He went to the door. "Pablo. I thought I saw you on your way here early this morning."

"Angelita came to the store asking about medicine. Gustavo's stomach is paining him. Rosa didn't have nothing so she sent me to find the *curandera*."

"Is she in the next village?" Hector asked. He hadn't heard of any *curanderas* in San Miguel.

"Teresa lives on the edge of town." Pablo tossed his head as if to indicate a direction. "She had to mix up a bunch of herbs. She pounds them in that rock thing. I had to wait so I couldn't come to help. I wanted to." Pablo shrugged as he nodded his head.

"Pablo, don't stand in the doorway," Inez called from the kitchen door, motioning him into the room.

"I don't trust those *curanderas*," Johanson said. "They got ways to make a person sick so they can charge to cure them. Bad as Yankee doctors."

"Teresa doesn't use any kind of magic or hex if that's what you mean," Alejandro said. "She's a cousin of Gustavo's so she'd never think to make him sick."

Hector scratched his head. He recalled two Teresas with children, or more likely grandchildren, at school. He couldn't call up a last name for either. "Which Teresa is Gustavo's cousin?"

"They're both his cousins. Everybody here is everybody's cousin." Inez dismissed any further inquiry with the tone in her voice.

"I've heard the *curanderas* use magic all the time," Johanson persisted. "They rely on superstition instead of the love of Jesus."

"You wouldn't think that if you knew Teresa," Inez said. "She's been a Christian all her life. At least, a Catholic."

"It's a matter of tradition," Alejandro interrupted. "Our ancestors learned a lot by trying one thing and another. Like what wild plants to eat. So why not what plants cure a stomachache? It's all tradition!"

Alejandro raised his voice to make his point. It was so unlike him that Hector felt tension in the air.

After moments of silence, Hector saw an opportunity."What kind of herbicide are you planning to spray, Reverend?"

"It's something new on the market. A friend's getting me a bargain price for it."

"Aren't herbicides dangerous to use on tomato plants that are so far along?" Hector cocked his head.

"I've seen this one used. Never caused any problems." Johanson dismissed further discussion with a nod of his head.

"It's been our tradition to hoe weeds," Alejandro said. "I wonder what will happen to us if we forget our traditions."

"You could forget that tradition about a giant snake in front of the girls, Ando. You'll scare them to death," Inez said.

135

Hector couldn't contain his curiosity. "Your ancestors did see the snake, didn't they? A large snake?"

"It was a good sized snake, I guess."

Maria and Marta looked up from their play. "What kind of snake, Granpa Ando?" Marta cried. "Did it have big fangs? Was it poison?"

"Just a snake," Alejandro said. "Nothing to worry about."

Inez muttered her disgust. "We don't have snakes in the mountains. It's too cold. You girls have nothing to worry about."

"This snake never leaves the spring, Marta. It will never hurt you," Alejandro said. "It's a good snake. I've only glimpsed it once in all my life."

"It's time for coffee," Inez interrupted. "Sit down, Pablo. I didn't have time to make decent cake, but here's something to go with coffee." She turned to Maria. "You girls can stay with your dolls."

✢✢✢

The coffee break proved a strain. Johanson insisted that *curanderas* represented remnants of pagan religions, and the practice ought to be halted. Alejandro said nothing so it was up to Inez to defend Teresa, but she hesitated to confront Johanson. Hector only spoke enough to be polite, insisting that the cake was better than Inez claimed. He searched his mind for a way to question Johanson about herbicides but could think of no way without offending Inez.

"The break was just what I needed," Johanson said. "You ready to go to work, Pablo?"

"Yes, Sir. Do you want me to sweep? I'm good at sweeping."

"We need to unload the truck. Did you see all that lumber on the truck in front of the house?"

"On that big truck out front?"

"What other truck is there, Pablo?" Johanson's sarcasm was lost on Pablo.

"We'll be out to watch, once we clean up," Inez said. "Ando is so good at drying dishes it won't take us any time at all."

Alejandro frowned but carried his cup and saucer along with Hector's to the sink.

"I thank you for your help this morning," Johanson said to Hector. "But with Pablo here, I won't need you anymore."

"What about those oak panels? They might be too much for just two people."

"Suit yourself," Johanson shrugged.

At the truck, Johanson studied what was left on the flatbed and what had been unloaded. "Let's move one of these flooring panels over there." He pointed to an opposite footing. "I want the oak here and the roofing panels over there."

"What are the floors?" Pablo asked.

Johanson grimaced. "Those boards there, Pablo. I want to put four of the nail kegs on them to support the oak paneling so it doesn't touch the ground. The other four barrels go there." He pointed with a finger. "We'll put the roofing panels on them and wrap everything in plastic. I don't know when I can start building."

The three each took a barrel and carried it to where Johanson wanted them. The second barrel Hector shouldered was much lighter than the first. "They've cheated you out of nails on this one," Hector said.

Johanson squinted. "That's the barrel with electrical outlets. I'm not sure what I got. The railroad auction doesn't specify things the best."

"You think the government will be running electric lines up here soon?" Hector asked.

"No," Johanson shook his head. "I've got my eye on a generator. Once the price is right, I'll have everything I need."

"You pick up all this lumber at railroad salvage?" Hector massaged his fingers as he straightened his back. He rubbed his hands along his waist.

"The lumber was at a going out of business sale. You can get real bargains if you're patient and keep an eye out."

"Watch out for that strapping, Pablo," Hector warned.

Pablo stepped on a piece and grinned as its entire length quivered. "Is it a rope? It's a funny rope."

"We don't know what it's made of, Pablo. It held panels together," Hector explained.

When Hector set his barrel down, Johanson repositioned it. He repositioned the other three also, moving one less than an inch, then shoving it back to where it had been.

He straightened up with a grin. "Are you ready for the oak paneling, Rector? What about you Pablo?"

"Ready," Pablo said. "Will it be done, then?"

"Almost." Johanson wrinkled his nose.

The three men went to the side of the truck with the panels. They tugged at the top one, sliding it to the edge of the truck. Johanson leaned over and pulled at the opposite side. The panel slid out to Pablo and Hector. The three balanced it among themselves and carried it to the barrels Johanson had set aside.

"I've got to get this truck back today, or it'll be my hide. The three of us can easily carry two of these. Make a little less work. What do you think, Pablo? You up to it?" Johanson ignored Hector with the question.

"Less work is good," Pablo said. "You still pay me twenty pesos?"

"Twenty pesos was for all day. Are you trying to cheat me?" Johanson grimaced.

"Pablo no cheat."

"He'll pay you ten pesos, Pablo. Is ten pesos okay?" Hector said.

"Ten is okay" Pablo paused in thought. "Twenty is better."

When the three men reached the truck, Johanson struggled to align two of the panels, pulling them to the edge. The three positioned themselves to equalize the weight. Once they man-handled the two panels off the truck, Hector almost dropped his side. He took a deep breath, counting each step to the barrels.

"Okay," Johanson grunted. "Now position these two over the one that's here. Easy. I don't want any chipped wood."

The three eased the panels into place. Hector wiped his brow with a handkerchief. "I think we'd do better moving one panel at a time."

"So, Hector the Rector isn't used to the hard life. All that time with the books has made you soft, is that it Rector?"

Hector shrugged. He pretended to ignore the baiting, but anger stirred within.

"He spend little time with books," Pablo said. "He's in fields with hoe. Everybody talk about the hoeing priest."

"That's the trouble, Pablo. You can't make a living anymore with a hoe. Too much machinery to compete with. In a few days I'm going to wipe out all the weeds in the tomato fields with a spray from my airplane. No need for hoes anymore."

Pablo looked puzzled but said nothing.

As the three men returned to the truck, Inez called from her porch. "You've done enough. That wood is so heavy. I'm making more coffee, but you need a water break now."

Maria and Marta appeared behind her holding a pitcher and glasses.

"We've only got two more panels to unload," Johanson called to her. "Then we're practically finished." He motioned to Pablo and Hector to position themselves while he tugged the wood.

Hector drew a deep breath as they lifted the load off the truck. He glimpsed Maria and Marta approaching, with Marta skipping ahead. Near the truck she froze.

"It's the giant snake," she screamed.

Hector realized the coil of strapping frightened her, but before he could speak, Pablo screamed and stepped back. His heel caught in his tattered pants leg, and he tumbled over backwards. Hector was caught off guard and twisted to the side. Johanson slid, and the panels fell on Pablo. He yelled in pain. Hector and Johanson scrambled to lift the wood off him.

"Damn, you, Pablo," Johanson screamed. "If you've chipped them, I'm going to kick the . . ." Johanson stopped in mid-sentence.

Inez had raced from the porch when Marta screamed and now stood beside Pablo. "Where does it hurt, Pablo? Are you bleeding?"

"No bleeding," Pablo whimpered. "Arm pains me."

Alejandro joined Inez, and the two examined Pablo. He winced when they moved his left arm, and a lump appeared mid-way up it.

"Rosa help Pablo," Pablo murmured.

"You can stay here tonight, Pablo," Inez said. "How would you like some of my green chili chicken?"

Pablo nodded. He said, "Pablo like."

Hector and Alejandro helped the young man to his feet, supporting him by the waist while they climbed the porch stairs. Inez sped ahead to spread sheets on the sofa bed.

When they came in, she whispered to Alejandro. "You can come up to my bedroom tonight so Pablo can sleep here. I'll go tell Rosa what happened."

Alejandro helped Pablo out of his shoes and pants and into bed.

"Pablo sleep?"

"That would be good, Pablo." Alejandro felt his forehead. "You rest, now. No fever."

Johanson and Inez were standing on the porch, but Hector heard them clearly.

"Can you take him to the hospital, Reverend, if his arm is broken?"

"The truck ride would make his arm worse, Inez. When they find out he doesn't have any money, they won't treat him any way."

"There's a Catholic hospital in Culiacan," Hector called. "They don't turn anyone away."

"I wouldn't take a pet dog there, Sister Inez," Johanson said. "I've heard terrible things about it."

"It sounds as if you just don't want to be bothered, Reverend." Inez put a sharp tone In her words.

"I do have to get the truck back tonight, but that's not it. It's that he'll be better off here under your care."

"I suppose that's true," Inez sighed.

When Pablo fell asleep, Hector went to the porch. Johanson was unloading the last of the building materials. Hector joined him as Johanson climbed into the truck.

"Pablo's asleep," Hector said. "You don't have to say goodbye."

Johanson nodded and slid behind the wheel. "You tell him goodbye for me."

"Aren't you forgetting something?" Hector said.

"I don't think so." Johanson frowned his puzzlement.

"The twenty pesos you promised him might make him feel better. At least ten.

"That damn dimwit didn't earn ten pesos. He damaged my panels. He's lucky I don't charge him ten pesos."

Johanson started the truck. As he reached to shift gears, Hector grabbed his arm. "He's got ten pesos coming!"

Johanson pulled his arms away, then thrust his hand in Hector's face. "You give him twenty pesos, you damn mackerel snapper. Your bishop can afford it."

Hector stood dumbfounded. He hardly felt the blow to his face, but 'mackerel snapper' left him perplexed. Johanson had used the English words. Hector didn't know what they meant, but he was certain Johanson had insulted him.

16

The next morning, Hector gnawed at an energy bar on his way to Inez'. Pablo was still sleeping so he promised Inez he'd return later. He went back to the Womb, carrying three warm tortillas Inez insisted he needed for breakfast. Hector didn't feel hungry, but he chewed a tortilla absent-mindedly while fidgeting on the edge of his cot.

When Hector flexed his fingers, he imagined them around Johanson's throat, breathed deep trying to dispel such thoughts. He studied the remaining tortilla to divert himself, instead imagined sitting on Johanson's chest, pummeling his face. Hector couldn't rid his mind of the English words, mackerel snapper, although they remained meaningless to him, but his major issue with Johanson was the man's promise to spray the tomato crop with herbicides.

Hector shuddered and evaded the issues by concentrating on a devout prayer for Pablo. Unable to concoct one worthy for such a sorrowful soul, he wondered if he'd ever be a deserving priest. His clenched fists clamored to relax. The tension reminded him of a meditation exercise from his days in seminary.

Visualizing a series of gardens the colors of the rainbow brought relief. Suddenly a voice echoed above him, "Father, forgive them, they know not what they do." Hector looked up into the eyes of Jesus, for a moment the figure's lips moved. He did not believe the voice had been imaginary, but he refused to accept the words as a miracle. He settled for a hallucination—perhaps divinely inspired.

Jesus' words made Hector realize he needed to forgive Johanson. His savior had provided the clue. Hector bowed his head and muttered words of forgiveness. They meant no more to him than the prayer he'd constructed for Pablo, but the effort reminded him of his fellow seminarians' discussion of forgiveness. The students were unsatisfied with a professor's explanation that they were duty-bound to forgive because God forgave them. A friend concluded that to turn the other cheek, did not constitute sufficient forgiveness. Priests must include reconciliation to achieve forgiveness.

What steps could Hector take to reconcile his differences with Johanson? Helping him build his church would not suffice. Hector shrugged, then promised himself to continue seeking reconciliation.

He rose and entered the church to stand before the altar. The Virgin sparkled at his presence. He wondered if she was trying to tell him something. Hector returned to the Womb and knelt before his cot, but he avoided the eyes of Jesus more than he focused on prayer.

Did he have to reconcile his differences with Johanson before finding relief from cravings for revenge? He took comfort from his mind's image of the Virgin surrounded by a radiant glow, her smile forgiving. He thought of his own mother and the constant support she gave him. A memory of tying the tails of two cats together and their ensuing fight haunted his thoughts. Their screeching cries echoed in his ears. His mother had thrown a blanket over the cats, calmed them, and insisted Hector untie their tails.

When he finished and the cats dashed off, he asked his mother if the cats would forgive him. When he saw a tear in her eyes, he asked if she would forgive him. She'd told him the first thing he had to do was to forgive himself.

Hector had thought about the incident many times, had confessed his prank often, but nightmares about the incident plagued him until seminary. The discussion in one of his first classes was about the need to forgive oneself before going into the business of forgiving and absolving the sins of others. Hector had spent that night in prayer, begging for forgiveness, until he realized that he did not need outside assistance. Only he could forgive himself.

He knelt before his cot for a minute more, reaching an inner peace, as he again forgave himself. When he rose, his mind floated free from thoughts of confronting Johanson or seeking revenge. Hector opened his top drawer to search for the wallet so seldom needed in San Miguel. He pocketed a twenty peso note and left to visit Pablo.

✞✞✞

Maria and Marta were playing on the porch. Marta raced down the stairs as soon as she saw Hector.

"Fly me, Father, fly me." Her smile tickled Hector's insides.

He twirled her around four times. When he put her down she stumbled in different directions. Hector's jaw dropped as he reached to steady her.

"She's teasing you, Fath . . . Mr. Cardenas. She's not really dizzy." Maria came to the steps and took her sister's hand. "Shame on you, Marta. You scared him."

Marta was undaunted. "I came close to heaven, didn't I, Father? I was like an angel."

"You're always close to heaven, my child." Hector brushed back his hair. "God is all around you. Around each of us."

Marta attempted to cross herself, but Maria grabbed her hand. "Mr. Cardenas has come to see Pablo, Marta. We shouldn't interfere with his duties."

"How is Pablo, Maria?"

"He says he feels fine, but he yells when he moves his arm. Mother has gone to find Rosa."

Maria opened the door for Hector, and he joined Alejandro sitting beside Pablo.

"Good morning, Father," Pablo said.

"I was about to say a prayer," Alejandro said. "It's better that you do."

"Why don't you say your prayer, Alejandro, and then I'll say mine. Two prayers will help twice as much."

Alejandro begged mercy from the Virgin and help from Jesus Christ. Hector recognized parts of Christian doctrine in the prayer, but most important was what originated in Alejandro's heart. Hector tried to match his friend's sincerity, but he felt inadequate.

Pablo bubbled with such gratitude for their concern over him that Hector extended his arm to pat Pablo's hand. Pablo moved his arm to take Hector's hand, winced, and groaned.

"It must be broken," Alejandro said.

"I can take him to Culiacan in my jeep, but the ride will be hard on the break."

"He'd have to wait all day to see a doctor at the clinic," Alejandro shrugged. "Poor Indians don't get much attention."

Just then Inez returned. "Rosa is going to get Teresa. She can set a bone better than any medical student at the clinic." Inez came to stand over Pablo. "We'll have that bone straight in no time." She patted Pablo's cheek. "You know Teresa can fix up bodies better than anyone for miles around."

Inez looked at Alejandro. "Have you offered Mr. Cardenas coffee?" Before Alejandro could reply, she said, "Of course not. That would be too much to expect." She looked at Hector. "If I remember, you don't like sugar."

"I take it black, too. Thanks."

"Tsk, tsk," Inez shook her head as she headed toward the kitchen obviously unable to imagine anyone not wanting sweetened coffee.

Inez called from the kitchen that Teresa must be on her way and for Pablo not to worry. She returned with coffee for Hector and herself. Alejandro brought a third chair for her, and she bombarded Hector with stories of ill treatment from the clinic that treated Indians—if attendants found the time.

A coughing at the door interrupted Inez. "That must be Teresa," she said and rose to meet her.

Hector recognized Teresa as one of the grandmothers who brought two children to school. Her eyes played leapfrog over lips that frolicked in an endless smile. She carried a bright colored bag with Guatemalan designs. Hector wondered what stories the bag could tell about its journey from so far south.

Teresa didn't waste time. "Don't move your arm, Pablo. Let me run my fingers over it." She lifted the arm carefully, but Pablo stifled a cry.

"It's good the bone is not sticking through the skin," Teresa said. "There's so much danger of infection when that happens."

"Is it broken?" Pablo asked.

"I'm afraid so, Pablo. It'll hurt when I straighten it. The more you relax, the less it will hurt."

Teresa retrieved two candles and a twist of rope from her bag. Inez found two candle sticks, inserted the candles, and put them at the head of the bed. Teresa lit them.

"We use candles in the church," Alejandro said to Hector.

When Teresa lit what looked like rope, Hector recognized a kind of twisted grass. The herb gave off a heavy, sweet aroma.

"It's tradition," Alejandro stammered as if defending the practice.

Hector offered a rationale. "It's a practice of the church, too—the use of incense. It reminds us all our senses can be aware of the presence of God." Hector felt his rationale was inspired. He'd never before given much thought to the church's use of incense.

Teresa hummed as she waved the glowing ember around Pablo. Hector expected the smoke to irritate his nose the way incense did, but instead it lulled his senses. He felt his whole body relaxing.

"Take a deep breath, Pablo, and let it out slowly," Teresa said, standing beside the young man.

When Pablo completely exhaled, Teresa took his wrist in one hand and his elbow in the other and pulled hard. Hector heard a click and saw Teresa's lips expand into an even wider grin. "It set good, Pablo. You'll be able to use your broom like always."

Pablo wiped away a tear. "Thank you, Aunt Teresa. You know so much. You do so good."

Teresa searched in her bag until she found a roll of bandage. "I forgot to get more." The sparkle in her eyes disappeared.

"I'll tear up an old pillow case," Inez said. "That ought to do."

Inez went upstairs and came down ripping a pillow case into lengths. Teresa took a small splint from her bag, and the two women wrapped the arm with care.

Teresa promised to return the next day, then started toward the door. Inez accompanied her. She slipped a bill into Teresa's bag and insisted she take a pound of sugar as well. The gesture reminded Hector that he had brought twenty pesos for Pablo.

"Will you say a prayer for Teresa?" Alejandro looked at Hector.

"After you," Hector said.

Alejandro asked a merciful Lord to watch over and reward Teresa. And to forgive her if any pagan practices survived in her services as a *curandera*.

Hector hadn't thought of Teresa as a *curandera*. He was puzzled as to why Alejandro thought any of her cures might be pagan. His curiosity interfered with the prayer he mumbled, but he followed Alejandro's lead in asking God to care for Teresa and reward her for her kindness.

"Teresa may be the best *curandera* in the whole valley," Inez said. "I don't know what put it in your head that she uses any pagan customs." She shook her head at Alejandro. "What made you think that?"

Alejandro hesitated. "Well, I don't know of any. Except maybe her chant. But I thought an educated priest might believe she relied on pagan ritual." He raised an eyebrow while looking at Hector.

"God is open to many different approaches, Alejandro. I realize the church was intolerant of Indian religions when the first missionaries came. They went too far in trying to eliminate them, but they did accept many Indian practices also."

Pablo followed the discussion with open mouth. "Uncle Alejandro, will you ask God to forgive me?"

"Pablo, why do you need to be forgiven?" Inez asked.

"I chipped that wood the Protestant loves."

Alejandro laid a hand on Pablo's good arm. "You didn't do anything bad, Pablo. If anyone needs a prayer of forgiveness, it's Johanson. He said awful things to you."

"I hope you can forgive him, Pablo." Inez said. "He was in such a rush, he made you work too fast."

"I'm sure Johanson is sorry for what he said to you, Pablo. You worked hard, and you deserve this." Hector showed the twenty peso note to Pablo before slipping it into a shirt pocket wearing away at the bottom.

"Can you forgive Reverend Johanson, Mr. Cardenas? For using such language." Inez put a hand on Hector's shoulder. "And you making up for his sins!" The gesture made Hector sure she understood that the twenty pesos came from him.

"I struggled to forgive him this morning. I found out something most interesting. I had to forgive myself first."

"What in the world did you have to forgive?" Inez asked.

"For being so angry at Johanson. At first, I thought all the anger was because of the way he treated Pablo. Maybe I should be angry at his language, too, but I'd heard most of the words before." Hector paused, looking at the three of them, feeling their presence. Confession in the confessional booth had never given him as much relief as he felt now. "My real anger at him must be because I see him as a threat to our San Miguel church. He could undo what missionaries have given their lives for." He looked at Alejandro. "What you have devoted your life to."

Alejandro responded as if by habit. He put a hand on Hector's head. "You are forgiven."

"And what about you, Ando?" Inez asked. "Don't you have to ask forgiveness from the Father?"

"What do you mean, woman?"

"He wanted you to plant your field in corn and beans. The one where you worked so hard, and then you go plant tomatoes on it. You ruined his experiment."

"I planted those tomatoes because you wanted me too, woman. I can do what I want with my land. And I wanted to please you."

"You wanted to please Father Hector, too, didn't you?"

"No. It's up to me what I do. I can't tell others what to do so they don't tell me. You forget you're an Indian," Alejandro snarled. "I guess you lived with that Mexican family too long."

"Don't you start on that." Inez returned the snarl. "I know you're jealous of my husband because of his wealth. How many times have I told you that money doesn't matter to me?"

"Well, I don't know what matters to you. I thought getting rich mattered. That's why I planted those damn tomatoes."

"If I mattered to you at all, you wouldn't curse in front of me. How many times have I told yom I don't want to hear such words? I'm sure Mr. Cardenas doesn't either."

"Why can't you call him, Father, like everyone else? You don't call that damn reverend, Mr. Johanson. It's always Reverend. Don't you realize you're kissing the ass of a false prophet?"

Inez leaped to her feet, her face a vivid red. She stormed into the kitchen.

"I think she's mad at you," Pablo said. "What's a false prophet?"

"It's someone who claims to speak for God when he doesn't know God," Alejandro said.

Hector fingered his chin. He should have been angry at Johanson for sowing such dissent between Inez and Alejandro instead of seeing the man as a threat to himself. He felt inept. A good priest would have defused such anger before it started, but he sat without saying a word.

"I made both tea and coffee to go with my cake. I think Pablo ought to have tea. Which will you have, Father? I know how much Ando likes his coffee."

"I'll have black coffee without sugar," Hector said.

"When did you have time to make cake, Inez?" Alejandro's tone showed his concern for her. "Taking care of me and Pablo. You have your hands full, but you can still make cake. What a remarkable woman you are."

Hector shook his head. Gustavo was right. The two could fight and make up in the same breath.

Alejandro praised Inez' cake to such length that she blushed. Pablo kept looking back and forth at the two of them, an anxious look on his face.

When Hector finished his cake and coffee, he mumbled an excuse to leave.

"Don't go before you talk some sense into this woman," Alejandro said.

"Now who's forgetting he's Indian?" Inez said. "You let me decide things for myself."

Her argument made Alejandro hesitate. Hector's curiosity piqued. He looked at Inez. "Can I help in any way?"

"Reverend Johanson needs someone to flag the tomato fields when he sprays for weeds."

"And she volunteered," Alejandro said. "Won't listen to reason," he grumbled.

"Maybe I can do it, if you show me how." Hector couldn't believe he had volunteered to help Johanson with his tomato venture.

"I'm afraid it's a matter of trust, Mr. . . . . Father." Inez replied. "We were counting on Alejandro, but with his back, he just can't."

"And she thinks she can." Alejandro shook his head.

"I've been farming all my life," Inez declared. "I can certainly mark a field by waving a silly flag."

"It's the poison, woman. I don't want you poisoned with all that spray."

"I have my husband's protective suit, and Reverend Johanson brought an inhalator, or whatever you call it, along with the flags."

"The way he buys things he probably got some Yankee bargain. Probably that terrible poison they used in Vietnam. What was that called, Father?"

"Agent Orange was horrible. I think it's been outlawed."

"You see, the Father agrees with me."

"Well, I want you to be careful, Inez," Hector said. "We should know what chemical Johanson plans to use. Alejandro is right about that. Herbicides aren't usually as dangerous as insecticides, but they can be harmful. Especially to . . ." Hector let his words trail off fearful his warning would be mistaken for disparaging Johanson. The man must intend to use something harmless, Hector argued to himself.

"That suit of her husband is too old. Probably full of holes. Who knows if it was any good when it was new? If it was any good, why did he die from the chemicals?"

"No one knows why he died," Inez said. "He hardly used the suit. It isn't like I'll be wearing it often."

"At your age, once may be enough. Anyway what happens when the bugs invade us. You'll be out there waving those silly flags so Johanson can't possibly miss dousing you with his poison."

"He won't douse the flagger. By the time we need the bugs sprayed, your back may be in shape so you can flag the fields."

Hector could see what was coming. He claimed he needed to look in on Gustavo and left, hoping Pablo would forgive him for abandoning him in the cross-fire.

17

A spitting rain greeted Hector on his way to the outhouse. The wet weather had excused him from the fields for a week, but if the forecast was correct he could survey the crops in the afternoon. Total summer rainfall for the mountains seemed higher than usual to him, but the radio station ignored such details.

Hector spent the morning reviewing church history, curious about the weather two hundred years ago. One missionary wrote that his teeth were rotting because of his daily diet of corn. Another priest hoped to construct a mill to lighten the load of women who spent their days grinding corn. Specific reporting on the weather was disappointing. Details on farming fared no better.

Hector put away the ledger and blew dust from other volumes before looking out the door. The sun sneaked from behind dissolving clouds. He put on old shoes, sharpened his hoe, and set off for the fields where twelve figures already bent over hoes or tied up tomato plants. As Hector got closer, he saw Gustavo, sweat dripping from his nose.

"Good morning, Father," Gustavo called. "Watch out for snakes!"

Hector chuckled. "So you heard what happened with Pablo and Johanson?"

"It's too bad about Pablo. But I saw him yesterday, and he's sweeping Rosa's floor. He'll be fine."

"How is Rosa taking it?"

"Oh, Pablo has broken bones before. Rosa knows Teresa can mend bones better than anyone in the valley. I'm sure your prayers helped, too."

Hector shrugged. "Alejandro's were even better."

"He and Inez told me about your remarkable sermon."

Hector's nose wrinkled in puzzlement. "What did they mean by a sermon? I didn't give a sermon."

"Your teachings on forgiveness, Father." Gustavo's head bobbed. "I'm sorry I missed it. Inez talked about how much it meant to her."

"Well, I wouldn't call it a sermon."

"Alejandro called it teaching. Doesn't a sermon teach?"

"I suppose it should." Hector looked at all the weeds that needed to be hoed. "Maybe I can teach more about forgiveness some Sunday morning."

He chopped at a cluster of grass threatening Gustavo's corn, and congratulated himself on his sharpened hoe.

Gustavo joined the effort, and the two finished a row before pausing to rest.

"The rain helps the weeds," Gustavo panted. "Too bad Angelita doesn't have a recipe that uses weeds."

Hector laughed. "I've been studying the corn and beans. They're both a rich green, hearty looking, taller than I expected for this time of year."

"It's been fine weather, Father. Everyone praises your prayers for rain."

It looks as if prayers have done more than any innovations I've tried, Hector thought. "So much for being an agricultural missionary," he muttered under his breath.

"What did you say, Father?"

"I hoped to help San Miguel more with my science. All that mulching you and Alejandro did might be a waste of time." He wiped his brow. "I hope you'll forgive me."

"That's funny, Father. A priest asking us sinners for forgiveness."

They laughed together before starting on the next row. When they finished, they were close to Gustavo's demonstration plot.

"I want to show you something, Father. You'll find out you don't need to be forgiven." Gustavo took off his hat and wiped sweat from his brow, waved his hat in front of his face, then did the same under his arms. Gustavo enjoyed teasing Hector's curiosity.

"Let's look at the corn and beans we mulched," Gustavo pointed to his field a few yards away. The plants weren't any taller than the others, but Gustavo insisted Hector examine their leaves.

"See how green they are. Look how the roots branch out. They're going to be remarkably strong." He stepped a few rows over and asked Hector to examine his beans.

"I'm not sure I see any difference," Hector said. "Maybe they're a little greener. They aren't any taller."

"Look for what you can't see," Gustavo said. He covered his chuckle with a hand.

Hector brushed back leaves on half a dozen plants but failed to note anything different. "I give up, Gustavo. What am I looking for that I cannot see?"

Gustavo giggled. "Let's go over to the big field and look at my beans there. Maybe you'll discover it then."

Hector's forehead furrowed. He feared he'd fail Gustavo's test. He turned over half a dozen bean leaves before an answer came to him. "You've got insects on these beans. I didn't see any bugs on the first plants."

"I've looked at all the beans in my demonstration plot, and I've found only one bug. If the mulching only did that, it would be worth it. We can't afford the chemicals to kill bugs."

"Do you mind if I show the men working out here how your beans resist bugs?"

Gustavo bellowed. "Oh, Father, it's not something I'd hide. I've already shown everyone how the mulching helps." He stopped laughing to speak seriously. "I thought the mulching would make paradise for the bugs, but now we can build up compost whenever we aren't busy with other work, like this hoeing." Gustavo spit at a flourishing nettle.

"Speaking of hoeing," Hector laughed. "Have you looked at Alejandro's tomatoes? How are the weeds there?"

"Do you know Johanson comes today to spray for weeds? Alejandro told me last night. His back's better, but Inez insisted she'd handle the flag. His back must bother him awful because he's going to let her do it. He hardly argued."

Hector swallowed. He had no idea what Johanson planned, but it was too late now for him to do anything about it. He adjusted his hat, and the two men wielded their hoes. They were nearly finished when the sound of an airplane roared toward San Miguel. Hector shielded his eyes with both hands to study an old bi-wing that circled overhead.

"Look at this ghost coming out to farm," Gustavo tugged at Hector's arm and pointed toward Inez' field.

A figure clothed in a faded white, baggy suit stumbled along in jumbo size boots, the face hidden behind a mask of goggles and an antiquated breathing tube going over the back to a canister.

"It must be Inez," Gustavo giggled. "It's not tall enough for Alejandro. The whole town will be joking about her."

Half way to her field, Inez stepped out of a boot and almost stumbled.

"I never saw a ghost trip," Gustavo laughed.

"Ghosts are supposed to float through the air," Hector said.

"I'm glad to know ghosts are as clumsy as I am."

Inez sat down to pull the boot on and trudged to the edge of her field. At the roar of the airplane, she shielded her goggles with a hand to look up. She waved just as Johanson hovered over the ground, streaking for her, engine screeching. Inez waved the flag as if her life depended on it. The motor missed twice and back fired once, but the plane came straight toward the field. Gustavo gasped as a cloud shot out the back of the plane while passing over Inez. Hector sucked in his lip. Johanson's early release enveloped Inez. He didn't stop the spray either as he flew past her field. Two men watching from their corn and bean fields had expected the plane to halt the spray, but the heavy mist continued. They bent low and covered their faces with their hands. The plane continued to the end of the fields. The sticky smell of herbicide that Hector expected didn't materialize. He prayed that the spray was indeed a harmless solution.

Johanson waved from the open cockpit as he circled and climbed. Hector couldn't tell if he waved at Inez or not, but she wielded the flag frantically.

"Inez will break her arm," Gustavo guffawed. "Unless the flag rips apart first."

"She should have set out another flag to show Johanson which way the wind is blowing," Hector said. "There are gusts."

"Maybe they planned to use their cell phones," Gustavo said. "Last night Inez told Alejandro he couldn't flag the plane because he won't use a cell phone."

Hector shrugged. "With that breathing contraption, she can't use a cell phone."

The plane came in even lower than the first time, but Johanson timed his release better so the spray missed Inez until a gust of wind blew a partial cloud back her way. Hector could almost hear what she must be saying into the inhalator.

Again the plane continued spraying to douse all the crops. Again, Johanson waved with enthusiasm as he circled. Again, he sprayed a farmer in a corn and bean field. The man had bent over to protect his face, but he looked up as Johanson circled and shook his fist at him. His lips were moving, but Hector couldn't hear him because of the airplane's roar. Hector quivered. If Johanson were using an herbicide, it would damage corn and beans as well as tomatoes.

"You'll have to forgive my cousin for all the cursing he's doing." Gustavo held his sides laughing. "He picked up a lot of swear words the year he worked in the lowlands."

"I can't imagine what Johanson is doing," Hector said. "He must know he's supposed to spray just the tomato fields."

"He's made a mistake, don't you think?" Gustavo raised an eyebrow. "He can't afford to spray all the fields—unless he found another of his bargains."

"And why isn't he paying attention to Inez?" Hector rubbed his chin. "It looks to me like she's positioned herself just right to show him where to spray."

Inez moved farther away for a third pass, jerking her flag up and down. Her breathing tube hung to her side. She appeared to be fumbling with something in her hand that she held to her mouth. Hector realized it must be a cell phone, but he couldn't imagine Johanson hearing anything in the open cockpit.

The plane roared down and released its spray beyond Inez, missing a quarter of her tomato field while continuing to spray to the edge of the cultivated area.

The men in the fields who had not been sprayed jogged toward Hector and Gustavo. Two stopped to pick up something. Their delay meant Johanson caught them on his next pass. This time Hector could not miss the curses.

"We better move away," Hector said. "I don't want a shower of herbicide."

"I can finish hoeing later if it doesn't rain," Gustavo said. "You've been a big help, Father. I owe you many hats."

Near the edge of the field they stopped to watch Johanson make another sweep of the total area. It was obvious he intended to spray all the corn and beans as well as the tomatoes even as Inez positioned herself on a neighboring tomato field.

The other men joined Hector and Gustavo. Their eyes were watering, but they had regained their usual good humor and bantered about Johanson doing their weeding for them.

The conversation turned sour, however, when one man asked the others if Johanson might charge them for the herbicide. Gustavo's cousin reminded them that the Protestant had promised to spray the tomatoes free if they planted them, but the corn and bean farmers had not been told of any free spraying. They asked Hector about herbicide prices. The figures he recalled worried the men.

They were getting sullen when Johanson made his last pass. His engine missed, coughed, and sputtered. The wings dipped from side to side. Two of the men cheered at the thought of his plane crashing.

The engine caught, and the wings steadied as Johanson climbed. He circled once more and waved. Hector guessed Johanson misread the arm waving of the men around him.

"I guess you better prepare that sermon on forgiveness this Sunday. These men will never forgive Johanson otherwise." Gustavo chuckled until saliva ran down his chin.

✞✞✞

A few days later Hector breathed relief. None of the fields Johanson had sprayed showed any signs of being poisoned. He guessed Johanson had known he'd used a harmless solution unless he had been hoodwinked himself. Hector wondered how he'd ever find out the truth.

He went to his room to prepare a sermon on forgiveness. He bogged down on Biblical admonitions, felt they did not suffice, and couldn't recall what points he'd made when he talked to Alejandro and Inez. Hector decided to talk to the two for help. Besides, he might find out why Johanson had sprayed all the fields.

When he reached Inez', he was surprised to see Adela and Rachel playing with Maria and Marta. The four were under the panels Johanson had stored for his church. The ends of the plastic wrapping protecting the panels flapped in a gust. The older girls sat under the oak paneling, Rachel and Marta crawled around under the other panels.

"Father," Marta cried as soon as she saw him. She scrambled out from the playhouse and dashed to him. "Fly me, please."

Hector lifted her above his head and twirled her around. When he sat her down, she took several drunken steps. "I guess I won't be able to fly you anymore, Marta. I make you too sick."

"No, no, Father. I was only kidding. Really." She clasped her hands as if praying to him. "Fly, Rachel, please."

Rachel crawled from under the panels and walked to Hector. She looked to her sister for approval, but Adela was engrossed with a doll. "Will it make me dizzy?"

"We'll have to see," Hector said, lifting and twirling her.

Rachel blinked her eyes when Hector put her down. She put one hand to her forehead. "I guess that was fun," she said. "But, it's scary, too."

"Come see our airplane hangar, Father." Marta seized Hector's hand and led him to the panels. "That's our house over there where we have our dolls. I mean our babies." She pointed to the barrels supporting the oak panels. "It's not much of a house. It doesn't have any sides. Maria says that flap of plastic is our wall, but it doesn't even make a good window." She went over to stand beside the flooring panels supported by barrels. "This is our airport. Uncle Ando said he'd build us a control tower. We don't need sides for a hanger. Do we Rachel?"

Rachel nodded, then she held out her arms and taxied to the runway, ran a few steps before jumping into flight. Marta followed, roaring almost as loud as Johanson's bi-wing had.

While the two girls ran around on the ground, Hector talked to Adela and Maria. "So, you're taking care of the babies while your sisters fly. Are they dusting crops?"

"Is that the same as spraying with poison?" Adela asked.

"Yes, it is. The herbicide is not exactly a poison. Well, it's poisonous to plants, but not to humans."

"It made my uncle sick," Adela said.

Hector wasn't surprised to hear that someone had gotten sick from the spraying. People had heard so much about herbicide and insecticide poisoning that psychological reactions were common.

"I'm sorry to hear that. I'll call on your uncle."

Adela gave him her uncle's name and described where he lived. She said Hector ought to hurry. Her aunt was going to call Teresa for help, and she would cure him right away.

"And how is your mother, Maria?" Hector asked. "I guess with all that protective clothing she wore she didn't get sick."

"She says she's fine, but Uncle Ando keeps kidding her about how much she scratches."

"Do you think she scratches a lot?"

Maria shrugged. "I don't know. Uncle Ando is a tease. But I saw her scratch her arms while she washed the dishes."

"How about your dolls?" Hector asked. "Are they itching or do they feel sick at their stomachs?"

Adela cocked her head with her mouth open. "They're just dolls, Father. Dolls don't itch."

Before Hector could reply, Marta and Rachel came zooming in for a landing. "Do you want to zoom me again, Father?" Marta asked.

"Don't you remember, Mama wants us to call Father, Mr. Cardenas?" Maria said. "I mean . . ." Maria reddened, then shrugged and said nothing more.

Inez called from the porch for the girls not to bother Mr. Cardenas and asked him if he wouldn't come in. She'd made coffee and promised not to add any sugar.

Hector called that he'd be delighted, said goodbye to the girls, and went to the house. The smell of coffee reminded him of how little he had eaten for breakfast. He imagined leftover cake with the coffee. Hector shook hands with Alejandro and squatted beside him.

"Your teaching about forgiveness impressed Inez," Alejandro said. "The next day she went over to Rachel's and Adela's mother and asked her forgiveness. I guess the two women made up. The next day Maria and Marta went to their house to play. Now they're here playing, and Inez can't bake enough cake to stuff them with." Alejandro chuckled. "You see how much we need a real priest."

Inez came out of the kitchen with coffee and cake. "You saw Rachel and Adela? I want you to know your sermon about forgiveness touched me deeply. I've made up with their mother, and the girls couldn't be happier. Thank you so much!" Inez served Hector before Alejandro.

"And have you forgiven yourself?" Hector asked.

"I'm working on it. I thought there would be nothing to it, but it's harder than forgiving others." Inez scratched at her arm before cutting the cake. Hector saw red welts on the other arm.

Alejandro chortled. "Next you'll have to forgive Johanson for giving you a rash."

Inez reddened. "Some bug bit me," she said to Hector. "Now Ando's blaming it on the spray."

"I saw how you got sprayed. I suppose Johanson was getting used to the controls."

"I did get covered, but I had protective gear on."

"That suit is full of holes," Alejandro said. "Two of them were so large I could poke my finger through them."

"Well, a little rash won't kill me. Now eat your cake, Ando."

Hector asked if Inez knew why Johanson had sprayed all the crops.

"He did that from the goodness of his heart." Inez seemed to force sincerity into her words.

"He got a bargain on the weed killer, that's why." Alejandro scowled. "The good friend who's always getting him bargains probably stole it."

"Ando," Inez screeched. "What a thing to say about Reverend Johanson in front of Father." Inez bit her lip as she added, "Mr. Cardenas."

"I guess we'll never know," Alejandro said. He looked at Hector. "Has anyone else in the village been sick?"

"A few itches and a few coughs," Hector said. "It's common after people are caught in a spray that they imagine aches and pains. So we may never discover what real damage the herbicide caused."

"At least the weed killer should help everyone," Alejandro said. "We'll pray for the health of all those who got sprayed."

"Your heart is in the right place, Ando. If you just weren't so stubborn . . ." A tear came to Inez's eye. "Sometimes I think it would be better if Reverend Johanson had never come to our valley."

Hector hid a smile when Inez started to cross herself.

18

Rosa had found the wood putty and oil that Hector requested, and she delivered the order the day after Johanson sprayed the fields. Now Hector was filling in the cracks that marred the massive oak doors of the church. He marveled at how well the hand-wrought planks fit together and how the oak had endured for more than two hundred years. Even if the can of putty was the smallest he had ever seen, it sufficed to plug the few cracks he found.

Hector hammered the putty lid in place to preserve what was left, then turned his attention to the iron hinges. The screws were pounded into place so that attackers could not remove them. Since the hinges had survived for two centuries, Hector didn't know why he bothered to oil them. He knew the new hinges on the small door did require oil. When school was in session the children loved to swing the door back and forth. Hector winced as he recalled the ear piercing squeal.

While he tested the hinges, he noticed two farmers approaching the church through the plaza. He brushed back loose strands of hair while trying to recall their names. They were not among his most faithful participants at mass. He recalled chatting about plant pests with one of the men but couldn't recall either man's name.

The two took off their straw hats as they climbed the stairs to the church. Their dress and size were much alike, but one had an unusual, round face, the other's contrasted in length. It narrowed to the point that his nose must have struggled for space to breath.

Round face held his stomach while he grimaced. Long face's grimace grew even grimmer. He walked with small, tight steps.

"Would you pray for us, Father Hector?" round face said. "The way Alejandro prays for sick people."

"Of course, my Sons." Hector searched his memory for names, but the effort proved fruitless. They were familiar faces, yet he failed to generate names for them.

The two men looked at each other for a moment as if puzzled. Finally, they dropped to their knees.

Hector knelt, too, but before praying he asked what troubled them.

"I can't keep anything down," round face said. "I've done nothing but vomit since that damn fool preacher sprayed us with his poison."

"Me, too," long face said. "But it's the other end, Father. I sleep outside to be near the outhouse. My guts are tied in knots. My wife threatens to stop feeding me."

"I'm sorry, my Sons." Hector sucked in a breath. None of the crops had suffered from Johanson's spraying so he was skeptical that the men were poisoned, but psychosomatic reactions were to be expected. He prayed for their health at length, helped them get to their feet, and asked if they felt better.

Round face rubbed his stomach. Both grimaced. Narrow face looked around as if searching for the nearest outhouse.

"When Alejandro prays for us, we kneel before the Virgin," round face said.

"Of course, my Sons. I wasn't thinking." Hector bit at his lip, realizing how much he still had to learn.

The three walked hurriedly to the altar. Hector knelt with the Virgin behind him, the two men facing them. He began a prayer, but their muttering interrupted him.

"What is it?" Hector asked.

"When Alejandro prays for us, we kneel in a circle," long face said.

"That way we are all equal in the eyes of the Virgin," round face said. "No one can head a circle."

The observation made perfect sense, and Hector filed it away in his memory for future use.

Hector prayed until sweat broke out on his forehead. He hadn't realized how engrossed he'd become. He took a deep breath and asked the two to join him in the Lord's prayer. When the three finished, he asked if they felt better. Both nodded, but round face put a hand to his stomach and massaged it.

"Perhaps you should see Teresa, too," Hector said.

"She's good," long face said. "Right now I don't have any money."

"What about the free clinic in Culiacan?" Hector asked.

Round face snorted. "To get there we have to go with Rosa. There's always a long wait at the clinic. She can't stay to bring us back."

"The last time I went, they sent me to a private doctor," long face said. "My son had sent me some money, but it was the time when the peso wasn't worth anything. The doctor wanted ten thousand pesos. I had only five so they turned me away."

"I'm sorry." Hector could think of nothing more to say. He guessed the ailments were psychological and prayer would help, but he worried that their illnesses might be physical. "I hope Teresa can help."

"I'd like her to settle with Johanson," long face said.

"What do you mean?" Hector asked.

"In the old days medicine people could make Johanson as sick as we are. All they needed was a little bit of his hair or some of his clothes—like his hat."

"You mean evil magic?" Hector asked.

"Not evil," round face said. "It was a way of getting justice."

Hector couldn't argue with the logic.

The two men thanked him for his prayers and promised to keep him informed as to how they felt. Both were massaging their stomachs as they left the church.

✝✝✝

Hector decided to see about Inez' symptoms. He didn't think she would be as susceptible to psychological ailments as the two men. When he reached her house, he found Alejandro on the front porch in a rocking chair. He was whittling a piece of wood but didn't volunteer to tell what he was carving.

"Where did you find a rocker?" Hector asked.

"Inez keeps it in her bedroom. It was a gift from her father-in-law, and she doesn't like to have it outside. But the weather's so good today, she's granted me the privilege. I think it has something to do with what you taught us about forgiveness, but she won't admit to it."

"How's she feeling?"

"She ought to be in the rocker. Her scratching would propel it like a rocket and maybe settle her stomach."

"You think it's the herbicide?"

"Has to be. She's never sick otherwise. She won't blame Johanson, but yesterday she was talking about having to forgive him." Alejandro chuckled. "Talking to herself, but I overheard her."

"You old eavesdropper."

"Yep, we're both getting old," he sighed. "Talking to ourselves, yapping about the old days. Pretty soon we'll be forgetting things."

"Well, you don't look old," Hector said. "And, I bet as soon as your back's in good shape you'll be out in the fields tying up tomatoes and picking off worms."

"The bugs may be a problem," Alejandro said. "Inez made it clear to Johanson that's he's not to spray the fields again. I heard her shout, no insecticides, on that cell phone of hers."

The two laughed. Before Hector could ask what Alejandro was carving, Inez appeared in the door and greeted Hector. For once, she didn't offer cake or coffee.

"Don't you wear out that rocker, Ando." Inez teased.

"This rocker could be made out of steel, it's so solid. Why don't you come and sit on my lap, and I'll rock you to sleep."

"Oh, Ando. You be careful what you say in front of Mr. Cardenas. He won't know what to think of us."

"He'll think we're an old married couple." He nodded to Hector. "Isn't that right, Father?"

"A happily married couple—perhaps middle age. Certainly not old."

Inez beamed. "I know people say we often fight. But I think we were made for each other."

"Then why won't you sit on my lap?" Alejandro patted his knees in an invitation.

"Your skinny old legs wouldn't hold me even if the rocker held us up."

Alejandro pretended to grumble. "Well, I wouldn't want to catch whatever rash it is that you have anyway. You kept me up last night scratching."

"If you were awake, who did all that snoring?" Inez scratched her neck.

"I don't snore," Alejandro snorted.

"And you talk in your sleep."

"Who talks in their sleep?"

"You do. I'm sure you were talking about Ana last night." Inez folded her arms over her chest. "It's always about Ana, isn't it?"

Hector heard a note of jealousy in Inez' voice, but most of her tone was teasing.

"What did I say about Ana?" Alejandro pretended to be gruff.

"Well, it's hard to know, I admit." Inez licked her lips. "I think you were talking Indian."

Alejandro guffawed. "You know I don't know any Yaqui." He turned to Hector. "My grandfather taught me a few words, but my grandmother only spoke Spanish. She'd tell him not to confuse me."

"That happened to a lot of people," Hector said. "I'm surprised how many persons still know an Indian language."

Inez excused herself to get a glass of water.

After Inez was inside, Alejandro and Hector sat in silence a while.

Finally, Alejandro said, "I suppose you're wondering who Ana was."

"I am curious," Hector said.

"We grew up together. We weren't closely related so we could have married, I guess."

"It must be hard in a small village where just about everyone is related to each other."

"We have to bend the church rules sometimes," Alejandro shrugged.

"When I served El Hidalgo, I thought it better to marry couples who lived together instead of telling them they couldn't be blessed by the Church." Hector paused. "Please don't tell the bishop I said that."

"I guess he'd think it wrong that I have married people for years," Alejandro said.

"The Church is forgiving." Hector held up both palms. "You did what you thought was right. No priests came here for two centuries. It's remarkable what you did—you and the men who came before you—to preserve the Catholic faith."

"I tried to do what was right. I guess the others before me did the same."

"They gave up a lot I'm sure." Hector brushed back hair from his forehead. "You must have, too."

Alejandro shrugged.

"I'm sorry you weren't able to marry Ana and have children," Hector said. "What happened to her?"

"Her family went to the city to look for work. Her father said he'd come back as soon as he earned a little money." Alejandro sat rubbing his chin. "But no one in the village ever heard from them again."

"Is that why you remained single?"

"Well, I waited a long time to hear from her. Inez and I saw a little of each other." Alejandro scratched his cheek. "She and Ana were the only two I could have married. Then Inez went off with her mother to work." Alejandro sighed. "I began to serve the men running the church. Between that and the farm, I kept busy. After a while, the men responsible for running the church got after me to go see the bishop to find out if I could be trained as a priest."

"And did you?"

"My mother wanted me to go, but my father needed me to help farm. It was a long way to go. No roads. We didn't have a horse. I could hardly read and write."

"It's what's in your heart that's important. I'm sure you had that." Hector knew Alejandro would make a fine priest. "But seminary does take a lot of reading and writing."

Alejandro sighed. "I wouldn't have Inez if I'd become a priest."

"That's right," Hector chuckled.

"Which isn't always such a good thing," Alejandro smiled.

"Until you remember her chicken and green chili soup."

"That mostly," Alejandro chuckled. "Oh, she has a good heart behind that tough exterior. It must have been hard raising twelve boys. And now two girls." He nodded his head. "That Marta is a handful."

"She needs a grandfather full time," Hector said.

Alejandro didn't answer, but a wry grin showed he agreed.

✝✝✝

Gustavo called a greeting from the steps. Inez came to the door, welcomed Gustavo, and said she'd leave the three men to themselves.

"I was in my field yesterday tying up tomatoes." Gustavo looked at Alejandro. "Could you use some help with yours, *Compadre*?"

"They'll be out of hand soon, no?" Alejandro sighed. "But my back's ready."

"I found only one tomato worm," Gustavo said. "Maybe we'll be lucky this year."

"Let's see if Father's eyes are better at spotting worms than yours." Alejandro used his arms to push himself up from the rocker.

When the three men reached Alejandro's field, the sun slid behind a cloud. A swarm of insects buzzed around Hector's head until a breeze took them away. Hector breathed deeply, his lungs enjoying the clean mountain air.

"The nights have been warm enough," Alejandro said. "The tomatoes will ripen just fine."

"The rainfall has been good, too." Gustavo looked at Hector. "Your prayers have worked a miracle."

Hector swallowed. He felt guilty because he had so seldom prayed for the crops. "It's your hard work that counts for the success. Are the corn and beans doing as well as the tomatoes?"

"We'll have one of our best harvests." Gustavo laughed, "The mice and birds will have a grand fiesta."

"There are new storage techniques," Hector said. "Low cost ones with cement foundations."

"It means everyone uses the same building, doesn't it?" Alejandro asked.

"It's the best way to keep costs down," Hector answered.

"Like a cooperative?" Gustavo asked. "I don't think San Miguel would cooperate like that."

"Cooperatives can start by doing just a few things. Maybe just one thing." Hector recalled the limited work of the co-op at El Hidalgo but how much it contributed to sustainable agriculture.

"Remember when that school teacher talked of co-ops?" Gustavo said to Alejandro. "What was his name?"

"*El Comandante!*" Alejandro laughed.

"Who was *El Comandante*?" Hector asked.

"That was our nickname for him," Gustavo said.

"He was a good man, but he kept telling other people what to do." Alejandro shook his head.

"Always giving orders," Gustavo sneered.

"He was trying to advise," Alejandro said. "Like you, Father."

"But sometimes I sound like I'm giving orders," Hector said. "Tell me when I do that, please."

"*El Comandante* knew a variety of corn that yielded more than ours. He grew a demonstration plot, like you showed us how to do," Alejandro said. "His corn did better than anyone's."

"The next year, some of us planted half our fields in the new corn," Gustavo said.

"That corn produced a lot more. *El Comandante* claimed it was fifty percent more." Alejandro beamed as he recalled the yield. "Everyone loved that corn."

"Too much," Gustavo said. "We didn't pay attention when the women complained that the meal wasn't right for tortillas. They had to mix it with old meal before it stuck together." Gustavo smiled.

"The next year, everyone planted their fields with *El Comandante's* corn. I can't remember its name." Alejandro fingered his chin a moment. "Well, we celebrated with fireworks because the harvest was so large. We invited a neighboring village to enjoy our success."

The two men laughed as they recalled the event.

"And what happened?" Hector asked.

"Everyone loaded up on beans!" Gustavo guffawed.

"The women couldn't make tortillas. The meal wouldn't stick together." Alejandro chortled. "That village still jokes about how San Miguel tortillas fall apart."

"They said they'd try to remember to bring glue the next time San Miguel gives a fiesta."

"So everyone quit that variety of corn," Hector said.

"Well," Gustavo reddened, "A few men grew it the next year. They took it to town to sell. But their wives didn't think much of that. Making trouble for other women. Even if they were city women."

"I can see why not many men wanted to try my mulching technique. I'm surprised as many did."

"They wanted to please you, Father," Gustavo said. "And Alejandro urged them to try it."

"In a way I feel like I'm *El Comandante*," Hector sighed. "He advised you—ordered you—to do something new, but he didn't stay around to suffer the consequences."

"Well, if anything goes wrong with the mulching, it can't cause much of a problem." Alejandro put his hand on Hector's arm. "And it didn't cost us any money. We had to pay a lot for that seed corn that couldn't make tortillas." Both he and Gustavo chuckled at the memory.

It reminded Hector of how Indians at El Hidalgo laughed away past misfortunes.

Alejandro plucked away two worms from one plant. "They're having a fiesta here."

"Maybe we should have Johanson spray for bugs after all," Gustavo said.

The three of them examined a dozen more plants but found no worms. "We don't need to spray," Alejandro said. "But I wish Johanson would do something about all that lumber he dumped in front of Inez'. She's made up with most of her neighbors, and their kids are swarming over that junk pile."

"Johanson wouldn't be pleased to hear you call it a junk pile," Hector laughed. "I wonder what he'll do if that precious oak paneling gets damaged."

"The way the kids are playing around it, something's bound to happen." Alejandro shook his head. "They've been building everything with it—except a church."

"You didn't help things when you built Marta a control tower out of the broken tomato stakes," Gustavo kidded. "They all loved that."

"I guess it didn't help," Alejandro nodded. "But Inez is so glad she's made up with the neighbors she won't interfere with the kids playing around that wood." He sighed. "Two older boys even dragged the bags of cement around to make a jail."

"Oh, no," Gustavo said. "What will Mateo and Marcos do when they find their mother has a jail in her front yard?"

"It's not to laugh about," Alejandro snorted. "Some kid is going to get buried in that junk heap."

19

Hector spent the next few days helping farmers search for pests. He learned that the two men whose health he'd prayed for had improved, but they were not yet working their fields. The lack of pests meant a break from the farm work.

The next day, Hector visited Alejandro and Inez. On the way, he heard the shrieks and shouts of playing children. In front of Inez' house most of his pupils were chasing each other around the piles of lumber, except for two who sat between sacks of cement. A scowling jailor twirling a nightstick guarded them. Hector wondered what crime the two had committed. He hoped it didn't involve drugs. At Marta's hanger he admired an adjoining three foot high control tower, patched together with broken tomato stakes and ingenuity. As Hector mused over the construction, he noticed two small wooden airplanes beside the tower. They were not only true-to-life, but each had its own character. The nose of one turned up as if to say, "You'll never find a faster airplane." The other had curving wings to proclaim the smoothest ride ever given. Hector reminded himself to look at Alejandro's figures that he carved for tourists.

"Father," Marta seized his hand. "Come see what we've built."

"The school can hold all of us." Rachel grabbed his other hand.

"My sister is a wonderful teacher," Marta said.

"Mine, too," Rachel echoed. "But she says Gatita can't attend."

Maria and Adela announced an end to recess. Except for Marta and Rachel, the children scurried to sit under an expanse of paneling. Maria and Adela knelt before them.

"Now we will begin with sums," Maria said. "Write on your blackboards 12 plus 16."

The children drew the figures on imaginary boards.

Maria waited a few moments before she asked, "Who has an answer?"

A few older boys at the side snickered.

A girl at the other side shot up her hand. "I know."

"It's a wonderful school, isn't it Father?" Marta looked up at Hector.

"It is," he said. But his brow furrowed as he worried about the children playing under the weight of the panels. "How long have you been in school?"

"This is the third day," Rachel said. "I'm getting kinda tired of it. Playing in our hanger is better."

"I'd like to be the teacher once," Marta said. "Don't you want to be the teacher, Rachel?"

"I guess. But I don't want to teach sums. I want to teach reading, and we don't have any books."

The comment reminded Hector that Edwardo had not responded to his request for school supplies. He'd have to write another letter.

"Marta," Rachel said. "We should go back to school now. What if everyone left when a visitor came?"

"Excuse us, Father?" Marta gave Hector a wide grin.

He nodded. "Study hard."

Hector watched Maria teach for a while. When Marta and Rachel took their seats, she led the class in a song. It registered on Hector that he had neglected musical instruction. Given the quality of his voice, he wondered whom he could get to assist him.

After listening to his students a few minutes, Hector continued on to Inez'. Alejandro sat on the porch, enjoying the rocking chair. As soon as Hector reached the stairs, Inez called from within the house to ask if he'd like coffee.

He said he would and pulled up a chair beside Alejandro.

"Every child in town must be here."

"From all that noise, I think every child in the next village must be here, too," Alejandro said. "They've built everything they can imagine with that lumber . . ." he repeated his joke "except for a church."

"What will they do when Johanson builds his church?"

Alejandro shook his head. "They'll be back in your school before that happens." He stared at Hector for a moment. "You will be here to start school, won't you?"

"I hope so," Hector said. "But I don't know what the bishop has in mind for me."

"It's been a miracle that you have been here as long as you have. You've done a lot in a short time."

"That's good of you to say, but I haven't helped as much with the farming as I wanted." Hector paused. "And the bishop wanted me to explain more about miracles to everyone—something I know little about. He thought miracles were too frequent in San Miguel "

"Here's your coffee." Inez carried three cups on a serving tray, served the two men, and took one for herself as she sat down. "Excuse me for butting in, but I couldn't help hearing you say something about miracles."

"I was telling Alejandro that part of my mission here is to explain that miracles are rare events. If they were commonplace, they'd no longer seem miraculous." The explanation was reasonable to Hector, but as soon as he'd uttered the words, he recognized the futility of his reasoning.

"We were blessed in the past with many miracles," Inez said. "But you can tell the bishop not to concern himself. We're no longer experiencing any."

"Well, some of those miracles you reported might not have been so miraculous," Alejandro said.

"When we all prayed over Gustavo's father?" Inez' nostrils flared. "You remember that? Nobody doubted that he was about to die. But our all night prayer vigil begged for his recovery. And he got well. No medicine. No help from Teresa. You said at the time it was a miracle."

"It did seem like one," Alejandro admitted. "But we prayed all night for your husband when he wasn't as sick, and he died."

"You could tell there were people in the congregation who didn't like him. They would have been insincere in their prayers. That one family didn't even stay the night."

"They had a sick baby, Inez. No one expected them to stay."

Inez shrugged but didn't give up. "Well, we had a committee that looked into every miracle that we reported. Right?"

"You were the committee, Inez. Those others never dared to contradict you. Besides, you could write better than anyone else so everyone supported you." Alejandro cleared his throat. "Almost everyone."

"I suppose you're going to bring up that chili." Inez glared at Alejandro.

Alejandro didn't answer. Finally, Hector asked about the chili.

"It's not important," Inez said.

Alejandro chuckled. "Pedro found a chili that looked like the Virgin. He passed it around the church and everyone agreed it looked like her. But no one talked about it being a miracle."

"Then it turned red." Inez' tone was defiant.

"And wrinkled," Alejandro guffawed.

"The man's a pagan," Inez grumbled. "Everyone else saw it. With the coloring you could see her eyes, especially her cheeks. It was the Virgin of Guadalupe. No doubt about it."

"And your committee report left no doubt about it."

"Well, it didn't convince the bishop." She gave Hector a dirty look.

"But it didn't keep you from writing more reports," Alejandro said.

"Did you believe most of those things were miracles or not?" Inez turned red.

Alejandro hesitated. "They were certainly unusual. I admit, we have had more than our share."

"Why do you think that is?" Hector asked.

"Because of God's blessing." Alejandro didn't hesitate to answer.

"Is there some reason San Miguel was blessed more than other villages?"

"God works in mysterious ways!" Inez's expression said she didn't need more of an answer.

"Our ancestors worked hard to maintain the faith." Alejandro drew a deep breath. "When the Jesuits left, how did any ignorant Indian know what to do? It's like that today. So many times I don't know what I should do when people need help. Should I marry these young people? What if I get the words wrong when I comfort dying people?" Alejandro sucked in his lips. "What bothers me most is when I baptize babies. I like to do it, but there's so much I'm not sure about."

"Prayer and blessing aren't dependent on words, Alejandro. I'm sure your heart is right, and you get across what it is that God wants."

"If that is so, why do priests study so long? Why do the words have to be Latin?" Alejandro looked perplexed.

"They don't have to be. The church used Latin for so long because people all over the world knew it then."

"Well, I think my ancestors worried about getting things right, and I do too. We all made mistakes, but God showed He cared for us by showering us with miracles."

"I'm sure he paid special attention to everyone when the Jesuits were expelled. Now that the people in the mountains aren't so isolated, God won't have to demonstrate his love by sending so many miracles."

Alejandro looked at Inez and chuckled. "Not since the committee turned Protestant."

"Oh, Ando. It wasn't just me. We all recognized the miracles. Other villages experienced miracles, too."

"I guess that's true. It's just that the other villages didn't have a committee to write letters the way you did." Alejandro smiled despite a wrinkled brow that showed concern for a serious matter.

"How did you select a committee to decide if something was a miracle?" Hector asked.

Inez deferred to Alejandro. "All the elders got together to talk it out. Whenever someone got sick, a *curandera* was called. If he or she didn't have a cure, then we all prayed over the person. If they got well right away, we knew it was a miracle."

"All this talk of miracles is making me thirsty," Inez declared. "We need more coffee. Sorry Mr. Cardenas, but I don't have any cake."

"Coffee is more than enough," Hector said.

"I think you're right," Alejandro reflected. "We're getting modern. God won't need to bless us with so many miracles as He did in the past." His tone didn't have much conviction, but his shrug said he didn't want to discuss the matter further.

He spoke instead of repairs the church needed, noted a few that would require purchases, and wondered if Hector had a budget that could help. Hector wrote down what was needed and promised to ask the bishop for aid.

✝✝✝

When Inez returned with more coffee, the three sipped in silence, content to watch the children play. The jailor tired of guarding his prisoners and freed them. The school children fidgeted so much that Adela took Maria's place as teacher. She spotted Gatita slipping out of Rachel's sack. Adela wagged a finger at her sister and told her to take the cat away. Rachel slipped from under the paneling and came to the house with Gatita. She asked Inez to watch her kitten. Inez held the kitten on her lap, scratching its ears. She was asking Hector about his experiences in seminary when a mouse darted across the porch. Gatita leaped from Inez' lap to chase it. The cat and mouse raced toward the jail, school house, and airport hanger.

Inez screeched. Hector couldn't tell if it was the mouse or Gatita's leap that startled her. She dashed from the porch after Gatita. Hector couldn't believe Inez' agility as she ran around the piles of lumber in pursuit.

The mouse headed for the airplane hanger with Gatita close behind. Inez almost caught up when her foot tangled in the control tower. She twisted around to free herself, backed into the panels that roofed the airport hanger, and staggered backward. Her arms flailed around as she struggled to regain her balance but to no avail. She went down among falling panels, one landing atop her leg. Her scream stretched over the valley.

Hector raced from the porch to see what he could do. Alejandro arrived almost at the same time, and the two men lifted a panel off Inez' leg. They both gasped. A sliver of bone protruded through a break in the skin. Blood spurted over the leg.

20

Hector and Alejandro hurried to get Inez inside where they would stop the bleeding. Alejandro bent over her and whispered something while getting an arm under her shoulders. Hector took the other side and slipped an arm under her waist. When Alejandro nodded, the two lifted her and headed toward the house.

"We'll carry her to my bed," Alejandro said.

"That was my mother-in-law's bed. Don't get blood all over it," Inez protested. "Maria, get that old comforter from upstairs to protect it."

"Yes, Mama." Maria had rushed to her grandmother's side when she saw the men carrying her. "I'll get it." She dashed up the porch stairs and disappeared into the house.

Alejandro and Hector positioned themselves at the foot of the stairs. Hector waited for Alejandro to direct.

"Take me up head first. Ando, you need to take half a step more before you start." Inez glanced at Hector. "Do you have a firm grip?"

Hector nodded, then concealed a grin at Inez' directions. How could she be totally in charge when she must be in so much pain? he wondered.

"Take me to the top of the stairs, and then rest until Maria can arrange the comforter." Inez' lips were turning blue.

Alejandro nodded at Hector. He gripped Inez a little tighter, and the two men did their best to keep her level as they struggled up the stairs. Inez gritted her teeth.

At the top, she called out. "Do you have the comforter spread out, Maria?"

"Yes, Mama."

"Are you rested?" Inez looked at Hector and Alejandro.

The two men maneuvered Inez through the door. In juggling her leg, she cried out for the first time, but she did not blame either man.

Inez breathed deep, trying to stay calm. She complimented Maria for the way she had arranged the comforter. "Pull the bed out from the wall, dear," she told Maria.

Hector and Alejandro did their best to keep the leg in place while they laid Inez on the bed.

"Thank you, gentlemen. I'll be comfortable now."

Hector noticed Inez bite her lip. Her face was a pasty white. "Let me get a better look at the break," he said.

The blood spurted, and Hector guessed broken bone had cut an artery. Alejandro bent over Inez, too, to examine the wound.

"You've cut an artery," Alejandro said. He managed to keep a calm voice, but beads of sweat broke out on his forehead.

"You'll have to make a tourniquet," Inez replied, her voice as calm as ever.

Hector felt his chest tighten, but he forced himself to appear as composed as Inez and Alejandro. When he shoved his palm into Inez' thigh, the spurts of blood slowed.

Alejandro came from the kitchen with a sash and a wooden spoon. He wrapped the sash around Inez' leg, but before he could do more, she insisted he reposition it farther up her leg. "You'll have to loosen it every twenty minutes. Or is it every thirty minutes?" She looked at Alejandro and then at Hector.

"We'll do it every twenty five," Alejandro said.

"I suppose that will do," she sighed. "Why do I have to remember everything?"

Alejandro tied the sash in a loose knot, inserted the wooden spoon in the knot and tightened the tourniquet. When Hector removed his palm to take the spoon, Alejandro went upstairs.

Hector brushed hair away from Inez' forehead.

"Is there any chance the blood will coagulate? Won't it spurt when we loosen the tourniquet?" Hector was surprised that Inez' voice trembled.

"We may have to tighten it and loosen it several times before the bleeding stops," Hector said. He couldn't remember anything about tourniquets from his short course in first aid. He did recall the dangers of infection from open wounds. Inez' wound was as open as he could imagine. "I have some penicillin in my first aid kit. I'll get it when Alejandro returns."

Alejandro came down as if on cue. He was fumbling with something in his hand.

"Ando! What are you doing with my cell phone? You've been scared to death to touch it before."

"I'm dialing Mateo and Marcos. At least, I'm trying to." Alejandro stumbled on the bottom stair but caught hold of the railing.

"That's good of you. But they're on the other side of the mountain. They told me I couldn't reach them." Inez turned to Hector. "They have a large order with a new customer. From the way they talked, I suspect it's Walgreen's. Isn't that a drug store giant in the United States?"

"I believe so," Hector said.

"They told me they were meeting in Columbus. I believe it's in New Mexico. Is there a large Walgreen's there?"

"I don't know," Hector said. "The only thing I know about Columbus is that's where Mexico invaded the United States."

"Oh, Mr. Cardenas!" Inez laughed. "You're trying to make me forget my pain. Mexico could never invade the United States."

"It wasn't much of an invasion, but Pancho Villa crossed the line with troops. And a famous United States general, Black Jack Pershing, came to fight him."

"Was it much of a war?" Alejandro asked.

"Not much. If I remember right, it was the first time the United States used airplanes in combat."

"Did they kill many Mexicans?" Alejandro said.

"No. They just used their planes—or maybe it was only one—to spy on our troops. I believe Villa rode in an automobile instead of on a horse. It was near the end of the Revolution."

"Airplanes can be dangerous weapons," Alejandro caught his breath. "I saw them using machine guns on people in a movie."

"Thank goodness they've never been used against us," Inez said.

Alejandro looked at her with mock concern. "Why it wasn't long ago that one sprayed you with poison gas." Hector hid his laugh while Alejandro guffawed.

Inez managed a rueful grin before berating Alejandro for ridiculing Reverend Johanson.

"Instead of joking we should be calling a hospital." Alejandro's features became serious.

"What hospital would send an ambulance to San Miguel?" Inez stated her question.

Alejandro shrugged.

"I'll call my friend at the bishop's. Surely he can talk a hospital into sending aid."

"It would be a Catholic hospital, wouldn't it?" Inez asked.

"Yes. One where the bishop has influence. I'm sure it would be a fine hospital. You'd get the best of care."

"No. I won't do that." It was obvious Inez wouldn't consider Hector's offer. "I'll call Reverend Johanson. He always told me I could count on him." She dictated the number to Alejandro who fumbled with the cell phone before handing it to her. She shook her head in disdain at his clumsiness but blew him a kiss.

"His answering machine says he's unavailable." Inez sucked in her lips.

"That's the fourth or fifth time he's been unavailable," Alejandro emphasized unavailable.

"He has many flocks," Inez said, but Hector heard distress in her voice.

"I'll get the penicillin." Hector rushed off to the Womb.

When he returned, Alejandro was tightening the tourniquet.

"It bled very little," Inez said. "I've got a bandage to apply. I'm sure the bone can wait until we hear from Reverend Johanson."

Hector got a glass of water from the kitchen and offered it to Inez along with the penicillin. He feared she might refuse it, but she took the pills and swallowed them with the water.

"Thank you, Sir. I'm much obliged."

"You don't have to be obliged. Not anymore than if we got you to a hospital. Won't you reconsider since we don't know when Reverend Johanson will answer?"

"And what if he expects to haul you to a hospital in a beat up old truck?" Alejandro said.

"A Catholic hospital is out of the question." Inez stuck out her jaw. "Let me have that phone again."

Alejandro pretended to hand it to her, then jerked it away. "What about

Father's offer, Inni? Please! This is an emergency."

Hector thought he saw Inez blush at Alejandro's nickname for her, but with her loss of blood he couldn't be sure.

"Reverend Johanson will take care of me." She dialed his number, got the answering machine, and explained what she needed. She handed the phone to Alejandro with a look of triumph. "Plug it into that large battery the boys brought. And don't worry about me. I'll be making you my chicken and green chili soup in no time."

✝✝✝

Hector went to Rosa's the next morning to see what medical supplies she had. She dusted off a box of bandages and charged it to Hector's account. He wondered how dusty the bandages inside might be as he made his way to Inez'. Five or six women milled around on the porch. Apparently she had made up with most of her neighbors. They all greeted Hector and thanked him for the care he had given Inez. He acknowledged their thanks but assured them he had done little.

Inside he found Teresa sitting beside Inez with a glowing twist of rope blowing smoke from it onto the broken leg. Someone must have taken off the wrap from the day before. Hector was relieved to see that the bleeding had stopped. Still, splinters of bone protruded, and Hector couldn't imagine Teresa setting such a fracture.

Alejandro greeted Hector before he could examine the wound further. "Johanson called this morning. He can't get here for three or four days. He didn't say what was keeping him."

"And Inez sent for Teresa?" Hector said.

"No. Teresa came late last night as soon as she heard about the broken leg. She had to go home for medicines but returned at dawn. She put some kind of powder on the leg to stop the bleeding. The incense helps, too."

"You mean the sweet grass."

"Well, native incense. What we had before the white man came." Alejandro shrugged.

"I'm sure it's as good as incense," Hector said. "What about a splint for the leg?"

"I've made two from Johanson's lumber. He shouldn't mind—since he's unavailable." Alejandro snorted his scorn.

179

"Will Teresa set the leg?"

"She takes care of most broken legs." Alejandro expressed confidence. "She's studying how to set Inez' leg now, not just waving that incense around. It helps her concentrate."

Hector waited and watched. It seemed a long time, but he realized it was only a matter of minutes until Teresa motioned to him and Alejandro to assist her.

"Hold her thigh as steady as you can, Alejandro. You take her hand, Father, and say a prayer." Teresa licked her lips. "Before you say one for her, say one for me."

Teresa held Inez' foot with one hand and maneuvered her leg with the other. Inez screamed a swear word before clenching her teeth. Alejandro handed her a smooth piece of wood to bite.

Inez closed her eyes. She might have fainted. At any rate, Teresa finished setting the leg without further outcry. The *curandera* wiped away the blood before wrapping the leg with a bandage. She nodded to Alejandro to bring the splints. The two placed the splints and strapped them to the leg with strips of dish towels. Hector went to the kitchen for a glass of water. When he offered it to Inez, she waved it away.

"There's some brandy on the top shelf of the kitchen cabinet, if you don't mind, Sir. Don't you think I deserve it? And maybe Teresa, too?"

"Absolutely. And what about Alejandro and myself?" Hector said.

"Pour four glasses." Inez' voice was weak, but she managed to make her words a command.

✢ ✢ ✢

Three days later Hector returned. The lumber had been laid flat on the ground so the children couldn't construct anything dangerous. Someone had nailed a few panels together to make a playhouse, and half a dozen girls tended dolls and dishes at the entrance. Two boys played with a top that suggested Alejandro's craftsmanship.

Alejandro sat on the porch watching the girls dress dolls and the boys compete to spin the top the longest.

"Inez is sleeping so I'm trying to keep the kids quiet."

"How is she?"

Hector climbed the porch stairs and sat beside Alejandro.

"The bleedings stopped, and there's no sign of infection." Alejandro shook his head. "She's sure prayer kept the infection away." He chuckled. "I'd bet on your penicillin."

"Can you tell anything about the leg? Does it look straight?"

"I saw Teresa push the bone together. She lined it up better than I thought possible."

"Is the skin around the break red?"

"A little. But I think it's part of the swelling around the break. Nothing like I've seen with infections."

"I'd be glad to call my friend on the bishop's staff. He might be able to persuade a doctor to fly up here in a helicopter."

"She'd never hear of it. More stubborn than anyone I've ever met. She'd claim she doesn't have the money to pay for it. If she doesn't, Mateo does. As long as he stays out of prison."

"What about any of the other sons? Might they come to help? You can't do everything by yourself."

"Gustavo and Angelita will help. The women Inez befriended the last few weeks are bringing food. Maria helps too. At least, she watches Marta." Alejandro smiled at his mention of Marta. "Most of the time she can keep her out of trouble."

Alejandro stared toward the road leading into San Miguel. A cloud of dust announced the arrival of a car or truck. In a few minutes, Hector saw a flatbed truck. Its age made him wonder how it survived the trip. When it rolled to a stop, Reverend Johanson stuck his head out the window.

"Where is Inez," he asked. "I'll take her to town if she can ride in the cab. Has Teresa really set a compound fracture? Inez should see a doctor. A real one, not just a *curandera*."

Alejandro went to the cab. "Inez is sleeping, if you haven't waked her."

"We could get to an emergency room before midnight." Johanson spoke in a quieter voice.

Hector joined the two at the truck. "Teresa did a terrific job."

"Well, if it isn't Hector the Rector on the spot." Johanson smirked at Hector. "What happened to the power of the Church? Is the Pope too cheap to send a helicopter up here?"

"Inez refused Father Hector's offer to help," Alejandro said. "She was counting on you." He spit out the you.

"What is all that ruckus?" Inez' yell was almost as loud as usual. "Did I hear Reverend Johanson?"

"You did indeed," Johanson called back as he climbed from the cab. He brushed by Alejandro and Hector and took the porch steps two at a time to enter the home without knocking.

Hector and Alejandro followed him inside.

Johanson was holding Inez' hand, but she returned the gesture with a frown.

"I'm sorry I was unavailable when you fell, my dear."

"Your answering machine wasn't much comfort, Reverend." Her voice was as icy as her look. "If it hadn't been for Teresa, I don't know what I would have done."

"It was regrettable, but—praise the Lord—I have wonderful news for you. At least, for you and the others at San Miguel who followed my advice." He patted her hand, glancing from Inez to Alejandro, relishing the anticipation he was building. "You'd never guess what happened on the coast." His smile spread across his face. "The Lord has blessed us. Hallelujah!"

"It can't be that the Lord favored you with a new truck." Hector regretted his sarcasm as soon as he spoke, but he appreciated Alejandro's swallowed guffaw.

Johanson frowned as he shot Hector a dirty look. "We can't all enjoy the wealth of the Pope." He turned back to Inez.

Before Johanson could say more, a knock came at the door. Gustavo burst in without an invitation. "It's the Virgin!"

"What about her?" Inez asked.

"It's remarkable," Gustavo exclaimed. "Angelita went with the other women this morning to clean the church. When they were dusting the Virgin, they saw bloody tears."

"What's remarkable about that?" Inez said with disdain. "She's cried as much blood as I just lost."

"Well, it was remarkable that the women all agreed it was blood. None of them argued that they were watery tears."

Hector rubbed his fingers over his lips to conceal a grin.

"So what if there is a dry spell, Gustavo?" Inez softened her tone. "Your corn doesn't need any more rain. It's almost ready to harvest."

"The beans could use one more shower, but the Virgin doesn't always warn just about drought." Gustavo hitched up his pants. "Remember that time she warned us about corn boers? Those worms destroyed our crop. She was right about that, wasn't she?"

"She was right," Alejandro said emphatically as if to end the discussion.

"Well the news can't be anything but good for us, the way the Yankees are buying up tomatoes." Johanson turned to Hector with a smug smile. "Everyone in San Miguel who planted tomatoes can pay off their debts and take a vacation." He bent over Inez and kissed her forehead. "What with the market the way it is and the way your tomatoes are after I sprayed the herbicide, you are going to be rich."

"What I want is to see a church in my front yard. With my profits I can hire the men in San Miguel to build our church. Since we have all the lumber right here, we can start soon. Alejandro can direct things. He's the finest carpenter in the valley."

"Well," Johanson paused, "He and I can work together on the plans. I know just how I want it to look. We can start as soon as we get the tomatoes to market."

"It'll be another week before most of the tomatoes are ripe," Gustavo said. "Unless you use that spray that makes them ripe."

"What spray is that?" Johanson raised an eyebrow.

"The one Father told me about." Gustavo hesitated. "Well, maybe it only works on Yankee tomatoes."

Johanson ignored Gustavo. "When do you think your field will be ready to pick, Alejandro? And Inez?"

"We've eaten a few. Less than a week should do it, but Roberto's field is ready now. He could half fill your truck, or more. So you don't have to go back empty."

Hector was surprised at how much enthusiasm Alejandro showed, but he recollected how few chances Alejandro had in his life to enjoy good fortune.

"Could Roberto start picking now? I'll stay overnight if we can finish loading by mid-morning." Johanson looked from Alejandro to Gustavo.

"We'll all help. Do you have boxes?" Alejandro said.

"You watch your back, Ando. Who'd take care of me if you throw your back out?"

"I'll be careful," Alejandro said.

"I have everything you need in the truck, plus my own strong back. We have a few hours of daylight left. Shall we start?" Johanson turned to Hector. "What about you, Rector? Will the Pope let you pick Protestant tomatoes?"

"Roberto's tomatoes are Catholic, Reverend. Did you forget?"

"After what he sells his tomatoes for, he may decide he's Protestant."

"And do you think he'll be able to buy his way into heaven?" Hector meant to be funny, but Johanson didn't laugh.

Alejandro eased the tension. "We could start picking this afternoon and finish by early morning."

✝✝✝

By mid-morning the next day, Roberto's early crop of tomatoes was loaded on Johanson's truck.

"I hope you'll come with me, Roberto," Johanson said. "So you know what we sell them for."

Roberto shrugged. "I trust you. I should stay here to watch out for worms on my next crop."

Hector laughed. "I'll bet it's been a long time since you've been to town, Roberto. I'll watch your tomatoes."

Hector's urging was all it took for Roberto to jump in the cab. "Tell my wife where I went, please."

"Besides keeping me honest, he can help me unload," Johanson said. "We should return tomorrow if buyers are close in. Otherwise, it may be a day or two."

"If the nights stay warm, Inez will have tomatoes to pick when you return," Alejandro said.

"Don't you let her out to pick." Johanson laughed louder than anyone else at his attempt to joke.

"You can cheer her up by making a fortune for Roberto. It'll be her turn next," Alejandro said.

Hector said a prayer under his breath that Johanson would find a good price for the tomatoes even if it meant a setback for the work he had done to show San Miguel farmers they could be independent from a merciless market.

21

Hector hadn't expected Johanson to return the next day, but felt certain he'd return by the second day. That morning he tarried over breakfast, uncertain about joining Inez and Alejandro to await Johanson. He paced the Womb twice before sitting down to a volume of church records. He'd turned several pages when he realized he'd failed to retain a word he'd read. He replaced the volume, then knelt before the crucifix and begged forgiveness for, at times, wishing the tomato crop to fail. Still troubled, he entered the church and knelt before the Virgin to pray for Johanson's successful marketing of Roberto's tomatoes.

When he felt further prayer to be counterproductive, he headed to Inez' home. He found Alejandro pacing back and forth on the porch, frequently glancing toward the road into San Miguel. Hector couldn't help turning in the same direction even though it was too early in the day for Johanson to arrive.

"Good morning." Alejandro nodded at Hector only to glance at the road.

"Surely, Johanson will return this afternoon," Hector said. "Won't he?"

"You never know where to find a buyer for the Yankee market. Too many speculators." Alejandro scratched at yesterday's beard. "Inez is praying that the Reverend won't have to travel too far."

"How is Inez?"

"Complaining about my cooking. Her new friends brought so much food, I haven't done anything but fry eggs," he snorted. "How do you keep fried eggs from being greasy?"

Hector licked his lips at the thought of fried eggs, especially greasy ones. Women had given him eggs a few times, but he had to depend on Pedro to fry them.

"Is that Father Hector?" Inez' voice from inside the house carried its customary authority. "Invite him in, Ando."

When Hector entered, he found Inez sitting up in bed, a piece of embroidery by her side.

"I see you're keeping busy even when you're bedridden," Hector chided. "May I see your work?"

"I wouldn't call it work. I'm so anxious to hear how Roberto did that I need the needlework to pass the time." She waved a hand to dismiss the cloth. "I was never any good with a needle. I learned enough as a maid to do a passable job of mending. Then my mother-in-law tried to teach me to embroider."

"It looks like a work of art to me," Hector said.

"She needs to rest her eyes," Alejandro turned to Inez. "Be sure to steady your leg. That's not the best splint in the world." Alejandro helped Inez lean forward and fluffed her pillow. He tucked the sheet around her waist.

"Oh, Ando, I'm not on my death-bed. I just wish we'd hear from Roberto." She looked at Hector. "What do you think, Mr. Cardenas? Is it good news or bad news that Reverend Johanson hasn't returned yet?"

Before Hector could reply, Inez went into detail as to why the delay meant good news. Her list of reasons ended in a cough. Alejandro left for a glass of water.

"Ando is so anxious to hear. That man deserves a break. Worked so hard all his life and has never had anything."

"His work for San Miguel must have meant a great deal to him," Hector said.

"Oh, of course. It's been his whole life. But he deserves a material reward. Though he'd probably give it to the poor."

"Another reward is your chicken and green chili soup," Hector smiled.

"Oh, Fath...uh, Mr. Cardenas," Inez sputtered. "Father Hector," she exclaimed. "One doesn't have to be Catholic to call you Father, do they? Even if the Reverend doesn't like it, you're going to be Father to me from now on." Her face reddened. "If that's all right with you?"

"It's fine with me, Inez. Do you mind if I don't call you my Child? I have a hard time calling Alejandro my Son. He's been like a father to me in so many ways."

"I'm happy you two get along. I think at first it bothered him when he heard a real priest was coming. He's served San Miguel as its priest for such a long time."

"Alejandro's got all the important qualifications for a priest."

"I wasn't gone two minutes, and I heard you two using my name. I hope it wasn't in vain." Alejandro returned with two glasses of water. "I put some fresh coffee on. Haven't got around to baking any cake, though."

"Father Hector has been making me laugh so hard you may have to re-splint my leg."

"If you can wait for my coffee, you won't need a splint. It'll work like penicillin."

"Oh, don't you start, Ando," Inez giggled. "Or I will need to have my leg reset."

The three sat in silence for a while before Alejandro cupped his ear with a hand. "Does anyone else hear a truck coming?"

"I'll look," Hector said. He went to the door and stared at the road for minutes before admitting that it was too early in the day for Johanson to return.

"Why don't you try him on your cell phone, Inni?" Alejandro handled the instrument as if it might give him an electrical jolt. "Once more won't hurt."

"His message machine said this morning he's 'unavailable.' If that's all I mean to him, we can just wait until he gets back here." Inez' brow furrowed. "I'd think he'd want to know how my leg is doing."

Hector realized everyone's mood would get worse the longer they waited. He supposed a good priest would console Inez and Alejandro, but he didn't know where to begin. Indeed, he felt so uneasy that he searched for a reason to leave.

"What if I go see how your tomatoes are doing? They should ripen quickly with a few warm nights."

"Please check both our fields, Father. I need Ando here with me while we suffer through this waiting." She muttered to Alejandro, "Why doesn't that man call?"

In Inez' field, Hector found a number of tomatoes with touches of red. They'd reached a good size and should be suitable for picking when Johanson arrived. Smaller, green tomatoes promised yields for weeks. Upper vines had blossoms on them. Hector walked on to Alejandro's field and found the same results. The plants showed no ill effects from Johanson's spraying, and Hector was convinced that the solution had been harmless. The early weeding seemed to have sufficed, and the weeds did little to threaten the crop. He wondered for a moment if his prayers had anything to do with the outcome, then kicked himself for thinking such vain thoughts.

At the end of another row Hector felt something amiss but couldn't put a finger on it. He retraced his steps and scrutinized the bottoms of a dozen leaves. Small white collections of minuscule balls, that he initially dismissed as a harmless fungus, proved to be egg masses. Inspecting another row, he found tiny mites on the ripening tomatoes. They weren't anything like the tomato pests he had studied in class, but upon examining the fruit, he saw that something was nibbling on it. He went back to the first field. It didn't take him long to discover the same problem. He hurried to Roberto's field and found egg masses on its tomatoes.

He bit his lip at the thought of telling Inez and Alejandro of his discovery. But what else could he do? He recalled how Alejandro had welcomed him to San Miguel. He and Gustavo. They had helped in so many ways. He kicked himself. How could he have forgotten Gustavo? The villagers likely had experienced the pest before. They'd have ways to deal with it. Whatever folk wisdom Gustavo possessed exceeded Hector's scientific knowledge.

Gustavo sat on a rickety chair next to his doorway. He bent over palm fronds weaving a hat. "Good morning, Father." Gustavo stood and motioned Hector to take his chair. "Has Inez heard anything from Roberto or the Reverend?"

Hector put a hand on Gustavo's shoulder to have him sit. "When I visited Inez this morning, she had heard nothing. Alejandro seemed even more anxious. Don't you think Johanson will return today? Does it usually take this long to find a buyer?" Hector ran a finger through his hair, prickly from the anxiety gnawing within himself.

"If he doesn't find a buyer, Inez and Alejandro will have to eat tomato soup for months." Gustavo forced a smile at his attempt to joke. Hector assumed even Gustavo's good humor couldn't handle thoughts of Alejandro's misfortune.

"I'm not sure they'll have such a harvest," Hector said. "I just came from their fields. Some kind of bug is eating the tomatoes. One I've never seen before."

Gustavo's mouth sagged. "The tomato worm? Is it a large green one?"

"No. It's a tiny pest. I didn't see any at first because I was looking for the green worm. In fact, I only saw the eggs. The first egg cluster I thought was a glob of spit. I had to look hard to discover the individual eggs. Whatever the pest is, it's nibbling on the fruit."

"I hope it's not that." Gustavo shook his head. He put aside his weaving. "We better go look."

On their way Hector told Gustavo about research into the use of natural predators. He described how laboratories were breeding Lady Bugs to control many pests.

"God seems to provide an answer for all our problems," Gustavo said. "If we wait long enough."

Hector wondered why he had never thought of it that way.

At the fields it took Gustavo only moments to recognize the eggs and find a tiny mite to show Hector. Hector had to squint. He guessed it might be related to a spider mite.

"We call it the Devil Bug," Gustavo shrugged. "I guess because it makes life hell for us." He laughed as he raised both hands. "Or maybe because it likes red things. Inez' husband planted strawberries a couple of times. The Devil Bug liked them, too. but mostly it likes tomatoes. When they start to ripen, the Devil Bugs plan a fiesta."

"I suppose Johanson planned to spray an insecticide to control it," Hector said.

"I don't know. It's been a few years since the Devil has troubled us." He paused a moment, before looking up at Hector. "It's strange that the Devil came when you did." He laughed as hard as Hector had ever heard him laugh. "Forgive me, Father. It's a poor joke."

"Well, it's a good time to have a priest, don't you think? But, I must admit I don't have enough experience fighting the Devil, and I don't know anything about fighting Devil Bugs."

"Maybe those laboratories are breeding some Angel Bugs as well as Lady Bugs. We could use them."

Hector laughed as hard as Gustavo.

"I was a young man when we were invaded by Devil Bugs. We weren't growing tomatoes to sell but for our own use. We had to pick them off. And you couldn't be sure you killed the Devils when you squeezed them. An uncle of mine told us to drop them in kerosene. The eggs, too."

"That sounds like good advice," Hector said. "I bet you won your fight against the Devil without a priest."

"Well, Alejandro's father served the village then."

"I hope I do half as well," Hector prayed under his breath.

"How is Alejandro's back, Father?"

Hector hadn't thought to ask Alejandro, but he recalled how slowly Alejandro had risen and how he had used his hands and arms when he rose to go for a glass of water. "I guess he still suffers, but I've never heard him complain."

"He shouldn't leave Inez alone for long, either." Gustavo paused as if in thought. "You and I can start giving the Devil his kerosene bath, but we won't be able to do it all. We'll need help. The Devil spreads fast if he isn't kept in check." Gustavo chuckled softly. "And prayer won't stop this Devil." He laughed out loud. "Forgive me, Father. I guess that's not right to say."

"I love your sense of humor, my Son. Prayer is always appropriate, but this Devil needs picking and dousing." He looked around at the village houses. "Do you think we could get others to help us?"

"I'm not sure. In the old days everyone helped everyone else. Now some people are jealous of Inez's wealth. And they don't like it that she became a Protestant. Maybe they'd want to help Alejandro, but not Inez."

"What if Inez paid them?"

"Maybe. But some people carry grudges. They didn't like it when she welcomed that Protestant. And now there's resentment against Roberto and Manuel because they may get rich. Manuel's field is full of tomatoes. If the price is high, Manuel will be rich."

"The first thing we must do is tell Manuel," Hector said. "Maybe he has relatives who will help."

"We all have relatives, Father. In fact, everyone in the village is related. But relatives have ways of avoiding their kin when there's nothing in it for them."

"My Son, aren't you being hard on your people?"

Gustavo shrugged his shoulders.

"At least, let's find Manuel."

Hector started at such a fast pace, Gustavo kidded about his legs outracing his body. When they reached Manuel's home, he was chiseling a piece of wood to serve as a chair leg. He stopped to welcome them and ask how they were.

Hector broke the news about the Devil Bug, and Manuel grimaced. "I haven't been to my field for a few days. My wife has been after me to repair our chairs."

"Father Hector found the Devils. I went with him just now to make sure, but maybe you should see for yourself."

"I'll get some kerosene. My wife was just filling our lantern. I wonder if Rosa has enough on hand."

The three men hastened to Manuel's field. It looked to Hector as if it were more infected than Alejandro's. They spent the rest of the day bathing Devil Bugs and their eggs in kerosene. Yet, the three had hardly started on Manuel's field when night fell.

"We have to have more help," Hector said as they walked back with Manuel. "Inez has a much larger field, and Alejandro planted as many tomatoes as you have if not more."

"We mustn't forget Roberto," Gustavo said. "He planted a large part of his field in tomatoes, too."

"But what if he's made his fortune already," Manuel said. "It wasn't fair that he got his tomatoes to market before anyone else."

"Someone had to be first, my Son. Anyway, he didn't have such a large harvest that it would make him rich."

Manuel looked at his feet. "Well, if we do his field, it should be last."

"Wouldn't Roberto work your fields if he were in your shoes?" Hector said.

"Oh, no, Father," Manuel shook his head. "He'd first take care of his own field. Why not? It provides for his family."

"What if we worked the fields in rotation?" Hector asked. "Wouldn't that be fair?"

Manuel replied with a blank stare. Hector waited in vain for Gustavo to back him up.

Gustavo changed tactics instead. "I'll have my wife tell all the women Inez has befriended. They'll get after their men to help out."

"The wives could work, too," Manuel said. "It doesn't take much strength to kill Devil Bugs."

"Maybe Inez could host a fiesta for everyone who helps." Gustavo looked at Hector. "Wouldn't that be a good way to repay the villagers for their work." His face brightened and he laughed. "And everyone will help if they're promised a fiesta."

✝✝✝

Hector wondered if Inez and Alejandro would be awake as he made his way to their home in starlight. He was glad to see a lamp burning in the front room window. His brow furrowed as he thought of breaking the bad news of an insect infestation, and he tried to imagine Inez's reaction to his request for a fiesta.

As he climbed the porch stairs, he heard Inez telling Alejandro that he should organize a procession to ensure good prices for their tomatoes.

Alejandro's voice quavered in response. "That would be like praying for money. The Virgin brings rain to keep us from starving. To ask her for money is sacrilegious. Shame on you, Inez. You'd know better if it weren't for that damn Protestant leading you astray."

"Don't you blaspheme Reverend Johanson, Ando." Inez' voice rose to a high pitch. "He wants to help us as much as Father Hector. Just in a different way. Think of all that money they have in the Vatican. The Pope must pray for money."

"I don't know anything about the Pope, but it would be blasphemy to hold a procession for money. Our ancestors have always prayed for rain. I read that even the Aztecs did, too."

"All right, Ando. We're on edge not hearing from Reverend Johanson. Let's remember that he found good prices just a week ago. The market couldn't change in a week."

"It's been a little more than a week," Alejandro said.

"True, the market doesn't often change much in a week—but it happens. At least, we can't get any worse news."

Hector took a deep breath. He had no option but to deliver worse news.

22

Hector cleared his throat to greet Inez and Alejandro, but he could think of no way to breach news of the Devil Bug.

"Do you think Reverend Johanson has worked a miracle?" Inez chuckled. "Well, not a miracle. But found a good price for tomatoes?" Inez looked at Hector as if sure of the answer.

But then she frowned. "What could have happened to him?" She fingered the embroidery cloth, unaware that she did. Her eyes darted back and forth between Hector and Alejandro waiting for an answer, but before either could speak, she continued. "Why wouldn't he come here first? If he's coming. He may have found such high prices that he and Roberto have headed North."

Alejandro chortled. "It would serve us right for being so greedy."

"Oh, Ando, it's not greedy to make a little money for once. On top of that we're helping to feed people. Tomatoes are very nutritious, aren't they, Father."

"They certainly are, Inez. A nice supplement to corn and beans—the really nutritious food when one needs calories." Hector gritted his teeth. How could he be lecturing on nutrition when he had to tell them about the Devil Bug?

He stammered. "But tomatoes can have problems when they're grown in large fields, no? Like those for export. If pests get in them, they spread rapidly."

Inez raised an eyebrow. "You're warning us a little late, aren't you Father?" She forced a laugh. "Besides, there's a wonderful crop in the fields ready to be picked, and the only thing we have to worry about is the market." She pursed her lips. "No?"

Hector scratched his chin, looked at the floor and then the ceiling before he cleared his throat.

"What is it?" Alejandro asked. "What is it that you have to tell us?"

"It's a problem with the tomatoes. Not the market." Hector's fingers curled. He was never any good at delivering bad news.

"I didn't hear what you said." Inez took her embroidery in both hands while staring at Hector.

"I looked at the tomato fields this morning to make sure there were no worms. There aren't." Hector took a deep breath. "But there is an infestation of Devil Bugs."

"Are you sure?" Inez gasped.

"I'd never seen them. Gustavo told me what they were when I showed him."

"It's been so long since we had any Devil Bugs around here, I don't know how they found us." Alejandro drew in a deep breath. "San Miguel wasn't meant for tomatoes. It's our punishment for chasing money."

"My husband had some luck with tomatoes, Father. Until Devil Bugs showed up." Inez turned to Alejandro. "Maybe you should lead a procession. The Virgin could save us."

Alejandro's jaw dropped. "What are you saying, woman? Protestants aren't supposed to believe in the Virgin's help. What's changed your mind?"

"I've seen the processions help so many times." Inez looked back and forth at Hector and Alejandro. "I don't care if it's a Catholic practice or not."

"What do you think?" Alejandro glanced at Hector.

"I don't know much about San Miguel processions, Alejandro." Hector longed to see another one now that he understood them better, but he feared the consequences if the ritual should result in another miracle. How would he explain to the bishop? What was he thinking? Saving the tomatoes was far more important than reducing the frequency of miracles.

"It would be like asking the Virgin's help to bring us riches." Alejandro interrupted Hector's thoughts. "She brings us rain to keep us from going hungry. It wouldn't be right to ask her to help us make money."

Alejandro's sincerity made Hector wonder how many Christians had ever prayed for wealth. Even, how many Christians right this minute were praying for money? Or ways to make more money?

"What do you think we should do, Father? You've trained in agriculture."

"I'm not sure, Inez." Hector shrugged. "Gustavo had a suggestion. We can pick off the eggs and the mites and douse them in kerosene."

"That worked in the past although we didn't have so many plants then," Alejandro nodded. "The real problem is that Inez and I have the largest fields of tomatoes. I'll do what I can with the two fields, but I can't come close to dousing all the Devil Bugs in them."

"You know you can count on Gustavo and me to help. You still have to watch out for your back, and you need to stay by Inez' side. We'll manage somehow."

"You do my field last, if you do it at all," Inez said. "I'm the one Reverend Johanson persuaded to plant tomatoes and convince others. I'm so sorry."

"Gustavo thinks your new friends will help out, Inez. He'd like to ask them if it's all right with you."

Inez sucked in her lips. Hector thought he saw a tear in one eye. She couldn't bring herself to speak, but she nodded her approval.

"We thought that if you promised a fiesta, the whole village might turn out." Hector forced as much enthusiasm as he could into his words. "It would be like the old days when everyone helped everyone else."

"Inez can't cook for the whole village," Alejandro said. "She'll still be in bed, maybe, when the harvest is finished."

"I can tell you what to do, Ando."

"You're good at that, Inni."

"Oh, don't you start." Inez pretended to be angry. "Maybe it wouldn't have to be right after the harvest, Father."

"I'm sure it wouldn't, Inez. Fiestas ought to come at the very end of the growing season anyway. After all the corn and beans are harvested."

"Just so there's enough help getting rid of the bugs," Inez said. "It'll be a grand fiesta."

"I'm sure Gustavo can round up more help," Hector said. "I'll go back to my room now so I can be ready for a full day tomorrow."

As Hector felt his way home, he wondered what he should pray for before retiring. If he prayed for sufficient help in the morning, would it be like praying for money? Clearly if he prayed for a good market, he'd be praying for money. Once more, Alejandro's thinking had troubled his thoughts.

✝ ✝ ✝

Hector wrestled with the Devil long before dawn. He faced an endless line of mites in a dream, engaged them in a hopeless struggle, and spilled the last of his kerosene in a wrestling match with a microscopic mite that morphed into a giant when he picked it up.

At first light he headed toward the fields before remembering to retrieve kerosene from his lantern. Once back on his way, he could see no one else headed to the fields and wondered what luck Gustavo had in persuading villagers to help. He decided to begin in Manuel's field. If they didn't clear one field at a time, there would be danger of reinfestation. Half way down a row, Hector spotted Manuel coming toward him. His wife trailed behind. Hector searched in vain for Gustavo.

"Good morning, Father," Manuel said. "You're early to do battle with the Devil."

Hector guessed he'd never hear the end of jokes about his profession and the Devil Bug.

"It's good to have help with the fight, my Son. I don't have much kerosene, but we can share what I have."

"That's good of you, Father, but my wife is bringing a can for each of us. She talked to a few of our relatives last night. We'll have more help soon."

"I wonder if Gustavo talked to many people. He told me he thought all of Inez's new friends would help us."

"Everyone will come—except those who find an excuse," Manuel chortled. "That may mean quite a few."

"I am surprised that Gustavo isn't here. He told me last night I could count on him."

Hector turned his attention to the tomato plants and searched diligently for mites and their eggs. Between the kerosene fumes and the difficulty of locating mites, Hector's eyes watered. He guessed for a moment, he would have welcomed a crop dusting plane loaded with insecticide. One stretch of plants held such numbers of the pests, Hector feared the fields could never be picked clean. But the next stretch gave him hope. He found only one mite and two egg clusters among dozens of plants.

Sweat worked its way down his forehead and overflowed his eyebrows. He tied his handkerchief around his forehead and kicked himself for forgetting his hat. He felt it must be noon, but after glancing at the sun he guessed that at most two hours had passed. He looked at the village homes, expecting to see Gustavo if no one else. He didn't see Gustavo, but half a dozen other figures were making their way toward the field. Most seemed to be women. Inez' new friends were coming to her aid.

One old man and three women came up to Hector, bidding him good morning. One of the women explained that they had come to help Inez with her pests, and she wondered why Hector was helping Manuel when Alejandro had a bad back and Inez had a broken leg.

Hector explained how all the fields would have to be cleared of the Devil Bugs, or their work wouldn't do any good. One of the women looked at Manuel out of the corner of her eye and asked why Hector had chosen to work Manuel's field first.

Hector didn't have a convincing answer, but his assurances that Manuel would help clear all the other fields once his field had been picked clean satisfied her. Still, one of the women exchanged sharp words with Manuel's wife. Hector chose not to hear what was said.

One or two others straggled to the field during late morning, and Hector thought that at least Manuel's field would be saved, and maybe some of Alejandro's. If only Gustavo had contacted the people as he promised, such a work force would have saved everything. Hector wondered if Gustavo could be so jealous of Alejandro's crop that he relished seeing it eaten by the Devil Bugs.

Hector blamed the pain in his back and his parched lips for ascribing malevolent motives to Gustavo. He guessed the sun was a little past overhead when his stomach competed with his back in complaining. He thought to tell Manuel that he needed to return to the Womb for more kerosene when two young girls approached carrying a pot between them with canteens strung over their shoulders.

The girls offered Hector a canteen first. It took utmost effort to insist that others drink before he did. The beans and tortillas were a little easier to resist, but once he drank his fill the meal proved to be more satisfying than the dinner he had with the bishop.

The simple food lasted him until dusk. He was about to head toward the Womb, wondering if he had enough energy left to bathe himself before dropping onto his cot.

"Father," a familiar voice called.

Hector turned toward the hillside to see Gustavo and his wife carrying bundles under their arms. He couldn't imagine what had taken them into the hills.

"Father Hector," Gustavo panted as he reached the field. "Our baby had a terrible night. We decided to look for Teresa. It was almost light when we found her. She told us what herbs she needed to make him right."

"And did you find them, my Son."

"We had to go into the mountains."

"I twisted my ankle, Father," Angelita said. "It's my fault Gustavo is late."

"The plants we needed only grow high up, Father. Angelita didn't rest very long."

"It doesn't matter, Gustavo." Hector put an arm on his friend's shoulder. "Did you get enough of the plants you need?"

"We had luck. We found more than enough. And there's time for me to visit Inez' friends tonight so they'll join us in the morning." Gustavo looked around at the people in the field. "Did you get much done while we were in the mountains?"

"We've almost finished Manuel's field. Tell people to bring kerosene with them." Hector spoke loud enough for everyone to hear, "With reinforcements tomorrow, we'll beat back the Devil from Inez' and Alejandro's fields. Right?"

The workers raised their fists and shouted victory calls.

"And Inez will host a fiesta in the fall for all who help," Hector roared. "San Miguel will feast and dance like never before."

More victory calls echoed, but most of the villagers were heading home.

The next morning, Hector rubbed sore muscles in his legs before massaging an aching back as he struggled into his clothes. He gnawed at a stick of jerky and drank an endless amount of water. He filled an empty bottle to take to the fields and clamped his hat on his head before treading his way to the outhouse. On his return he couldn't stop imaging a plate with half a dozen sizzling fried eggs on it accompanied by a side of bacon. He vowed never again to complain about greasy eggs.

As he started for the fields, Hector saw most of the villagers leaving their homes carrying cans of what he assumed to be kerosene. By mid-morning, the workers finished Manuel's field. They asked Hector where to begin next. He hesitated to choose between Alejandro and Inez, settled on Alejandro's because his field was closest to Manuel's.

The morning passed quickly for Hector with so many people working and joking together, but he welcomed the noon day break when the girls appeared with water and food. He breathed deep while surveying all that had been done. The workers had nearly cleared Alejandro's field. If everyone continued as they did today, Inez' and Roberto's could be finished in less than four days.

Just as they resumed their fight with the Devil, Gustavo called out that a truck was coming. Everyone agreed that it must be Johanson, but a dispute broke out over whether he brought good news or bad, and Hector heard bets being wagered. Everyone left the fields, almost racing to Inez'. They gathered before the porch. Alejandro was already standing on it staring toward the road. Moments later, he waved to the crowd and thanked them for their help. He cupped his hand to his ear at something Inez called from inside, then told the people to expect a celebration like no other San Miguel had seen before.

Johanson's pickup arrived amidst cheers meant for Inez. His face beamed as he rolled down the window and held up fingers in a victory sign. The crowd cheered again. Roberto climbed down from the other side, grinning and waving to everyone.

"It was a good price," he called over and over.

Johanson joined Alejandro on the porch, motioned for silence and then screamed out the exact figure he had found for Roberto. Hector brushed back hair. It wasn't the highest price ever paid for tomatoes, but it beat the average. Hector's shoulders sagged. Perhaps, sustainable agriculture wasn't the answer to San Miguel's poverty.

"I had to return the flatbed, I'd borrowed," Johanson announced. "But I have cartons so we can fill my pickup." He looked around at the people. "Is everyone ready to harvest tomatoes?" The few token cheers were not what Johanson had expected. "Who wants to make money?" he called out. He received only polite acknowledgement.

Alejandro explained to him that people were exhausted from picking pests off the tomatoes. Their work was being done out of friendship. They'd not profit from whatever the price of tomatoes might be.

Johanson looked down at his feet, rubbing his forehead.

Alejandro turned to the people. "For all you have done to help with the tomatoes, I promise to share with you half my profits, whatever they are."

Hector heard Inez call something from the living room. Alejandro motioned from the porch once more for quiet. "And Inez promises to do the same!"

The cheering went on for some time. When it ceased, Roberto and Manuel could do nothing less, and their promises were greeted with deafening applause.

"So let's pick tomatoes," Johanson yelled. He climbed onto the back of his pickup and started tossing empty cartons to the villagers. One of them yelled back, "Where do we begin?"

"Pick the ripe ones," Johanson said.

Everyone hesitated. Hector spoke up. "We should harvest Manuel's field which is free from mites and then the part of Alejandro's field that we just worked." He looked around. "We don't all need to harvest. Half of us can go back to dousing mites."

"What are you talking about Rector?" Johanson said "Don't you want your congregation to be rich? They'd no doubt give some of their wealth to the Pope."

Before Hector could answer, Alejandro took Johanson by the arm, obviously explaining about the Devil Bug. He then escorted Johanson inside.

Hector tried to think how best to assign people to harvesting or picking bugs, but before he could decide, the men began retrieving cartons and the women headed toward Alejandro's field with cans of kerosene.

As Hector went to get a carton, Roberto touched him on the arm and asked to speak to him. "Father, I don't know if it's important, but I want to tell Alejandro and you something."

"Let's go join Alejandro, my Son." Hector led Roberto toward the porch. Johanson remained in the house with Inez.

"I meant to join you this morning," Alejandro said, one arm on his back. "But Inez was in a lot of pain."

"Looks like your back might not be in the best shape," Hector said.

"Oh, it's not bad, I guess." Alejandro grimaced as he straightened his back.

"Roberto wants to tell us something."

"Can he hear?" Roberto pointed to the living room with his chin.

"You mean Johanson?" Alejandro asked. "Not if we don't yell."

"We were gone so long because he searched and searched for the highest price. We got a good offer right away, but the Protestant drove all the way to Hermosillo before he was satisfied." Roberto shrugged. "He had to pay in gasoline for the little extra he got. Do you think he'll charge me for it?"

"I think he wanted to impress us with the highest price he could get," Alejandro replied. "I suppose we can't expect as high a price with future deliveries. Too many tomatoes will be coming to market."

"Still," Hector admitted. "With even a ten percent drop over the season, you stand to make a decent profit."

"You mean it makes a difference when we deliver our crop?" Roberto looked perplexed.

"The sooner the better," Alejandro told him. "And if we have to depend on Johanson's pickup truck, we may be in trouble."

Just then, Johanson opened the door. "Inez is her charming self. I hope the leg continues to mend." Instead of joining the men, he headed toward his truck. "I'll see if any cartons are left so I can help pick. I'd like to be on my way early tomorrow."

"Gentlemen," Inez called. "Could you join me?"

Inez was pretending to embroider when they reached her bedside. She told them she realized Johanson could take what tomatoes were ripe at present, but soon they would need better transport.

"Bring me my cell phone, Ando, please."

Alejandro raised an eyebrow but looked for the phone. "Do you know some trucking firm?" he kidded.

"I don't, but my boys may." She soon had Marcos on the phone and explained what was needed.

Her smile told them her boys would resolve the problem. "They promised to take our tomatoes to market. We'll soon be rich, and the villagers will have a little employment before they have to harvest their corn and beans."

"And all without a procession," Alejandro said.

"My boys are all we need."

Hector hoped she was right, but he wondered what would happen if their drug lord needed them when ripened tomatoes had to be delivered.

23

The next day, Alejandro joined the villagers to attack the Devil Bugs in Inez' field. They half finished their work before it grew dark. Alejandro left first, headed to Inez', holding his back. Hector followed Alejandro soon afterwards to secure a pledge from him that he'd rest until his back healed.

Hector veered toward the Womb, but Inez had struggled to the porch on what looked like homemade crutches. Standing almost as straight as usual, she called to him. "Father, I hope you watch out for Ando. His back hurts him more than he lets on."

Hector pretended not to hear but waved. His own back ached, and he looked forward to straightening it out on his cot before he bathed. He wondered how much longer he could put off washing his clothes.

Inez yelled louder. "Father Hector! Has there been any word on Manuel and Reverend Johanson?"

"Not yet, Inez," Hector stopped and faced Inez to return her call. During the day, a dozen people had asked him the same question. "If they don't come tomorrow, it'll be the next day I'm sure." Unless Johanson searches for the highest bidder in all of Sonora, Hector thought.

"Well, I'm sure Marcos and Mateo will be here tomorrow to haul away a load. You can count on my boys, you know." Inez' voice cracked from her effort. She almost stumbled as one crutch seemed to give way. Alejandro raced to her and helped her into the house.

Hector made his way to the Womb, stretched out on his cot and almost fell asleep before recovering enough to bathe himself. He dropped to his knees beside his cot out of habit, sorting out what to pray about. He recalled Johanson and Manuel. Hector refused to pray that they find a high price for the tomatoes, but he did ask for their success and safe return. Alejandro might criticize him, pointing out that success equated with a high price. Hector shrugged. He was too tired to argue the point, even in his own mind, but before he crawled into bed, he prayed that Mateo and Marcos would arrive safely.

✞✞✞

The next morning it seemed to Hector that everyone in the village had come out to rid Inez' field of Devil Bugs. He found Gustavo and congratulated him on the turnout. By early afternoon, everyone finished, but instead of returning home, the villagers gathered around Hector as if expecting further assignments.

"We're not sure what to do next, Father," Gustavo said. "Everyone's feeling good because we accomplished something important. I guess they expect you to say something."

Hector was stymied for anything to say when Alejandro came limping toward the field. It looked to Hector as if Alejandro were wearing a corset.

"I want to thank everyone who has helped with the tomatoes." Alejandro glanced at the people close to him before waving to others farther away. "It is like old times when the whole village joined together to solve our problems." He paused as if searching for the right words. "Inez is grateful, too. She doesn't know how she can thank you." His studied gaze took in everyone. "Even the grandest fiesta can't repay what you have done for us."

"Is she going back on her promise to pay us wages with her profits?" a voice called from behind Hector. "A fiesta won't pay our debts."

Hector grimaced, but he had experienced the practicality of people in poverty when he worked at El Hidalgo.

"We're glad to help you, Alejandro. And Inez, too." The voice added. "But our children are going hungry."

"I know. I know," Alejandro said. "We can all use money. You have my word that we will share whatever profits we make." Alejandro clutched his back. Beads of sweat gathered above his lips.

"It that corset too tight?" a woman close to Alejandro asked. "I can loosen it for you."

"Inez told me it was a back brace," Alejandro scowled. "What makes you think it's a corset?"

Most of the women giggled loud enough for all to hear. The woman who volunteered to help Alejandro said, "I never saw a back brace before. I'm sure that's what you have on." She covered her mouth with a hand. "But it looks like a corset."

Alejandro's face flushed. He thanked everyone again and turned to leave.

Just then a black van appeared on the road into San Miguel. The crowd fell silent as all the villagers watched its progress.

"Look!" a voice called. "There's a second one."

"I can't believe it," Gustavo said. "Two Ford Explorers coming to San Miguel. The same day. It's a mira . . ." I mean, it's remarkable."

"Truly remarkable," Hector chortled. "Do you think Mateo and Marcos mean to haul tomatoes in them." He couldn't help snickering at the thought.

"I just hope they don't deliver them to their regular buyers." Gustavo held his sides laughing. "Well," he added, "I don't know many pharmacies that sell tomatoes."

Everyone close by laughed. Hector guessed the whole village knew of Mateo and Marcos' enterprise.

The villagers made their way to Inez' to greet the two vans. Mateo and Marcos seemed taken aback by the reception and stayed close to their vans. When Hector told them the village was waiting for them, they nodded a greeting. The two wore their dark, expensive sunglasses, but they had changed to work clothes. Their shoes were as sturdy as any Hector had ever seen, showing little sign of wear.

Inez had hobbled onto the porch, this time supported by a cane. When she greeted her sons as heroes, the villagers responded with a cheer. Marcos kept glancing back toward the road, but eventually he smiled at the assembly as much as his mother did.

"We were expecting you in a truck," Alejandro said to them. "How are you going to haul tomatoes in a car like that?"

"We've brought cartons, and we took out all the seats," Mateo answered. "We'll pile the boxes to the roof. It's the best we could do on such short notice."

Hector wondered if they had in mind combining some of their own deliveries with those of San Miguel but decided he was being overly skeptical. They were dutiful sons, whatever their vices.

"We could buy only new cartons," Mateo announced. "What if everyone folds them into shape while it's still light so we can fill them in the morning? It's important we leave by noon." He looked at his mother. "Is that all right, mama?"

"At least I'll have you overnight," Inez beamed. "I showed Alejandro how to make my chicken and green chili soup so I can feast you tonight."

"You didn't, by chance, pass Reverend Johanson and Manuel on the road, did you?" Alejandro said. "We're expecting them any time now. The Reverend drives an old pickup. Or he may have a dilapidated flatbed."

"We didn't pass anyone on the road." Marcos glanced back at the road the moment he spoke.

Hector wondered what demons pursued him besides drug officials or members of other gangs. He tucked into his mind a thought to pray for Mateo and Marcos. They were certainly loyal to their mother, whatever their other virtues were.

"Here are the cartons," Mateo said as he opened the vans' doors. "Let's get started."

Men crowded forward to fold the boxes and pile them along the path to the fields. It was barely daylight when they finished, but the people did not disperse until Mateo and Marcos disappeared into the house after locking their vans. The village seldom experienced such excitement.

✞✞✞

Hector rose early the next morning, massaged his back while he dressed, and thought about Alejandro's back. By the time he started toward the fields, numerous figures were heading in the same direction.

Half way there, Gustavo caught up with Hector. "Good morning, Father. We're getting an early start on the Devil, no? Do you think we'll catch him asleep?"

"I've heard the devil never sleeps, Gustavo. If he does, what kind of bed do you think he might use?"

"It couldn't be made of straw, like mine!" Gustavo chuckled over his joke.

Hector turned serious. "Are we weeding this morning, or picking tomatoes."

"We're picking, Father. That way, we'll be taking food from the Devil's mouth, no?"

"Even before he can say a blessing," Hector quipped. Gustavo hesitated a moment before he caught on, then guffawed.

The two walked a few steps in silence before Gustavo asked if Hector thought Johanson and Manuel would return by afternoon. Hector shrugged and shook his head.

"Perhaps, you could organize a lottery, Father. Everyone in the village is sure he knows when the two will return. It would be a way to raise money for the church, no?"

"The church seems to be doing all right with what money it has."

"But we need a budget to buy you some food. Rosa is telling everyone that you must constantly fast, judged on what little you buy at her store."

"Well, I'll fill up on tomatoes now," Hector laughed. "And soon I'll feast on corn and beans."

"If the birds and mice don't feast first." Gustavo laughed but Hector knew his jest hid a practical worry. Peasant farmers experienced tragic loss to their crops while in storage. In some cases birds and rodents took more of a yield from bins than they did in the fields.

"I hope for your sake Alejandro has a few tomatoes left over. When Manuel returns with his riches, it'll be tempting to send every tomato to market." Gustavo smiled but the usual twinkle in his eye was missing. "You do think Manuel and the Protestant have found a market, don't you? A good market?"

"I hope Johanson hasn't driven all over Sonora to find the highest bidder. Once we fill the two vans, it won't be long before more tomatoes will be ready."

When they reached Inez', Alejandro joined Hector and Gustavo. The three picked up as many cartons as they could carry and headed toward the fields. Alejandro called loudly enough for everyone to hear. "I think we should pick the ripest fruit from all the fields. We don't want any to go to waste."

"Look out for the Devil," Gustavo called. "Once we've picked, we'll have to battle him."

Hector was impressed at how villagers sorted themselves out among the four fields of tomatoes without anymore direction from Alejandro. He guessed they all knew that it was in their best interest to get the greatest yields they could, ignoring ownership of the fields.

"Why don't you look for Devil Bugs, *Compadre*," Gustavo said. "You wouldn't have to bend your back so much."

"I have to make up for Inez' field as well as my own, *Compadre*," Alejandro answered. But at the next step, he grimaced and clutched his back.

"Gustavo and I will work twice as hard." Hector reached for two tomatoes as he spoke. The fruit was ideal for eating, and his mouth watered at the sight and smell. He hoped they weren't too ripe for packing.

"Look Alejandro," Hector said. "These tomatoes are just right for the Devil's fiesta. The best help you can give us will be to locate where we need to attack the mites as soon as we finish picking."

Alejandro nodded agreement and walked the rows checking for the pest. When Hector and Gustavo finished picking their rows, they carried the full boxes to Inez'. Mateo and Marcos stuffed paper around the sides of the cartons to protect the fruit they had picked. Hector noted that some of their harvest was not ripe enough, but he said nothing.

"We need the ripest fruit, *mihijitos*," Gustavo said. Mateo and Marcos scowled at Gustavo before breaking into grins. His use of "little sons" must have surprised them, but it also reminded them of times when they were young and Gustavo had taken them under his wing.

"You're right, Gustavo," Mateo said. "We'll do better with the next batch. But we do have a drug consignment waiting for us that can't be put off. You don't know what our competition is like."

"I've heard the drug business is cut-throat." Gustavo managed his comment without any hint of a smile.

Mateo scowled at him, but Marcos seemed to take his words as sincere. "You'd never believe what we have to put up, my friend."

Hector thought it best to avoid further word play. "Do you know first-hand any tomato brokers?"

"We have cousins who still farm," Mateo said. "They've given us names. They told us the market has been good—so far, at least."

"You can never tell about cash crops, though," Marcos added. "The bottom can fall out any time. But farmers scaled back production along the coast, so we think prices will hold."

"If we get the tomatoes to market," Mateo grumbled.

"One more load should do it," Marcos replied.

Well before noon the vans were crammed with cartons of tomatoes.

Marcos and Mateo hugged their mother, promised to return with proper crutches and a new cane. The two vans roared off.

✝ ✝ ✝

Reverend Johanson called on his cell phone to say he was more than half way to San Miguel. Inez insisted Hector stay for left-over chicken and green chile soup so he was on hand when the Protestant drove in.

A backfire announced his arrival. No one wanted to speak first. Manuel stayed in the cab with his window rolled up. Johanson stepped down but remained by the pickup's door, reluctant to close it.

Hector, followed by Inez and Alejandro stepped from the porch. Inez bit her lip before speaking. "What is it, Reverend? Bad news?"

Johanson stared into his dashboard. "We drove to every buyer I've ever met. Spent all the money I had on gasoline. Believe me, I looked everywhere. You can ask Manuel." He glanced at Manuel, but Manuel didn't move. "I gave the tomatoes to a soup kitchen. It didn't make sense to bring them back here."

"I don't understand," Inez' voice cracked. "My sons told me the coastal farmers didn't plant as many tomatoes as usual. What happened?"

"Every buyer we found told us that Florida had a record crop this year. There are so many staked tomatoes to be had, that a lot of them are going for catsup."

Inez sobbed. Hector put an arm around her shoulder and led her up the porch. Johanson bounded from his cab and took Inez' hand. "Let's pray to Jesus for guidance, Sister. He's always there in our hour of need."

24

Inez kneeled briefly but got up with a gesture that dismissed Johanson. Alejandro comforted her with an arm around her waist and the two went into her house. Johanson started toward the door, but Alejandro slammed the door in his face.

Hector hid a grin. "You can bed down in my room, Reverend, "if you don't mind sleeping on the floor."

"I'm fine in my truck bed, Rector. When it rains, I sleep in the cab. Spent many a night sitting up sleeping. Just so long as I know the Lord is with me." Johanson paused to look into the sky. "Evangelists don't have a Pope to provide room and board for them."

"How do you sustain yourself?" Hector asked. "You spend a lot on gas, and you brought in all that lumber and cement to build a church. You purchased all that herbicide." With his mention of herbicide, Hector stared into Johanson's eyes. For once, Johanson's eyes betrayed him. They narrowed to slits as he fixed on Hector's chest.

"God provides." Johanson stammered. "He and friends I've made. I earn some money crop dusting, too. I used left over herbicide from a job I had earlier. Had to dilute it a little to provide enough for everyone." He cleared his throat. "But it was top quality to begin with."

Hector thought that he protested too much. Perhaps he'd confess if pressed. "You added enough water that the herbicide wouldn't kill nearly full grown plants." Before Johanson could reply Hector went on. "You thought you'd convert more people by spraying all the fields, didn't you?"

"The crops were in good shape. I didn't do anything wrong. I just inspired hope. What's wrong with that?" Johanson flushed but stared into Hector's eyes. "If the Pope had saved the tomatoes, it would only be so he could tax people for his ten percent."

"What makes you so certain that the Catholic Church doesn't save souls?"

Johanson sneered. "Well, a few priests may be interested in souls as much as enriching the Pope. But look at history. The Vatican has amassed so much wealth the Church could eliminate world poverty, could stamp out disease, could . . ."

"If the Church did have the wealth you think it has—and it doesn't—where would it begin? Do you really believe the Church has more wealth than the United States or the World Bank?"

"Governments are the Devil's hands. They have no heart. They're only interested in power. In accumulating more wealth."

Hector realized it was futile to argue with Johanson. When they reached his truck, Hector bid him a curt good night and treaded his way to the Womb. He didn't know where to start with his prayers so he limited them to a plea for guidance.

✠ ✠ ✠

In the morning Hector busied himself with repairs to the church, chores postponed during the growing season. So few serious tasks faced him that he marveled again at how well San Miguel had been built. Even the Womb, whatever its original purpose, could have served as a stronghold.

The next day, Hector kept an eye out for Mateo and Marcos. He had little hope they'd find a market for their tomatoes, but he doubted they'd quit looking until they exhausted every contact.

The two must have started toward San Miguel at the crack of dawn the next day because Hector heard their approach around noon. He hurried to Inez' along with the villagers. He could see that both vans were crammed full with cartons, seemingly even fuller than when they left because their front seats were piled high with cardboard.

Hector jogged beside the vans as the two drivers wove their way among people on what passed for a road to their mother's home. He guessed they were in no rush to bring Inez bad news. By the time Mateo and Marcos parked and got out, Hector and dozens of farmers had gathered. Inez, braced on crutches, waved with both hands from the porch. Alejandro supported her with an arm, watching impassively. Johanson stood beside the steps of the porch, as if ready to flee.

"We know it's not your fault." Inez screeched to her boys so everyone would hear. "Reverend Johanson searched all over and couldn't find a buyer. The Florida growers have ruined us."

"There's a chance you won't lose everything." Mateo addressed the villagers as well as his mother. "But it's going to take hard work."

People waited while Mateo looked over the crowd, demanding full attention from the farmers.

Finally, Alejandro said, "We all know hard work, Mateo. We're not afraid of it. What do you have in mind?"

"You need to fetch every pot and pan in the village," Mateo said.

Marcos burst in. "Men should gather fire wood. Women will cook the tomatoes into salsa."

"The village doesn't have enough firewood," someone at the back objected.

"We realized that," Mateo said. "We've brought a few propane stoves and some large pots, but they're not enough if we're going to salvage the harvest."

"We'll be cooking all day and night for the next couple days," Marcos called.

"Everyone can help." Mateo might as well have said, "Everyone will help, or else."

"Excuse me," Hector stepped forward. "Did you look into a market for salsa? The North Americans have mechanized salsa and catsup production. I doubt San Miguel could compete even if wages here are not a factor."

"We have contacts in Mexico City." Mateo frowned at Hector. "You can believe we know about markets."

"Even along the coast we will sell salsa," Marcos added.

"How do you boys propose doing that?" Inez called from the porch. "I know you can sell your pharmaceuticals all over the country, but where did you learn how to sell salsa?"

Mateo answered his mother with a mumbled reply, while he called on villagers to help him unload the vans. Hector guessed that Mateo would rather not discuss his marketing practices, wondering if the two intended to coerce buyers.

Someone behind Hector snickered, a low voice suggesting they produce a marijuana based salsa. Similar jests made their way through the gathering. The twittering annoyed Mateo whose face grew as red as the tomatoes ripening in his van.

Before Mateo could say anything, Johanson proclaimed, "I've been praying to Jesus asking him for guidance. He revealed to me that Mateo is doing the right thing. We should trust in him, just as we trust in Jesus."

Hector took a deep breath. He wondered if Johanson figured supporting Mateo was a way to work himself back into the good graces of Inez. What more did the minister have to lose, anyway? Hector thought. Johanson's advice to plant tomatoes would make him an outcast unless Mateo found a way to rectify the disastrous market conditions.

"The Reverend is talking sense," Mateo shouted. The crowd quieted. "We trust the Lord, and if we work hard, like Alejandro said, we can salvage the tomatoes." He looked to Inez as if seeking approval. "Our opportunity is in bottling the product."

Everyone around Hector looked at everyone else. Hector's confusion was as great as theirs.

"We got a bargain on bottles for the salsa, and we obtained labels at cost. So we can compete in the market. We've already lined up one grocery chain."

"Maybe when they lined them up, they threatened to shoot them, too." Hector didn't recognize the low voice whose words obviously weren't intended for Marcos or Mateo.

Alejandro left the porch to oversee the setting up of two propane stoves. Gustavo had joined Marcos to unpack a pair of large pots. Farther away two men were arranging stones for a fireplace. Hector assumed others must be gathering firewood. He joined two men unloading the vans. Underneath cartons of bottles, he came upon three boxes of labels for the salsa. They had been printed at a Hermosillo press shop.

Inez called to several of her new friends, and they went into her house. Moments later they appeared with more pots for cooking the tomatoes. Johanson stood around the propane stoves as if offering advice. Mateo seldom looked at him, but a few times motioned for him to step back.

Hector joined the men preparing a stone fireplace where Gustavo was adjusting a homemade grill. The men wanted to know how a bottle or jar could affect the price of anything in it.

Gustavo looked at Hector with a twinkle in his eye. "Are there bottles of a certain shape that hide foreign matter better than other bottles?"

Hector had to chuckle before explaining Gustavo's joke to the other men. From their looks, Hector guessed his explanation failed. One laughed politely, but the others busied themselves arranging the stones.

Hector turned serious and said he had read reports that large food companies spent much money determining what packaging consumers preferred. From the blank looks of the men, Hector knew he hadn't convinced them.

Gustavo came to his aid. "Once in one of those large stores where they sell only groceries, I found a whole shelf of nothing but peanut butter. I was young and didn't know what peanut butter was. The labels were in English so I couldn't read them, but they had a picture of a squirrel. I thought the jars must be full of squirrel shit." The workers burst out laughing, then jested about what might be found on Rosa's shelves.

Several women interrupted the joking to arrange pans around the fireplaces and to hang pots over the fires. Other women brought cleaned tomatoes from Inez' to fill the vessels. Gustavo kept asking Hector if he was going to add any foreign matter. By the end of the day, almost half the jars and bottles had been filled and placed on racks to cool. Inez called to people that she had only tortillas and beans to feed them, but everyone was welcome.

The aroma of boiled tomatoes was so thick in the air that the tortillas and beans tasted like tomato stew. Everyone proclaimed the meal to be the best they'd had in weeks. They all thanked Inez and promised to return early the next morning.

✟✟✟

Hector had trouble sleeping that night wondering how Mateo and Marcos could possibly market salsa on such quick notice and with no experience. He prayed that they would not resort to intimidation or violence before he fell into a fitful sleep.

By the time Hector returned to Inez' the next morning, half the village was stewing tomatoes and adding enough other ingredients so that the contents could pass for salsa.

Hector looked around to see what was needed. Johanson and Gustavo

215

were pasting labels on bottles before packing them into cartons. Hector joined them to help.

"Mateo says this strange-looking gringo will sell our salsa," Gustavo said. "I don't see how."

Hector stared at an Anglo face with a huge handlebar mustache, the head half-swallowed by a gigantic sombrero. The stereotype irritated Hector until he studied it further. He recognized the face of a movie star, but couldn't name him until he read Paul Newman's signature. He recalled that the actor shared profits from his products with the poor so Hector swallowed his concern about stereotypes.

Mateo left off supervising the new pots of boiling tomatoes and walked over to watch the men attaching labels.

"Be careful with them," he advised. "The ink sometimes runs."

Suddenly, it dawned on Hector that the labels from the Hermosillo press packages were counterfeit.

"Mateo," Hector said. Mateo scowled at him. "Do you have permission to use the Paul Newman label?"

"Yeah, the Hermosillo press has it in writing. You can check it out with them."

"Don't you think the Newman organization would only authorize first class printing? If these labels run when they get wet, the Newman company wouldn't authorize them."

"Look, Father." Mateo seemed reluctant to address Hector as Father. "Without this Yankee label, how many bottles of this swill do you think we're going to sell?"

Johanson stopped his labeling to look at Hector. "This actor is using his fame to sell his salsa that's no better than our salsa. Anyway, his company is never going to notice the few sales we take away from him. Right?"

Alejandro must have noticed the confrontation between Hector and Johanson. He had left the porch and joined them, looking askance at Hector.

Before Hector could say anything, Gustavo said, "Father, we don't have any foreign matter in our salsa. Won't people be better off eating it rather than the real thing?"

Hector swallowed. Gustavo had a point, but the use of counterfeit labels amounted to stealing, no matter how little the theft involved.

Alejandro asked what was going on, and Hector explained.

"It seems to me like stealing," Alejandro said. He turned to Johanson. "Wouldn't you call it stealing, Reverend Johanson?"

"Think of Roberto and Manuel, if not yourself and Inez. You've invested everything in tomatoes. What will you do if you lose your investment?"

Inez' curiosity led her to join Alejandro and the others. She wobbled off the porch on her crutches and hobbled toward Alejandro. "Are you discussing how to market our salsa?"

"The Rector is suggesting that your sons are thieves," Johanson said.

Inez glared at Hector but held her tongue, looking at Alejandro for an explanation.

"Mateo may have made a mistake with the labels. They seem to belong to someone else." Alejandro didn't take his eyes off Mateo while he spoke.

"What is he saying, Mateo?" Inez fixed Mateo with a stare as if he were a grade school child.

"Mama," Mateo whined. "If we don't use a popular label—a Yankee one—we'll never sell our salsa. The coast people, especially, they prefer anything from the North to what Mexico has to offer."

Inez raised an eyebrow. Before she could speak, Johanson started. "There's nothing wrong about borrowing a movie star's name and fame, Inez. People do it all the time. Your sons have done nothing wrong. All they want to do is save your investment and help San Miguel."

"What do you think, Father?" Inez turned to face Hector.

"The labels are counterfeit. We don't have permission to use the Paul Newman brand label."

"Don't listen to him, Inez. He's got the Pope's money to fall back on. You'll lose everything!" Johanson's brow trickled sweat.

"We've never been dishonest, Inni." Alejandro took Inez' hand. "We won't start now. Not over a few tomatoes."

"It's more than a few tomatoes," Johanson screamed. "What about Roberto and Manuel if you won't think of yourselves. They have everything to lose."

"They have relatives. The village will share. We'll make it somehow." Alejandro waved a hand over the men standing close by as if blessing them. No one voiced disagreement with him.

"You're all mad. You've got to market the tomatoes one way or another," Johanson shrieked. "And it's you who led them astray." He pointed a finger at Hector. Hector stepped toward Johanson to calm him, reached out to put a hand on his shoulder.

Johanson backed away, as if from the Devil. "Do you think you're Jesus that you can forgive me? I wanted the tomatoes to make people rich. Lord knows, San Miguel deserves it." He looked around, sweat breaking out on his brow. "It's not my fault the Florida growers done us in."

"Then whose fault is it?" Mateo growled.

Johanson's face turned purple. Hector took another step to reach out to him. Johanson clenched a fist and hit Hector on the cheek with a right cross. Hector dropped to one knee. He wasn't aware of it, but when he rose he turned his other cheek. Johanson was about to hit him again but had second thoughts. He spat on Hector, then fled to his pickup.

"When you turn your backs on me, you turn them on Jesus," Johanson screamed, and he climbed into the cab.

Hector had never seen a face so contorted with anger.

"You'll all burn, you sinners." As Johanson slammed the door shut, he taunted, "And good riddance."

His tires screeched as he backed the pickup toward Hector. Hector jumped away. Alejandro called to Johanson, "Don't forget your lumber."

"You can stick it, you know where," Johanson yelled.

✝✝✝

Inez and Alejandro directed the bottling of the last of the salsa. Villagers would have a supply of stewed tomatoes to last them into the next year. Alejandro and Hector even agreed that the villagers could apply the last of the labels for their own use if they felt Paul Newman and his sombrero improved the taste of their salsa.

Everyone joked about Johanson's abrupt departure until people considered the plight of Roberto and Manuel as well as Alejandro and Inez. A hush settled and everyone gathered around Hector. He realized they expected him to step up to the challenge, but any solution eluded him.

Alejandro turned to Hector. "We've made it through hard times before." He put a hand on Hector's shoulder. "We'll work this out."

"It's good we have a priest to pray for us this time," Gustavo chimed in. "It's remarkable, Father, that you're here."

Hector's innards growled. How can I help? he wondered. I should have talked them out of cash crops in the spring. I could have done a better job of warning them. I could have . . . The list seemed endless. He felt as sorry for himself as he did for the villagers.

"At least, the tomatoes will last throughout the winter," Gustavo said. "We can have corn and tomatoes one day and beans and tomatoes the next."

"And tomatoes and tomatoes when the corn and beans are all eaten," Alejandro said with a long face. "It's going to be a long winter."

As Hector shook his head in despair, he noticed the piles of lumber that Johanson had bequeathed to the village. A laugh rumbled up from his lungs before he spoke out. "Gustavo has a point," he said. "With tomatoes in the diet, we'll have enough beans and corn to last if we don't have to share our harvest with the mice and birds."

"How do we do that, Father?" Inez asked. "Are you thinking of poisoning them? That's helped before, but people got sick from it. Many mothers know better."

"From what Johanson said when he left, I will swear an oath that he's given his lumber and supplies to Alejandro, no?"

For the first time, Hector saw a smile cross Mateo's face. "We can raise a little money with it," Mateo said. "I know a builder who owes me—if he's got any cash."

Hector wagged a finger at Mateo. "I was thinking we could use the cement footings and build a first class storage shed with the lumber." He looked at Alejandro. "Don't you think Johanson would approve? He wouldn't want his wood go to waste."

"I don't expect to see Johanson back here, ever again." Inez spoke up before Alejandro had a chance, but Alejandro echoed his agreement.

"Will you oversee the work?" Hector asked.

"I'll draw up plans in the morning." Alejandro's smile could not have been any broader. "If you will advise me on new methods of storage."

25

The communal spirit that blossomed with the attempt to save the tomato harvest buoyed everyone's interest in a pest-proof storage facility. A hush settled over villagers as they listened to Hector's description of new types of storage. Villagers had a dozen question for him. Still, murmurs of reluctance reverberated when villagers realized their corn and beans would be stored in a common bin.

"My sweat watered my beans when I hoed them," one man said. "I nursed individual corn stalks to feed my grandchildren. I want them to eat the food I raise."

"So do the mice and birds," Gustavo quipped.

Most farmers laughed, but a few mumbled resistance. Cries of agreement went up for the necessity to consume one's own food.

"We all know that it's Mother Earth that feeds us." Alejandro took off his hat as he spoke. "She and Father Sun." He glanced at Hector, as if seeking approval, before turning back to the people gathered around him. "Of course, God directs everything. We must never forget that."

"But we plant the corn and beans, fight the weeds, and harvest whatever there is. The outcome all depends on how hard we work. What about the person who is lazy?"

Hector couldn't identify the man who spoke, but he heard a note of hesitation in the voice. Alejandro must have planted a seed of doubt among the villagers.

"Don't we all put our souls into our work?" Alejandro said. "Don't we sweat over our plants? Is one man's sweat better than another man's?"

Gustavo followed Alejandro's lead. "We help each other plant and weed and harvest whenever someone is in need. Is it right to talk about 'our' corn just because it came from our field?"

"Let's hear what Father Hector has to say," a voice called.

Hector knew this problem was one for the villagers to solve for themselves. He did his best to avoid deciding for them as he explained the merits of new storage bins and pest management. His emphasis upon avoidance of pesticides stirred the women to murmur their approval. Several mothers recalled the miseries of their children from the use of pesticide poisoning in their households.

Alejandro asked for a show of hands on who would help build the bin. As far as Hector could tell everyone waved an arm in the air. Alejandro warned that it would take long days and hard work to finish construction before harvest. No one protested.

✞✞✞

That evening Hector wrote Edwardo asking him to send the steel mesh needed for pest-proof storage bins, assuring him that San Miguel had the other supplies it needed. He conveyed his excitement about the growing cooperative spirit at San Miguel. Hector concluded that if Edwardo felt it necessary to secure the Bishop's cooperation, he should remind him that San Miguel had experienced no more miracles. As a final touch, Edwardo could report to the bishop that the villagers had banished the Protestant missionary.

Two weeks later, Hector joined Alejandro at Inez' to draw up plans for the bin. He didn't need to explain to Alejandro that the storage space had to be protected from rain while well ventilated to ensure proper drying of the corn. Alejandro had many ideas about accomplishing both objectives, and Hector's knowledge of new materials simplified the task. Hector mused over the completed drawings when Alejandro finished. The work couldn't be mistaken for blueprints, but Alejandro conveyed all the information necessary to direct unskilled labor.

Alejandro called the villagers together and laid out tasks for them. With the footings that Johanson had constructed, the flooring went quickly. Next, side walls were nailed together that could be erected once the pest-proof webbing arrived.

A few days later Edwardo arrived at Inez' in a stick shift pickup, begrimed and sweating. His truck settled into a rut a few yards from the construction site. The noise of his spinning tires drew Hector and the workers to watch.

"You're right on time," Hector said. "Or you would have been had you come two days earlier."

"It took me a day to fill out all the requisition forms our new bookkeeper has devised. His only goal seems to be making life miserable for everyone else."

"You have to requisition rich widows, now?" Hector laughed.

"Look at this pile of junk I'm driving, you fiend. I borrowed it from a friend rather than fill out a hundred forms for a truck rental." Edwardo stepped down from the truck to kick a tire.

"Just so you have all the netting we need."

"I think it's all here. Thank the Lord I have only one friend who makes such demands."

Hector put an arm on Edwardo's shoulder. "Seriously, I do appreciate it. I didn't expect you to make the delivery personally."

"I had to see your face when I told you." Edwardo waited for a response.

Hector's brow furrowed. "Okay. Told me what?"

"The bishop is so elated with your work here that he's decided to congratulate you in person."

Hector half smiled. "I'm sure I've made his day. I'm also sure he'd never come here unless he needed to fill his lungs with the cleanest air in all of Mexico." Hector took such a deep breath that Edwardo had to imitate him.

"Well, you're half right," Edwardo said. "We've had a heat wave on the coast. The bishop plans to escape it by coming here, even if it means camping out."

Hector's mouth dropped open. "You are kidding, aren't you?"

"No. The bishop put San Miguel on his calendar a week ago. Don't be surprised if a few others accompany him. He intends to show off your progress in agriculture although he's most curious how you convinced San Miguel people that miracles aren't as frequent as they once thought."

"The lack of miracles is pure luck, Edwardo. I haven't done anything to change people's outlook. Let me explain. No, you wouldn't understand. Look. Is there any way you can dissuade his holiness from coming up here?"

"His first priority is getting away from the heat so I can't do anything about that. Besides, I've heard him tell others how impressed he is with the way you've changed beliefs among his Indians." Edwardo laughed as he nodded. "One time I heard him say that you could teach applied anthropologists a thing or two."

"But I haven't done anything." Hector bit at his lip in frustration. He realized it was futile to argue. "So when does he plan to come?"

"He's ready now, what with the heat wave, but I convinced him you ought to have a week's notice."

"A week! Are you crazy? We can't have the storage bin built by then." Hector was overwhelmed, and he had no idea how the villagers would respond to a visit by the bishop.

He didn't have time to think further before Inez joined them. "I hope you and your friend will come to lunch, Father," Inez said.

"We can unload the truck right away." Alejandro raised an eyebrow to ask Hector if he should call men to unload.

"I can get out of this rut with a push," Edwardo said. "Just show me where to park."

Alejandro waved a hand and half a dozen men came to help. They shoved the truck free, and unloaded the webbing in no time, but the villagers lingered to examine the novel material.

"I have beans and tortillas ready." Inez turned to Hector and Edwardo. "Will you two join us?"

The four of them walked to Inez' porch. Inez' friends had taken charge of the kitchen and were dishing beans onto tortillas to the men who had gathered. Inez went to the kitchen while Alejandro arranged four chairs around the dining room table. She returned with tortillas covered with beans and a few jalapenos. "If I had known you were coming, Father Edwardo, Alejandro would have made my famous chicken and green chili soup."

"We're too busy for anything fancy," Alejandro said to Edwardo. "We need to finish our storage bin before harvest."

"Do you think there's any chance we can finish it in a week?" Hector said.

"It would take a miracle," Alejandro said matter-of-factly.

Edwardo choked on his bite of tortilla, then doubled over holding his sides. Hector could have punched him. Instead he pummeled him on the back. "Edwardo isn't accustomed to such good corn tortillas, only the soft wheat ones they eat in the cities."

Both Alejandro and Inez looked skeptical. Alejandro asked why they needed to finish in a week.

Edwardo looked at Hector with a raised eyebrow. Hector nodded an okay. "The bishop has taken an interest in what San Miguel has accomplished. It may serve as a model for further work in the highlands. So he's decided to visit San Miguel next week."

Inez and Alejandro sat speechless. A few beans dripped from the tortillas Inez was holding midway between mouth and plate. The furrows on Alejandro's brow deepened.

Inez put down her tortilla. "You mean the bishop is coming to San Miguel? In one week?" Her voice rose to a high pitch.

Alejandro said nothing, but his lips quivered.

"He can't stay in the Womb!" Inez was indignant.

"He's planning to camp," Edwardo said.

"Out of the question," Inez stomped her foot. "We'll make room for him here." Then she bit her lip. "But surely, he won't come alone. How many will be in his party?"

"His holiness would be comfortable here," Hector spoke before Edwardo could. "The others can camp or share the Womb with me." Hector found humor in the situation as he pictured Mateo and Marcos delivering an assortment of wines to their mother while she hosted the bishop. For a moment he imagined the archbishop reacting to the bishop's involvement in a drug bust.

"I'm sure we can work things out," Edwardo stammered. "It's very kind of you to offer your home, señora. I'll relay your invitation to the bishop's secretary. He makes all the arrangements."

"Please give him my telephone number, Father Edwardo." Inez reached for the instrument to read off the number. "I don't call myself much, so I never remember my own number," she laughed.

The phone buzzed as she held it, and she dropped it in surprise. "Must be one of my sons. Excuse me. They're such dutiful boys." She flipped the top to answer, then frowned as she listened. "No," she replied, "that's not possible." She shook her head. "It's being used. After all, you gave it to us."

The words coming from the phone couldn't be understood, but it was an angry voice that uttered them.

Inez answered smugly. "Nevertheless, I do think you ought to come for a visit next week. You can meet the bishop. He'll be my guest." She paused to listen. "Of course, the Catholic bishop."

Hector thought he heard a curse from the phone before it went dead.

Inez beamed. "I just invited Reverend Johanson to meet the bishop, but I believe he's declined."

26

The flurry of activity in the week preceding the bishop's visit reminded Hector of Mexico City traffic. He and the few able-bodied men worked with Alejandro mornings to erect a framework for the storage bin. The steel netting proved difficult for Alejandro to arrange the way he wanted it, but Alejandro soon saw the netting's advantages and demonstrated to others how to install it. Even if incomplete, the building should impress the bishop.

In the afternoons when Hector joined the women working in the church, they refused to let him dust or mop. The faction of women who thought the Virgin cried blood sewed new garments for her and polished the wood molding on her case until it gleamed. Every day they seemed to scrub the glass. The salty tears faction unearthed a can of wax from Rosa's shelves and rubbed its contents into the altar until it glowed. The elderly men white washed every stone in sight, then aligned them to usher everyone into the church from all directions.

Hector stopped at Inez' once where he found Alejandro berating her for scrubbing the kitchen floor on her hands and knees. She complained that the foolish man had been standing on a ladder to wash windows. Hector excused himself before they could feud further, claiming he needed to wash his cossack.

The evening before the bishop was to arrive, Hector held a meeting in the church to describe the roles of bishops and archbishops. Twice he worked up to the subject of miracles, but each time he managed to evade their discussion. He reasoned to himself that the bishop could do a better job of explaining their rare occurrence.

The next morning Hector awoke with a start. He knew the day was critical, but for a moment he couldn't recall why. Then he remembered that the bishop and his entourage were to arrive in early afternoon. He muttered a short prayer asking that no miracles occur while the bishop visited. He trusted that God would understand he meant his prayer as a joke and not sarcasm.

Hector lit a candle on the chest of drawers next to his bed and reached for his freshly washed cassock. He looked askance at the large jar of red wine that reflected the sparkle of the candle, but Edwardo had insisted on an ample supply for the communion the bishop would offer.

As Hector slid the garment over his head, his feet searched for his sandals. When he reached to fasten them, his fingers cramped. He massaged both hands a minute, adding a sincere prayer that the bishop never suffer arthritis.

He left the Womb for the outhouse, wondering what experience the bishop had with sanitation in rural villages. Even Inez had an outhouse. As he sat, he gave thanks for the warmth of the seat. In another month or two he'd have to clench his teeth before taking his place. Then, it struck him. The bishop might assign him elsewhere after the visit. Hector worried his talents might be wasted.

A rooster awakening the sun ended Hector's anxiety. The Womb was a little warmer than the outside, but it didn't tempt him to return to bed. He washed his hands and combed his hair, worried a moment the bishop would notice he needed a haircut.

Outside, around the plaza, a few women were sweeping the front of their houses. He knew that inside, villagers were shaking out their best clothes and smoothing wrinkles with their hands. No doubt, Alejandro searched for his best hat. The rooster crowed again. Hector glanced at the sun although he knew the bishop wasn't scheduled for a few more hours.

✝✝✝

In early afternoon, Alejandro greeted Hector at the bell tower. He wore a new hat Gustavo had made. "It would be an honor to pull the rope, Father."

"An honor for me, too, Alejandro. Let's pull together."

The two men reached for the bell rope and gave it a tug. On its first swing the clapper barely touched its bronze housing, but their next heave brought forth a jubilant tone. Both men chuckled as they became one with the rhythm of the swinging bell.

"We'll announce the bishop's visit to the next valley," Hector said.

"And to the valley beyond it," Alejandro laughed.

It wasn't long before villagers filled the plaza outside the church. Children covered their ears. Two dogs on the far side of the plaza began to yowl their annoyance at the bell's peal. Alejandro let up on the rope. He had to put a hand on Hector's arm to signal a stop.

A mild breeze stirred luke-warm air so Hector addressed his congregation from the church steps. The men and women filling the plaza grew quiet while children and dogs romped on the edge. Hector shouted out his thanks for all his people had done to prepare for the bishop's visit. He felt compelled to tell them something about miracles, but once again words failed him. Surely, the bishop would know what to say.

He started to repeat what he had said about the work of bishops when two jeeps and an SUV appeared in the distance. Hector ended with a blessing which no one heard because of all the murmuring. He saw Gustavo at the foot of the stairs and joined him.

Gustavo was speaking to his wife, "The bishop in San Miguel. It's a miracle."

✞ ✞ ✞

Edwardo was all business. He jumped from the SUV when it slowed and opened the door for the bishop when it stopped. A young priest appeared out of nowhere and offered an arm which the bishop refused. The bishop greeted Hector with effusive congratulations and told him he'd meet with the villagers inside the church once his party had a chance to walk out all the jolts from the road.

He introduced his entourage to Hector who in turn introduced everyone to Alejandro, explaining how he and his forebears had served the church for generations. Alejandro blushed, cutting short the accolade by turning to the villagers and inviting them into the church.

While the bishop's party stretched, Edwardo pulled Hector aside and whispered to him that a highland rancher had invited the bishop to his lodge. The party intended to depart by late afternoon. He hoped Inez and the congregation wouldn't be hurt by so short a visit.

"You have no idea how much it will hurt," Hector grumbled. "Look around at all the work these people have done." His anger grew so much he didn't trust himself to say more. As Hector accompanied the bishop to the front of the church, his fingers twitched in torment.

Before the altar, Hector looked over the crowded church. Everyone was present—except for Inez. He whispered to Alejandro to ask where she was. Alejandro assured him she was on her way. Hector had to break the news of the bishop's abbreviated visit to her beforehand, or Inez would feel even more slighted. He whispered to Edwardo that the communion wine was on his dresser in the Womb. Edwardo whispered back that the bishop didn't intend to serve communion. Hector muttered a curse under his breath while he hastened to the back of the church to stand behind the bishop. His heart raced and his innards turned somersaults. Bile flooded his mouth. He feared his anger would turn to vomit. He excused himself, explaining he needed to greet a late arrival. Inez deserved that much, at least.

At the door he shielded his eyes to look toward the Yepiz house. Inez was almost to the church, her head enveloped in a blossoming black hat. Her white dress glowed to show off a red and yellow floral print. Hector shuddered as Inez tottered along on high heels. Maria and Adela walked alongside Inez as if to prop her up if she swayed too much. Marta and Rachel skipped along in the lead.

At the altar Edwardo was introducing the bishop and his party to the congregation. The bishop touted the resume of a young priest praising a book he had written on miracles, even if he had never witnessed one. Hector's stomach did a double somersault. Why would a bishop think an inexperienced youth could influence people who equated wisdom with age?

Before he could worry more, he greeted Inez and took her arm. Maria and Adela stayed close behind as if expecting Inez to fall at any time. Rachel and Marta had bounced up the far side of the stairs, Marta half waving to Hector as the two girls slipped into the church.

"Inez, I know how hard you've worked for the bishop's visit. It touches my heart. I'll be forever grateful." Hector held her arm with both hands.

"What's wrong, Father? Come out with it!"

Hector choked but managed to speak. "The bishop can't stay overnight. He has to leave this afternoon."

"He wouldn't dare." Hector had never heard such an icy tone. "If he knew who my mother-in-law was . . ."

"It's another invitation." Hector felt he was lying and his face reddened.

"It's one more time the bishop has let me down. What am I'm going to tell my friends? And Maria and Marta? You can't believe how much work Maria has done. It isn't fair." Despite her anger, a tear came to Inez' eye.

Hector led Inez to the front of the church where her friends had reserved a place for her. The bishop paused at the interruption. Inez whispered to Hector that he would have to tell Maria.

Maria and Adela had squeezed between the women standing close to Inez. Before Hector could reach Maria, Marta tugged at his cassock.

"Father Hector, please!"

"What is it, my child?"

"Will you ask the bishop to bless Gatita. We asked grandma to do it, but she said no."

Rachel stepped out of nowhere and pulled Gatita from her blouse. "Please, Father, please." She handed the kitten to Hector.

Hector didn't know how to refuse a blessing, his mind focused on talking to Maria. His fingers cramped, and the cat slipped from his hand. She darted for the door at the front of the church. Hector envisioned Rachel and Marta, and who knows how many other children, dashing after it. He warned the two girls he'd only ask the bishop if they stayed where they were while he retrieved Gatita.

He ran as fast as he could, wondering what the bishop must think of him dashing from the church. Gatita paused a moment at the top of the stairs, then leaped down the steps two at a time. Hector had run half way into the plaza before he caught the kitten. He couldn't help petting her when she began to purr, and he paused a moment, trying to think what to tell Maria.

The rare sound of an airplane distracted him. He looked up to see where it was going, unconscious that he continued to pet Gatita.

A bi-plane circled high above. Hector thought the pilot leaned from the open cockpit to study San Miguel. Hector waved but doubted the pilot could see him, marveling at the vintage of the craft. The only time he had seen a bi-plane was Johanson's crop duster. The memory wrinkled his forehead in a frown.

The airplane ended its circling and dived straight toward the San Miguel church. Hector half expected the plane to release a cloud of pesticide. As it drew near, a blazing scar marked the pilot's face. Hector thought a bitter Johanson meant to disrupt the bishop's greeting with the roar of his engine.

When the plane pulled up at the last minute, Johanson flashed Hector the finger.

Hector's insides exploded.

What if Johanson's extra tanks were filled with gasoline? Hector's legs wobbled before he got them in motion. He raced to the outside door of the Womb. He had to get the congregation inside it. If he warned them of the impending disaster, they'd head for the front door and death. How could he get people into the Womb? He'd yet to see a villager hasten to comply with entreaties of any kind.

Hector threw open the back door so hard it slammed shut behind him. He tossed Gatita on his cot and dashed through the tunnel into the church. His cassock caught on a nail as he pushed through the door. He ripped the garment from the nail, bumping his head despite bending low.

The bishop's voice struck him as he entered the sanctuary. "Miracles prove God's existence, but we don't need proof when we have faith."

"It's a miracle," Hector screamed. "A miracle in the Womb."

As soon as the words were off his tongue, he imagined the bishop damning him, but he screamed even louder. "Everyone to the Womb! To witness the miracle. Who knows how long it will last?" His screeching scorched his throat.

Young boys squealed and dashed forward. The girls followed. Young mothers with toddlers trailed behind. The older women hustled arm in arm, a few crossing themselves while they shuffled along. Teresa tottered at the tunnel entrance. If she fell, she'd block the passage way. Hector grabbed an arm and propelled her toward the Womb. She turned to give him a look, but at least she kept moving. Alejandro understood the urgency in Hector's voice. He bellowed at the men who hesitated. They donned their hats as they ran toward Hector, glancing back at Alejandro who was shaking a fist. Hector guessed Alejandro might have heard the plane. If the men didn't trample one another, they'd make it to safety.

But, the bishop and his entourage remained frozen in place. When the bishop did turn his head, his stare was the blackest scowl Hector ever experienced. For a moment, it immobilized him. But only for a moment. He leaped to the altar platform, grabbed the bishop with one arm and pulled.

With his other hand on the bishop's back he pushed. The bishop would say later it felt like being shot from a cannon.

"Move, damnit," Hector yelled to Edwardo and the others. He cupped hands to his mouth and roared. "You'll never see another mass, if you don't get out of here." Hector would never know if it was his command or the roar of the plane's engine at full throttle diving toward the church that made Edwardo and the others run. They caught up with the bishop as he stumbled into the Womb. Hector was right behind. He slammed the door as the sanctuary exploded. The force of the blast, more than its sound, made Hector's knees buckle. He grabbed the door latch to stay upright. The floor beneath him trembled. The walls of the tunnel vibrated so hard Hector thought they'd tumble.

He gasped at the thought of the Womb crashing in on his villagers. Its blackness exaggerated sound and vibration. A scraping sound on one wall threatened doom. The eerie sound ended in a crash, sending another tremor through Hector's sandals and up his spine. He visualized cascading adobe bricks, yet the room remained as black as ever. The dome hadn't even cracked.

The odor of burning gasoline penetrated the Womb. When Hector felt the door's heat, he feared it might be burning. He wrapped his hand with his cassock to grasp the latch and open the door a crack. A flush of red and searing heat forced him to slam it shut. Oily fumes made him gag.

Another shudder followed, one so strong that Hector guessed the church walls must be crumbling. A rumble of falling adobe shook Hector's body, seared his soul. The clanging of a bell followed, its clapper sounding like a wounded dog. The tower had collapsed, with the bell tumbling into the plaza. An eerie silence followed. For a minute the only sound Hector heard was his own breath. Children began to whimper, but none of the infants cried. Nor did the old women make any noise.

"Shall I light your candles, Father?" As usual, Alejandro took charge.

"There are matches on my chest of drawers," Hector said.

"They're all wet." The puzzlement in Alejandro's voice matched Hector's own. He had no idea the chest might be wet.

"There are more matches in the top drawer, Alejandro. On the right."

A flame followed the scratching of a match. Hector blinked. The first candle did little to dispel the Womb's darkness. Alejandro lit two more. The three candles made it possible to recognize people in the room. The bishop and his entourage were across from Hector, cringing against the wall. The women had grouped themselves on the far side with the children. The men began to shuffle, anxious to examine the damage to their church.

"It's a miracle," a woman's voice broke the stillness.

Hector gasped. In the lighted room, he saw that the heavy crucifix above his chest of drawers had loosened and worked its way to the ground. The four huge spikes that had held it in place had dug deep furrows in the adobe wall as the crucifix skittered down the wall to crash behind Hector's chest of drawers. It would have crushed his cot if he hadn't moved it. The container of wine on the chest was half empty. The cross must have jarred it, Hector thought. Its contents had soaked his chest of drawers.

"Stigmata," an elderly voice gasped.

A dozen voices echoed, "Stigmata!"

When the children joined in, Hector wondered if they had any idea what a stigmata was. He wondered even more which of the adults had been cut.

The crucifix caught his eye as he looked around for someone bleeding. His mouth dropped open. Blood was dripping from Christ's feet. Even a few places on his body and arms were dripping a wine red.

Hector breathed deep considering how to rationalize the stigmata, reconsidered, and decided the bishop or his neophyte could explain away the miracle.

But who would explain how the congregation had escaped an inferno worthy of the Devil?

EPILOGUE

More than a year after Johanson crashed his plane into San Miguel, the bishop remained convinced the Finger of God had saved everyone's lives—except for the Protestant—and allowed so little damage to the church. However, personal animosities between the bishop and the archbishop held up the requisite paperwork to begin proper investigation of the miracle.

The bishop assigned an architect to draw up plans for a new entrance, and she included completion of the second bell tower. Edwardo convinced one of his widows to fund construction and to purchase a second bell. Despite deep dents in the old bell, villagers installed it in the tower. The second bell was misdirected to a San Miguel church in Guatemala.

Villagers considered Hector's suggestions for organizing a co-op, enlisting Gustavo as a temporary secretary. Then, they filled the position on a rotating basis. The two factions of women resolved their differences long enough to convince the men that they should be included in the rotation.

Alejandro found extra space over the Protestant's footings to build a classroom behind the new storage bin. Inez insisted that Johanson's expensive paneling be used to cover the smoke stained vigas of the church ceiling. The blackened roof beams, in contrast with the oak paneling, took on a luster Hector had never seen in any other church.

The priests in the bishop's entourage wanted to conduct a fund-raising campaign to purchase pews, but Hector discouraged them. His congregation insisted that since their ancestors had stood, they were meant to stand.

Inez held out a month before Alejandro convinced her to return to the Catholic faith. Gustavo claimed Alejandro had to ask Inez to marry him before she returned, but Hector discouraged such speculation. Hector was overjoyed when Alejandro asked him to conduct the wedding. Gustavo spent all the money he earned weaving hats to purchase fireworks when Alejandro selected him as best man. Maria served as bridesmaid. Rumor had it that she convinced Inez at the last minute to go through with the ceremony. Marta, of course, was flower girl. In her exuberance, she emptied the flower basket half way to the altar. Inez winced to see Gatita curled up in the bottom of the basket, but Hector and Alejandro could not suppress a laugh. The whole congregation roared when the church bell rang and Gatita dashed to the door with Marta in pursuit.

Mateo and Marcos sacrificed time from their drug business to round up their other brothers for the wedding. Only two, who had gone North, couldn't make it. Marcos explained to his mother the pair had obligations to the United States government, but the two promised to visit as soon aa they could. Inez said she knew her sons would find secure positions in the United States.

Jesus' arrival highlighted the wedding for Inez. When she learned that Jesus had devoted himself to working with the poor and the downtrodden, she begged forgiveness for calling him her Judas. She swore to keep San Miguel spotless as her penance. Jesus gave her away. His wedding gift to his mother was an ivory rosary that the Knights of Columbus gave him for his work with AIDS victims.

Mateo and Marcos served as ushers although they had little to do since men went to the right as always while women went to the left. The two men had more responsibility presiding over the wedding feast. They brought a beef carcass that Gustavo and two villagers quickly skinned and butchered. Gustavo later told Hector that his cousin in a neighboring village reported that a friend in the next village lost a cow about the time of the wedding. The brothers brought bags of rice to vary the diet of corn and beans. When Hector smelled a sweet odor from the burlap bags, he hoped the marijuana hadn't affected the rice. Everyone had a high time, but Hector couldn't be sure if it was because of the remnants of marijuana or the joy everyone felt for Alejandro and Inez.

Mateo's and Marcos' cases of wine carried a French imprint, but Hector noticed the bottles were missing labels. Although the wine tasted like any other to Hector, Inez insisted the French watered whatever they shipped to Mexico.

Gustavo's fireworks began with Cherry Bombs that roused every dog in the village. Their yowls carried to the next valley. Marta could not find Gatita for two days. The explosions were followed by rockets bursting into umbrellas of green, white, and red. The display brought thunderous cries of awe from the onlookers until sparks ignited the grass in Inez' back yard. Mateo put out the fire with two bottles of wine. Every villager told Hector that they had never experienced such a wedding. Gustavo said to him that he must have done a remarkable job before the wedding in counseling the couple. They had never gone so long without an argument.

The journalists, Isabela and Yolanda Mendoza, returned to the village when they heard an airliner had crashed in the village, but a Protestant missionary had led everyone to safety in the Catholic church. Hector corrected the story as best he could, and Gustavo showed them the salvaged bell. Villagers had polished it until it looked like new—except for the dents. Yolanda shot most of a disk posing each villager with the bell. She used the rest of the disk to shoot Alejandro and Gustavo after Hector explained how they and their ancestors had led the church for centuries.

Weeks later a photo of Gustavo beside the bell appeared in a leading Culiacan newspaper. A photo editor cropped the picture to exclude Alejandro, probably influenced by Gustavo's grin. His teeth gleamed more than the bell. Gustavo was chagrined when he noted Alejandro's absence until he read that the paper identified him as Alejandro Guichuca, the descendant of a Yaqui general. On a slow news day, three frontier papers on the United States border picked up the story and the photo. The two *compadres* became international celebrities.

A paper in Hermasillo reprinted the photo accompanied by a story with the headline, TOO MANY MIRACLES. Editorial follow-up poked fun at San Miguel and Catholicism in general. The notoriety didn't escape the attention of the archbishop. He and the bishop resolved their differences long enough to decide that Hector needed to continue his work in the highlands.

Hector spent a week with Edwardo and his computer writing a grant to fund development work in sustainable agriculture. The project employed indigenous people to experiment with their own demonstration plots as well as to construct appropriate storage facilities.

Johanson's vision of San Miguel as a visionary center came true. Young men from a dozen different villages in the valley were supported by the Rodale Foundation to work with Hector for a year. While they studied elements of agronomy, they planted various indigenous crops in their home village, relying on a combination of their elders' wisdom and the latest scientific knowledge.

Hector had never been happier. The only thing lacking in his life was the crucifix with Jesus watching over him. The villagers insisted on locating it in the church alongside the Virgin. While presiding over mass, Hector often overheard "stigmata" whispered, but he never learned of anymore miracles.

Hector missed them.

www.ingramcontent.com/pod-product-compliance
Lightning Source LLC
Chambersburg PA
CBHW020553020726
47494CB00006B/2047